GARDNER

- Cited by the *Guinness Book of World Records* as the #1 bestselling writer of all time!

- Author of more than 150 clever, authentic, and sophisticated mystery novels!

- Creator of the amazing Perry Mason, the savvy Della Street, and dynamite detective Paul Drake!

- THE ONLY AUTHOR WHO OUTSELLS AGATHA CHRISTIE, HAROLD ROBBINS, BARBARA CARTLAND, AND LOUIS L'AMOUR *COMBINED*!

Why?
Because he writes the best, most fascinating whodunits of all!

You'll want to read every one of them,
from
BALLANTINE BOOKS

Also by Erle Stanley Gardner
Published by Ballantine Books:

The Case of the

Drowning Duck

Erle Stanley Gardner

BALLANTINE BOOKS • NEW YORK

Copyright © 1942 by Erle Stanley Gardner
Copyright renewed 1970 by Erle Stanley Gardner

All rights reserved under International and Pan-American Copyright Conventions. Published in the United States of America by Ballantine Books, a division of Random House, Inc., New York, and simultaneously in Canada by Random House of Canada Limited, Toronto.

ISBN 0-345-37868-7

This edition published by arrangement with William Morrow & Company.

Manufactured in the United States of America

First Ballantine Books Edition: January 1994

Cast of Characters

1 DELLA STREET
secretary extraordinary and alter ego

2 PERRY MASON
lawyer famous for his lack of interest in ordinary litigation

2 JOHN L. WITHERSPOON
a rich man with a problem

5 LOIS WITHERSPOON
his daughter, who knows when she is in love

20 MARVIN ADAMS
who has doubts about his past but none about Lois

25 PAUL DRAKE
head of the Drake Detective Agency and a willing backer of any Mason hunch

30 MRS. ROLAND BURR
a slinky type who's been around

32 GEORGE L. DANGERFIELD
a man with respect for his wife's skill

39 RAYMOND E. ALLGOOD
detective agency owner

Chapter 1

Once when Della Street, Perry Mason's private secretary, had asked him what was the most valuable attribute a lawyer could have, Mason had answered, "That peculiar something which makes people want to confide in you."

Certainly Mason possessed this power to a marked degree. When he walked across a room, people instinctively followed him with their eyes. When he seated himself in a hotel lobby or on a train, persons who were seated next to him almost invariably started a casual conversation and wound up baring their innermost secrets.

As Mason himself had once said, a lawyer either has this quality or he hasn't. If he has it, it's as much of a natural gift as having a good ear for music. If he doesn't have it, he shouldn't practice law.

Della Street insisted that it was merely the instinctive reaction which people gave to one who could comprehend human frailties, and extend sympathetic understanding.

Mason seldom needed to ask questions. At times, he even seemed uninterested in the confidences which were being poured into his ears. His very indifference stimulated people to go to even greater lengths. But Mason always was understanding and sympathetic. He always made allowances for human weaknesses, and frequently had said that every man who has lived enough to be more than a stuffed shirt, has a closed chapter in his life. If he hasn't, he isn't a man.

There on the veranda of the hotel at Palm Springs, Della Street, standing under the steady, unwinking stars which were blotted out here and there by the silhouetted fronds of tall palms, could look into the hotel lobby and see the man who had seated himself next to Perry Mason. She knew, with what amounted to absolute certainty, that this man was getting ready to tell Mason something so important that it had previously been kept as a closely guarded secret.

1

If Mason realized this, he gave no sign.

He was stretched out comfortably in the deep leather chair, his long legs thrust out before him, the ankles crossed, a cigarette between his lips. His face, usually granite-hard, was relaxed into the grim mask of a fighter who is at rest.

It was only when the man at his side cleared his throat as a preliminary to speech that Mason apparently became aware of his existence.

"I beg your pardon. You're Mr. Mason, the lawyer, aren't you?"

Mason didn't, at once, turn to survey the man's face. He let his eyes slide obliquely over to look at the other's legs. He saw black dress trousers that were creased to a knife-like edge, expensive black kid dress shoes that were as soft as gloves.

The man on his right went on, "I'd like to consult you," and then, after a moment, added, "Professionally."

Mason turned then all the way for a brief appraisal. He saw a shrewd face with a high forehead, prominent nose, a long, lean mouth which indicated decision, and a chin which was almost too prominent. The eyes were dark, but steady, with the calm confidence of power. The man was in his late forties, and his clothes, his manner, and the fact that he was staying in this particular hotel at Palm Springs indicated wealth.

Any sudden effusive cordiality would have frightened this man as much as too great a reserve would have antagonized him. Mason said simply, "Yes, I'm Mason," and didn't so much as offer to shake hands.

"I've read quite a lot about you—your cases—in the newspapers—followed them with a great deal of interest."

"Indeed?"

"I presume you lead a very interesting and exciting life."

"It's certainly not monotonous," Mason agreed.

"And I guess you hear many strange stories."

"Yes."

"And are the recipient of many confidences which must, at all costs, be treated as sacred?"

"Yes."

"My name's Witherspoon, John L. Witherspoon."

Even then Mason didn't extend his hand. He had turned

his head back so that the other had only the benefit of his profile. "Live here in California, Mr. Witherspoon?"

"Yes, I have a place down in the Red River Valley, down in the cotton section of the valley—a mighty nice place, fifteen hundred acres."

He was talking hurriedly now, anxious to get the preliminaries over with.

Mason seemed in no hurry. "Gets rather hot down there in the summer, doesn't it?" he asked.

"Over a hundred and twenty some of the time. My place is air conditioned. Most of the houses in the valley are. It's really marvelous what they're doing to make the desert livable these days."

Mason said, "It must have a splendid winter climate."

"It has. . . . I wanted to talk to you about my daughter."

"You're staying here at the hotel?"

"Yes. She's here with me."

"Been here long?"

"I came up specifically to see you. I read in the Indio paper that you were staying here at Palm Springs. I've been studying you for the past hour."

"Indeed! Drive up?"

"Yes. I don't want my daughter to know why I'm here or that I've consulted you."

Mason pushed his hands down deep in his trousers pockets. Della Street, watching him through the huge plate-glass window, saw that he didn't even turn his eyes toward the other. "I don't like routine cases," Mason said.

"I don't think this would be uninteresting—and the fee would be . . ."

"I like excitement," Mason interrupted. "Some particular case appeals to me, usually because there's a mystery connected with it. I start plugging on it, and something develops which leads to excitement. I usually try to cut a corner and get in hot water. It's the way I'm built. Ordinary office practice doesn't appeal to me in the least. I have all the work I can do, and I'm not interested in ordinary litigation."

His very indifference made Witherspoon the more anxious to confide in him. "My daughter Lois is going to marry a young chap who's going into the Engineering Corps as soon as he finishes college."

3

"How old?"

"My daughter or the boy?"

"Both."

"My daughter's just twenty-one. The boy's about six months older. He's very much interested in chemistry and physics—an unusually bright chap."

Mason said, "Youth really stands a chance these days."

"I'm afraid I don't follow you—not that I'm unpatriotic, but I don't relish the idea of having a prospective son-in-law sent off to war almost as soon as he gets back from his honeymoon."

"Prior to 1929," Mason said, "kids had too much of everything. Then after the crash, they didn't have enough of anything. So they became too much concerned with economic problems. We began to think too much about sharing the wealth, instead of creating it. Youth should create something, and it should have something to create.

"The modern youngsters are coming into a different scheme of things. There'll be heartaches. There'll be fighting, and hardships—and death—but those who survive will have been tempered in a crucible of fire. They won't put up with makeshifts. Make no mistake about it, Witherspoon, you and I are going to be living in a different world when this war is over, and it's going to be different because of the young men who have suffered, and fought—and learned."

"I hadn't thought of youth in that way," Witherspoon said. "Somehow, I've never seen youth as a conquering force."

"You must have seen it in uniform in the last war, but then its back wasn't against the wall," Mason said. "The 'youth' of 1929 is middle-aged today. You're due for a surprise. . . . This young man of yours interests me. Tell me more about him."

Witherspoon said, "There's something in his past. *He* doesn't know who he is."

"You mean he doesn't know his father?"

"Neither his father nor his mother. Marvin Adams was told by the woman whom he'd always considered his mother that he had been kidnapped at the age of three. She made that statement when she was on her deathbed. Of course, the disclosure, which came about two months ago, was a great shock to him."

"Interesting," Mason said, frowning at the toes of his shoes. "What does your daughter say about that?"

"She says . . ."

A feminine voice from the second row of chairs which sat back to back, and directly behind Mason's chair, said, "Suppose you let her say it for herself, Dad."

Witherspoon jerked his head around. Mason, moving with the leisurely grace of a tall man who carries no extra weight, got to his feet to look down at the animated girl who had now turned so that she was kneeling on the seat of the chair, her arms flung over its leather back. A book slipped to the floor with a hard thud.

"I wasn't eavesdropping, Dad, honest. I was sitting here reading. Then I heard Marvin's name—and—suppose we have it out."

John Witherspoon said, "I see no reason for discussing this in your presence, Lois. There's nothing for us to have out—yet."

Mason looked from one face to the other, said, "Why not? Here's my secretary, Miss Street. Suppose the four of us go into the cocktail lounge, have a drink, and discuss it in a civilized fashion. Even if we don't reach an understanding, we won't be bored. I rather think, Witherspoon, that this might be an interesting case."

Chapter 2

Lois took the conversational lead from her father easily and naturally. "After all," she said, "this problem primarily concerns *me*."

"It concerns your happiness," her father said curtly. "Therefore, it concerns me."

"*My* happiness," she pointed out.

John Witherspoon glanced at Mason almost appealingly, then lapsed into silence.

"I'm in love," Lois said. "I've been in love before. It was a lukewarm emotion. This time I'm playing for keeps. Nothing anyone can say, nothing anyone can do, is going to change it. Dad's worried about my happiness. He's worried because there are some things about the man I'm going to marry we don't know, things that Marvin himself doesn't know."

"After all," John Witherspoon pointed out, somewhat lamely, Mason thought, "family and background are important."

Lois brushed the remark aside. She was a small-boned, vivacious girl with intense dark eyes and a volatile manner. She said, "About five years ago Marvin Adams and his mother, Sarah Adams, came to live in El Templo. Sarah was a widow. She had a little property. She put Marvin through school. I met him in high school. He was just another boy. We both went away to college. We came back for winter vacation and met again, and . . ." She snapped her fingers. "Something clicked."

She looked at the two men as though wondering if they would understand, then shifted her eyes to Della Street.

Della Street nodded.

"My Dad," Lois went on, pouring out the words, "is nuts on family. He traces our ancestry back so far it makes the *Mayflower* look streamlined. Naturally, he was interested in finding out something about Marvin's parents. He ran up

6

against a snag. Mrs. Adams was very secretive. She'd come to the valley because she had tuberculosis, and thought the change of climate might help. It didn't. Before she died, she finally admitted that she and her husband, whose name was Horace, had kidnapped Marvin. Marvin was then a child of three. They had held him for ransom. They didn't get the ransom. Things began to get too hot for them, and they cleared out and came West. They became attached to the child, and finally decided to keep him and bring him up. Horace died when Marvin was about four years old. Mrs. Adams died without ever telling anyone who Marvin really was. She said he came from a good family and a wealthy one, and that was all she'd say. Marvin gathered, from what she said, that the kidnaping had taken place somewhere back East. She said his real parents were dead.''

"That was a public statement?" Mason asked. "Made to the authorities?"

"Definitely not," Witherspoon said. "No one knows about it except Marvin, Lois, and myself."

"You're a widower?" Mason asked him.

He nodded.

"What do you want?" Mason asked.

Again Witherspoon seemed less positive than one would have expected.

"I want you to find out who the boy's parents were. I want to find out all about him."

"Exactly why?" Lois asked.

"I want to know who he is."

Her eyes locked with those of her father. "Marvin would like to know, too," she said. "But as far as *I'm* concerned, Dad, I don't care whether his father was a ditchdigger or a Vermont Republican. I'm going to marry him."

John Witherspoon bowed in a silent acquiescence which seemed altogether too docile. "If that's the way you feel about it, my dear," he said.

Lois looked at her watch, smiled at Mason, and said, "And, in the meantime, I've got a date—a party of us going for a horseback ride in the starlight. Don't wait up for us, Dad, and don't worry."

She got to her feet, impulsively gave Mason her hand, and said, "Go ahead, do whatever Dad wants. It will make him

7

feel better—and it won't make one darn bit of difference to me." Her eyes turned from Mason to Della Street, and something she saw in Della Street's face caused her to turn hurriedly back to look at Mason. Then she smiled, extended her hand to Della Street, said, "I'll see you again," and was gone.

When she had left, Witherspoon settled down with the air of a man who is at last free to speak his mind. "It was a very nice story that Sarah Adams told," he said. "It was told to forestall any inquiry on my part. You see, that was only a couple of months ago. Lois and Marvin were already in love. It was a great sacrifice made by a dying mother. . . . It was a dramatic statement. On her very deathbed, she forfeited her son's love and respect to secure his future happiness. Her statement wasn't true."

Mason raised his brows.

"That statement was made up out of whole cloth," Witherspoon went on.

"For what possible reason?" Mason asked.

"I've already employed detectives," Witherspoon said. "They find that Marvin Adams was born to Sarah Adams and Horace Legg Adams, and the birth certificate is duly on file. There's no evidence of any unsolved kidnaping taking place at about the period mentioned in Mrs. Adams' spurious confession."

"Then why would she have made any such statement?" Della Street asked.

Witherspoon said grimly, "I'll tell you exactly why. In January of 1924, Horace Legg Adams was convicted of first-degree murder. In May of 1925, he was executed. The story Mrs. Adams told was a pathetic, last-minute attempt to save the boy the disgrace incidental to having that matter made public, and having him lose the girl he loved. She knew that I was going to try to find out something about the boy's father. She hoped her story would forestall that investigation, or turn it into a different and unproductive channel."

"The boy doesn't know, of course?" Mason asked.

"No."

"Nor your daughter?" Della Street inquired.

"No."

Witherspoon waited a moment while he twisted the stem of a brandy glass in his fingers; then said positively, "I am

8

not going to have the son of a murderer in the Witherspoon family. I think even Lois will appreciate the importance of the facts when I tell them to her."

"What do you want *me* to do?" Mason asked.

Witherspoon said, "I have a transcript of the evidence in the entire case. To my mind, it proves conclusively that Horace Legg Adams was guilty of willful, first-degree murder. However, I want to be fair. I want to give Marvin the benefit of the doubt. I want you to look over the transcript of that case, Mr. Mason, and give me your opinion. If you think Marvin's father was guilty, I shall tell my daughter the whole story, give her your opinion, and absolutely forbid her to see or speak with Marvin Adams again. It will be a shock to her, but she'll do it. You'll see why when you read the transcript."

"And if I should think he might have been innocent?" Mason asked.

"Then you'll have to prove it, reopen the old case, clear the record, and get a public recognition of the miscarriage of justice," Witherspoon said grimly. "There will be no blot on the Witherspoon family name. I positively won't have the son of a convicted murderer in the family."

"A murder that's eighteen years old," Mason said thoughtfully. "That's rather a large order."

Witherspoon met his eyes. "I will pay rather a large fee," he announced.

Della Street said, "After all, Mr. Witherspoon, supposing the man *was* guilty. Do you think that your daughter would change her mind because of that fact?"

Witherspoon said grimly, "If the father was guilty of that murder, there may be certain inherited tendencies in the son. I have already seen some things which indicate there are such tendencies. That boy is a potential murderer, Mr. Mason."

"Go ahead," Mason said.

"If those tendencies are there," Witherspoon went on, "and if my daughter won't listen to reason, I will put Marvin in such a position that those inherent weaknesses of character will come out. I will do it in such a dramatic way that Lois will see them for herself."

"Just what do you mean by that?" Mason asked.

Witherspoon said, "Understand me, Mason, I'll do anything to protect my daughter's happiness, literally *anything*."

"I understand that, but just what do you mean?"

"I'll put the young man in a position where apparently the only logical way out is to commit murder; *then* we'll see what he does."

"That will be rather tough on both your daughter and the person whom you happen to pick as a prospective victim," Mason said.

"Don't worry," Witherspoon said. "It will be handled very adroitly. No one will actually be killed, but Marvin will *think* he's killed someone. Then my daughter will see him in his true light."

Mason shook his head. "You're playing with dynamite."

"It takes dynamite to move rock, Mr. Mason."

For a moment, there was a silence; then Mason said, "I'll read over that transcript of the trial. I'll do that to satisfy my curiosity. And that's the only reason I will read it, Mr. Witherspoon."

Witherspoon motioned to the waiter. "Bring me the check," he said.

Chapter 3

Rays of early-morning sunlight flashed across the desert until, striking the mountain barrier on the west, they burst into a golden sparkle which tinged the towering peaks. The sky was beginning to show that blue-black which is so characteristic of the Southern California desert.

Della Street, attired in tan frontier pants, cowboy riding boots, and a vivid green blouse, paused as she walked past the door of Perry Mason's room, tapped tentatively on the door.

"Are you up?" she called softly.

She heard the sound of a chair moving back, and then quick steps. The door opened.

"Good heavens!" she exclaimed. "You haven't even been to bed!"

Mason brushed a hand over his forehead, motioned toward a pile of typewritten manuscript on the table. "That damned murder case," he said. "It's got me interested. . . . Come in."

Della Street looked at her wrist watch, said, "Forget the murder case. Slip into your riding things. I ordered a couple of horses for us—just in case."

Mason hesitated. "There's an angle about that case I . . ."

Della Street walked firmly past him, opened the Venetian blinds, and pulled them up. "Switch off the lights," she said, "and take a look."

Mason clicked off the light switch. Already the vivid sunlight was casting sharp, black shadows. The intense illumination reflected back into the room with a brilliance that made the memory of the electric lights seem a sickly, pale substitute.

"Come on," Della Street coaxed. "A nice brisk canter, a cold shower, and breakfast."

11

Mason stood looking out at the clear blue of the sky. He swung open the window to let the crisp air purify the room.

"What's worrying you?" Della Street asked, sensing his mood. "The case?"

Mason looked toward the pile of transcript and folded, age-yellowed newspaper clippings, and nodded.

"What's wrong with it?" Della asked.

"Almost everything."

"Was he guilty?"

"He *could* have been."

"Then what's wrong with it?"

"The way it was handled. He *could* have been guilty, or he *could* have been innocent. But the way his lawyer handled it, there was only one verdict the jury could possibly have brought in—murder in the first degree. And there's nothing at all in the case, as it now stands, which I could point out to John L. Witherspoon, and say, 'This indicates conclusively that the man was innocent.' The jury found him guilty on that evidence, and Witherspoon will find him guilty on that evidence. He'll go about wrecking the lives of two young people—and the man *may* have been innocent."

Della Street remained sympathetically silent. Mason stared out at the cruel, jagged ridges of the steep mountains which towered almost two miles above sea level, then turned, smiled, and said, "I should shave."

"Never mind that. Get into some riding boots and come along. Put on some overall pants and a leather jacket. That's all you need."

She went over to Mason's closet, rummaged around, found his riding boots and jacket, brought them out, and said, "I'll be waiting in the lobby." The lawyer changed his clothes hurriedly, met Della in the lobby, and they went out into the cool fresh air of the desert morning. The man who was in charge of the horses indicated two mounts, watched them swing into the saddles, and grinned at Mason.

"You can tell what a man knows about horses the way he gets on one," he said. "Those are pretty good horses, but you'll have better ones tomorrow."

Mason's eyes showed that he was interested. "How can you tell?"

"Lots of little ways. The tenderfoot tries to tell you how

12

he always rode bareback as a boy, and then he grabs hold of the horn and cantle." He snorted disgustedly. "Now, *you* never touched the cantle with your hand. Have a good ride."

Mason's eyes were thoughtful as they trotted away from the hotel and up the bridle path.

"What now?" Della Street asked.

"That talk about getting on a horse made me think—you know, a lawyer must always be on the alert for details."

"What does getting on a horse have to do with it?" she asked.

"Everything—and nothing."

She reined her horse close to his.

"The little things," Mason said, "little details which escape the average observer, are the things that tell the whole story. If a man really understands the significance of the little things, no one can lie to him. Take that wrangler, for instance. The people who come here have money. They're supposed to be intelligent. They've had, as a rule, the best education money can buy. They usually try to exaggerate their ability as horsemen in order to get better mounts. And they're utterly oblivious of the little things to do which give the lie to their words. The wrangler stands by the hitching post, apparently sees nothing, and yet can tell to a certainty just how much a person knows about a horse. A lawyer should appreciate the significance of that."

"You mean that a lawyer should know *all* of those things?" Della Street asked.

"He can't know them all," Mason said, "or he'd be a walking encyclopedia, but he should know the basic facts. And he should know how to get the exact knowledge he needs in any given case to prove a man is lying when his own actions contradict the words his lips are uttering."

She looked at his somewhat drawn countenance, the tired weariness of his eyes, said, "You're worrying a lot about that case."

He said, "Seventeen years ago, a man was hanged. Perhaps he was guilty. Perhaps he was innocent. But just as certain as fate, he was hanged *because a lawyer made a mistake*."

"What did the lawyer do?"

Mason said, "Among other things, he presented an inconsistent defense."

"Doesn't the law permit that?"

"The law does, but human nature doesn't."

"I'm afraid I don't understand."

Mason said, "Of course, the law has been changed a lot in the last twenty years, but human nature hasn't changed. Under the procedure, as it existed in those days, a person could interpose a plea of not guilty, go into court, and try to prove he wasn't guilty. He could also interpose a plea of insanity which was tried at the same time as the rest of the case, and before the same jury, and as a part of the whole case."

She studied him with eyes that saw deep beneath the surface, seeing those things which only a woman can see in a man with whom she has had a long, intimate association.

Abruptly, she said, "Let's forget the case. Let's take a good, brisk canter, soak up the smell of the desert, and come back to business after breakfast."

Mason nodded, touched his horse with the quirt, and they were off.

They left the village behind, rode up a long winding canyon, came to water and palms, dismounted to lie in the sand, watching the purple shadows seek refuge from the sunlight in the deeper pockets where the jagged ridges offered protection. The absolute silence of the desert descended upon them, stilled the desire for conversation, left them calmly contented, souls purified by a vast tranquillity.

They rode back in silence. Mason took a shower, had breakfast, and dropped into a deep, restful sleep. It wasn't until afternoon that he would see John Witherspoon.

Della and Perry met him on the shaded veranda which furnished a cool shield against the eye-aching glare of the desert. Shadows of the mountains were slowly stealing across the valley, but it would be several hours before they embraced the hotel. The heat was dry but intense.

Mason sat down and began to review the case dispassionately.

"You're familiar with most of these facts, Witherspoon," he said, "but I want Miss Street to get the picture, and I want to clarify my own perspective by following the case in a

14

logical sequence of events; so I'll run the risk of boring you by dwelling on facts you already know."

"Go right ahead," Witherspoon said. "Believe me, Mason, if you can satisfy me the man was innocent . . ."

"I'm not certain we can *ever* satisfy ourselves," Mason said, "at least not from the data we have available at present. But we can at least look at it in the light of cold, dispassionate reason."

Witherspoon tightened his lips. "In the absence of *proof* to the contrary, the verdict of the jury is binding."

"In 1924," Mason said, "Horace Legg Adams was in partnership with David Latwell. They had a little manufacturing business. They had perfected a mechanical improvement which gave promise of great potential value. Abruptly Latwell disappeared. Adams told his partner's wife that Latwell had gone on a business trip to Reno, that she would doubtless hear from him in a few days. She didn't hear from him. She checked the hotel records at Reno. She could get no trace of him.

"Adams told other stories. They didn't all coincide. Mrs. Latwell said she was going to call the police. Adams, confronted with the threat of a police investigation, told an entirely different story, and told it for the first time. Mrs. Latwell called in the police. They investigated. Adams said that Latwell had confessed to him his marriage was unhappy, that he was in love with a young woman whose name didn't enter into the case. She was referred to in the newspapers and in court as 'Miss X.' Adams said Latwell told him he was going to run away with this woman, asked him to stall his wife along by telling her he'd gone to Reno on a business trip, that Adams was to carry on the business as usual, hold Latwell's share of the proceeds, give an allowance of two hundred dollars each month to Latwell's wife, and wait until he heard from Latwell as to what to do with the rest. Latwell wanted to get completely away before his wife could stop him.

"At that time, Adams told a convincing story, but because of his early contradictory statements, police made a thorough investigation. They found Latwell's body buried in the cellar of the manufacturing plant. There was a lot of circumstantial evidence indicating Adams was guilty. He was arrested. More

15

circumstantial evidence piled up. Adams' lawyer evidently became frightened. Apparently, he thought Adams wasn't telling him the whole truth, and that, at the time of trial, he might be confronted with surprise testimony which would make the case even more desperate.

"The prosecution closed its case. It was an imposing array of circumstantial evidence. Adams took the stand. He didn't make a good witness. He was trapped on cross-examination—perhaps because he didn't clearly understand the questions, also perhaps because he was rattled. He evidently wasn't a man who could talk glibly or think clearly in front of a crowded courtroom and the stony faces of twelve jurors. Adams' lawyer put on a defense of insanity. He called Adams' father, who testified to the usual things a family can dig up when they want to save a child from the death penalty. A fall in early childhood, a blow on the head, evidences of abnormality—principally that Horace Adams had a penchant as a youngster for torturing animals. He'd pull the wings off flies, impale them on pins, gleefully watch them squirm—in fact, that animal-torturing complex seemed to be the thing on which the defense harped.

"That was unfortunate."

"Why?" Witherspoon asked. "It would indicate insanity."

"It antagonized the jury," Mason said. "Lots of kids pull the wings off flies. Nearly all children go through a stage when they're instinctively cruel. No one knows why. Psychologists give different reasons. But when a man is on trial for his life, you don't stand much chance with a jury by dragging in a lot of early cruelties, magnifying them, distorting them, and trying to show insanity. Moreover, the fact that Adams' lawyer relied on an insanity defense, under the circumstances of the case, indicated that he himself didn't believe Adams' story about what Latwell had told him.

"Circumstantial evidence can be the most vicious perjurer in the world. The circumstances don't lie, but men's interpretation of circumstances is frequently false. Apparently no one connected with the case had the faintest knowledge of how to go about analyzing a case which depended simply on circumstances.

"The district attorney was a shrewd, clever prosecutor

who had political ambitions. Later on, he became governor of the state. The attorney for the defense was one of those bookish individuals who are steeped in the abstract lore of academic legal learning—and who knew nothing whatever about human nature. He knew his law. Every page of the record shows that. He didn't know his jurors. Almost every page of the record indicates that. Adams was convicted of first-degree murder.

"The case was appealed. The Supreme Court decided that it was a case of circumstantial evidence, that, thanks to the care with which Adams' lawyer had presented his points and bolstered his arguments with decisions, there were no errors of procedure. The jurors had heard the witnesses, had seen their demeanor on the stand, and, therefore, were the best judges of the facts. The conviction was affirmed. Adams was executed."

There was a certain touch of bitterness in Witherspoon's voice. He said, "You're an attorney who has specialized in defending persons accused of crime. I understand you have never had a defendant found guilty in a murder case. Yet, despite your viewpoint, which is naturally biased in favor of the defendant, you aren't able to tell me that this man was innocent. To my mind, that is conclusive of his guilt."

"I can't say that he was innocent," Mason said, "and I *won't* say that he was guilty. The circumstances in connection with the case have never been thoroughly investigated. I want to investigate them."

Witherspoon said, "The mere fact that you, biased as you are, can't find anything extenuating . . ."

"Now, wait a minute," Mason interrupted. "In the first place, it wasn't a case which would have appealed to me. It lacked all the elements of the spectacular. It was a sordid, routine, everyday sort of murder case. I probably wouldn't have taken Adams' case if it had been offered to me. I like something which has a element of mystery, something which has an element of the bizarre. Therefore, I'm not biased. I'm fair and impartial—and I'm not satisfied the man was guilty. The thing of which I *am* satisfied is that this man was convicted more because of the way his lawyer handled the case than for any other reason."

Witherspoon said, almost as though talking to himself, "If

he was guilty, it's almost certain that the boy will have inherited that innate streak of cruelty, that desire to torture animals."

"Lots of children have that," Mason pointed out.

"And outgrow it," Witherspoon commented.

Mason nodded his agreement.

"Marvin Adams is old enough to have outgrown it," Witherspoon went on. "I think first I'll find out something of his attitude toward animals."

Mason said, "You're following the same erroneous course of reasoning which the jury followed back in 1924."

"What's that?"

"That because a man is cruel to animals, you think he's a potential murderer."

Witherspoon got up from his chair, walked restlessly over to the edge of the veranda, stood looking out at the desert for a moment, then came back to face Mason. He seemed, somehow, to have aged, but there was clear-cut decision stamped on his face. "How long would it take you to investigate the circumstances of the case so that you could pass on the circumstantial evidence?" he asked Mason.

Mason said, "I don't know. Eighteen years ago, it wouldn't have taken very long. Today, the significant things have been obscured. Events which went unnoticed at the time, but which might have had an important bearing on the case, have been snowed under by the march of time, by the sheer weight of other events which have been piled on top of them. It would take time, and it would take money."

Witherspoon said, "I have all the money we need. We have very little time. Will you make the investigation?"

Mason didn't even look at him. He said, "I don't think any power on earth could keep me from making the investigation. I can't get this case out of my mind. You furnish the expenses, and if I can't come to a satisfactory conclusion, I won't charge you any fee."

Witherspoon said, "I'd like to have you do this work where you can exclude everything else—every possible interruption. We have only a few days—and then *I'm* going to act. . . ."

Mason said in a low voice, "I don't need to tell you, Witherspoon, that that's a dangerous way to feel."

18

"Dangerous to whom?"

"To your daughter—to Marvin Adams—and to yourself."

Witherspoon raised his voice. A flush darkened his skin. "I don't care anything about Marvin Adams," he said. "I care a lot about my daughter's happiness. As far as I'm concerned, I'd be willing to sacrifice anything to keep her from being unhappy."

"Has it ever occurred to you," Mason asked, "that if young Adams knew exactly what you were doing and the reason back of it, he might do something desperate?"

"I don't give a damn what he does," Witherspoon said, emphasizing his words by gently striking the top of the table with blows of his fist at measured intervals. "I tell you, Mason, if Marvin Adams is the son of a murderer, he is never going to marry my daughter. I'd stop at nothing to prevent that marriage, absolutely nothing. Do you understand?"

"I'm not certain that I do. Just what do you mean by that?"

"I mean that where my daughter's happiness is concerned, I'd stop at nothing, Mason. I'd see that any man who threatened her happiness ceased to be a threat to that happiness."

Mason said in a low voice, "Don't talk so loud. You're making threats. Men have been hanged for but little more than that. You certainly don't mean . . ."

"No, no, of course not," Witherspoon said in a lower tone, glancing quickly over his shoulder to see if his remark had been overheard. "I didn't mean that I would kill him, but I would have no compunctions whatever about putting him in such a position that the inherited weakness of character would become manifest . . . Oh, well, I'm probably working myself up needlessly. I can count on Lois to look at the situation sensibly. I'd like to have you come down to my house, Mason—you and your secretary. You could be undisturbed and . . ."

Mason interrupted to say, "I don't want to be undisturbed."

"I'm afraid I don't follow you. When a person is concentrating . . ."

"I told you," Mason went on, "that from the data available and evidence in the record itself, Horace Legg Adams might well have been guilty. I want to uncover evidence which *wasn't* in the record. That's going to take more than undisturbed solitude. It's going to take action.''

"Well," Witherspoon said, "I'd like to have you near me. Couldn't you at least come down now, and . . .''

Mason said crisply, "Yes. We'll leave right away. I'll go down and look your place over. I want to see something of your background. I want to see a little more of your daughter and of Marvin Adams. I take it he'll be there.''

"Yes. And I have two other guests, a Mr. and Mrs. Burr. I trust they won't disturb you.''

"If they do, I'll move out. . . . Della, telephone Paul Drake at the Drake Detective Agency. Tell him to hop in a car and start for El Templo at once.''

Witherspoon said, "I'll find my daughter and . . .''

He broke off as he heard the sound of running steps, the lilt of a woman's laughter; then the youngsters came pellmell up the steps, and were starting across the veranda, when they saw the trio at the table.

"Come on," Lois Witherspoon called to her companion. "You've got to meet the famous lawyer.''

She was wearing a playsuit which showed the girlish contours of her figure, an expanse of sun-tanned skin which would have resulted in a call for the police twenty years earlier. The young man with her wore shorts and a thin blouse. He was beaded with perspiration, a dark-haired, dark-eyed, intense young man with long, tapering fingers, nervous gestures, and a thin, sensitive face which seemed, somehow, older than Mason had expected. It was a face that mirrored a sensitive mind, a mind that was capable of great suffering, one that a great shock might unbalance.

Lois Witherspoon performed quick introductions. She said, "We've had three sets of fast tennis, and I *do* mean fast! My skin has a date with lots of cold water and soapsuds.'' She turned to Perry Mason and said, almost defiantly, "But I wanted you to look us over, perspiration and all, because—because I didn't want you to think we were running away.''

Mason smiled. "I don't think you two would run away from anything.''

"I hope not," she said.

Marvin Adams was suddenly very sober. "There's no percentage in running away from things, war, fighting, or—anything else.''

"Away from death," Lois added quickly, "or—" meeting her father's eyes—"away from life."

Witherspoon got heavily to his feet. "Mr. Mason and his secretary are going back with us," he said to Lois, and then to Mason, "I'll go and make arrangements to check out. If it's all right with you, I'll have your bill added to mine, and then you won't need to bother with it."

Mason nodded, but his eyes remained on Marvin Adams and did not follow John L. Witherspoon through the door into the lobby.

"So you don't believe in running away?" Mason asked.

"No, sir."

"Nor do I," Lois said. "Do *you*, Mr. Mason?"

The question made Della Street smile, and that smile was Lois Witherspoon's only answer.

Marvin Adams wiped his forehead and laughed. "I don't want to run, anyway. I want to dive. I'm as wet as a drowning duck."

Della Street said, half jokingly, "You have to be careful of what you say in front of a lawyer. He might get you on a witness stand and say, 'Young man, didn't you claim that ducks drown?' "

Lois laughed. "It's a favorite expression of his ever since his physics professor performed a classroom experiment. Down at the ranch a few nights ago, Roland Burr, one of the guests, called him on it. Tell them what you did, Marvin."

The young man seemed uncomfortable. "I was trying to show off. I saw Mr. Burr was getting ready to call me on it. Shucks, I was away out of line."

"Not a bit of it," Lois defended. "Mr. Burr was actually insulting. I jumped up, ran out, and got a little duck, and Marvin actually drowned it—and he didn't even touch it. Of course, he took it out in time to keep it from *really* drowning."

"Made a duck drown?" Della Street exclaimed.

"Right in front of all the guests," Lois boasted. "You should have seen Mr. Burr's face."

"How on earth did you do it?" Della asked.

Marvin quite apparently wanted to get away. "It wasn't

21

anything. Just one of the more recent chemical discoveries. It's nothing but a spectacular trick. I put a few drops of one of the detergents in the water. If you folks will excuse me, I'll go shower. I'm awfully glad to have met you, Mr. Mason. I hope I see you again.''

Lois grabbed his arm. "All right, come on."

"Just a minute," Mason said to Lois. "Was your father there?"

"When?" she asked.

"When the duck was drowned."

"He wasn't drowned. Marvin took him out of the water after he'd sunk far enough to prove his point, wiped him off, and . . . pardon me, I guess I'm digressing. No. Father wasn't there."

Mason nodded, said, "Thanks."

"Why did you ask?"

"Oh, nothing. It might be as well not to mention it. I think he's a bit sensitive about using live things in laboratory experiments."

She looked at Mason curiously for a moment, then said, "All right, we won't breathe a word of it. The drowning duck will be a secret. Come on, Marvin."

Della Street watched them walk across the porch, saw Marvin Adams hold the door open for Lois Witherspoon. She didn't speak until after the door had gently closed; then she said to Perry Mason, "They're very much in love. Why were you wondering about whether Mr. Witherspoon had seen the performance of the drowning duck or might hear about it?"

Mason replied, "Because I think Witherspoon might have been biased enough to see in it, not the experiment of a youngster interested in science, but the sadistic cruelty of the son of a murderer. Witherspoon's in a dangerous frame of mind. He's trying to judge another man—and he's terribly biased. It's a situation that's loaded with emotional dynamite."

22

Chapter 4

It was quite evident that John L. Witherspoon was proud of his house, just as he was proud of his horses, of his car, of his daughter, and of his financial and social position. Strongly possessive, he threw about everything which came within the sphere of his influence an aura of prideful ownership.

His house was a huge structure built on the western edge of the valley. Off to the south was the black slope of Cinder Butte. From the front windows could be seen the waste of desert which rimmed the fertile stretch of the irrigated Red River Valley. East of the house were green irrigated acres. Far to the west were jagged mountains of piled-up boulders.

John L. Witherspoon proudly escorted Mason and Della Street around the building, showing them the tennis courts, the swimming pool, the fertile acres of irrigated land, the 'dobe-walled enclosure within which the Mexican servants and laborers lived.

Long purple shadows creeping outward from the base of the high mountains slipped silently across the sandy slopes, flowed gently down across the irrigated acres.

"Well," Witherspoon demanded, "what do you think about it?"

"Marvelous," Mason said.

Witherspoon turned and saw that the lawyer was looking out across the valley at the purple mountains. "No, no. I mean *my* place here, the house, my crops, *my* . . ."

"I think we're wasting a hell of a lot of valuable time," Mason said.

He turned abruptly and strode back to the house where Della Street found him at dinner time closeted in his room, poring once more over the transcript of that old murder case.

"Dinner in a little over thirty minutes, Chief," she said. "Our host says he's sending in some cocktails. Paul

23

Drake has just telephoned from El Templo that he's on his way out."

Mason closed the volume of typewritten transcript.

"Where can we put this stuff, Della?"

"There's a writing desk out here in your sitting room. It's Mission type, good and strong. It'll be a nice place for you to work."

Mason shook his head. "I'm not going to stay here. We leave in the morning."

"Just why *did* you come down here?" she asked curiously.

"I wanted to see a little more of those kids—together. And to size up Witherspoon in his own back yard. Met the other guests, Della?"

"One of them," she said. "Mrs. Burr. We can't meet Mr. Burr."

"Why not?"

"He lost an argument with a horse shortly after you came in and buried yourself in that transcript."

Mason showed quick interest. "Tell me about the horse, and the argument."

"I didn't see it. I heard about it. It seems he's quite an enthusiast on fly-casting and on color photography. That's the way Witherspoon met him—at a camera store in El Templo. They got talking, found out they had a lot of interests in common, and Witherspoon invited him out for a couple of weeks. . . . I understand Witherspoon does things that way—likes to show off his big house here. He claims he either takes to a man at first sight, or never likes him at all."

"A dangerous habit," the lawyer commented. "When's Burr's two weeks up?"

"I think it was up a couple of days ago, but Witherspoon suggested he stay on a little longer. It seems Burr is going to open up a business here in the valley. He found he needed more additional capital and sent East for it. It's supposed to be here tomorrow or next day—but he'll stay put for a while now."

"On account of the horse?" Mason asked.

"Yes."

"What happened?"

"It seems Burr wanted to take a color photograph of one

of the mares. A Mexican vaquero was backing her out of the stable to take her over to the spot Burr had designated. She was nervous and high-strung. The Mexican jerked at her head. Burr was standing beside her. The doctor left about fifteen minutes ago."

"Take him to the hospital?"

"No. He's staying here in the house. The doctor brought out a trained nurse and left her in charge, temporarily. He's going to send a regular nurse out from town."

Mason grinned. "Witherspoon must feel he's like the host in that play where the man broke a hip and . . ."

"Witherspoon was the one who absolutely insisted on his staying here," she said. "Burr wanted to go to a hospital. Witherspoon simply wouldn't listen to it."

"You certainly do get around and keep your ears open," Mason said. "How about Mrs. Burr?"

"Mrs. Burr is a knockout."

"What sort?"

"Light reddish hair; large, slate-colored eyes; a perfectly wonderful complexion, and . . ."

"No, no," Mason interrupted, grinning. "I meant what sort of a knockout."

Della Street's eyes twinkled. "I guess it's what they call a technical knockout. She hits below the belt. She . . ."

The door opened. Paul Drake came breezing into the room.

"Well, well," Drake said, shaking hands, "you sure *do* go places, Perry! What's it all about?"

Before Mason could answer, the door opened again, and a soft-footed Mexican servant glided into the room, carrying a tray on which was a cocktail shaker, and three filled glasses.

"Dinner is in thirty minutes," he said in faultless English as he passed the tray. "Mr. Witherspoon said please do not dress."

"Tell him I won't," Mason said, grinning. "I never do."

They clicked the rims of their glasses as the servant withdrew.

"Here's to crime," Mason said.

They sipped their cocktails, making something of a ceremony of it.

"You certainly pick swell places, Perry," Drake commented.

"It depresses me," Mason told him.

"Why? It looks like the guy who owned it had invented a way of beating the income tax."

"I know," Mason said, "but there's something about it I don't like—an atmosphere of being cooped up."

Della Street said, "He doesn't like it because there isn't any excitement, Paul. When he works on a case, he wants to go out and drag in the facts. He can't stand to stay put, waiting for the facts to come to him."

"What's the case?" Drake asked.

"It isn't a case. It's a post-mortem."

"Who's your client?"

"Witherspoon, the man who owns the place."

"I know, but who are you trying to prove didn't commit the murder?"

Mason said gravely, "A man who was hanged seventeen years ago."

Drake made no effort to conceal his disgust. "I presume he was executed a year or so after the crime was committed. That would make the clues at least eighteen years old."

Mason nodded.

"And you think he was innocent?"

"He may have been."

Drake said, "Well, it's okay with me, just so I get paid for it. Gosh, Perry, who's the acetylene torch?"

"Torch?" Mason asked, his mind still on the murder case.

"The straw-headed lass in the seductive white outfit that fits her like the skin on a sausage. You can take one look at that and know she hasn't anything underneath it except a pleasing personality."

Della Street said, "She's married, Paul. But don't let that cramp your style. Her husband got mixed up with a horse this afternoon. I understand he's now filled full of morphine and his leg's wrapped in a plaster of Paris cast, and a weight is dangling from . . . ."

"She's married!"

"Yes. Why so startled? Good-looking women *do* get married, you know."

"Then she must be related to the big-chested chap with

26

the paunch and the air of ownership—what the devil's his name?"

"No. That's Witherspoon. She's Mrs. Roland Burr. They became acquainted a couple of weeks ago in El Templo. Burr and Witherspoon are fly-fishing cronies and camera fiends. I've picked up all the gossip already, you see."

Drake whistled.

"Why, Paul. What's the matter?"

Drake said, "When I stepped out of my room into the corridor just now, I opened the door rather quietly, and this baby in white was leaning up against the big guy. She tilted her lips up. The last I saw, as I silently eased back into my room and waited for the coast to clear, was the paunchy party getting ready for a smear of lipstick. My entrance was delayed by a good thirty seconds."

"After all, Paul," Della Street pointed out, "a kiss doesn't mean a lot, these days."

Drake said, "I'll bet this one meant something. It would have to me. If she . . ."

There was a knock on the door. Mason nodded to Della Street. She opened it.

Lois Witherspoon came marching into the room. Marvin Adams, looking somewhat embarrassed, hung a pace or two behind her.

"Come on in, Marvin," Lois said, and, looking at Paul Drake, said, "I'm Lois Witherspoon. This is Marvin Adams. You're the detective, aren't you?"

Drake glanced obliquely at Mason, seemed almost taken aback for a moment, then said in his slow drawl, "Why? Did I drop a magnifying glass or did you notice some false whiskers clinging to my chin?"

Lois Witherspoon stood in the center of the floor. She had that reckless defiance, that utter disregard of consequences which is a part of youth. She spoke with hot-headed rapidity. "I bet you've heard the whole story, so don't you try to stall! You can't cover up. Your automobile is sitting out in front. The registration is 'Drake Detective Agency.' "

Drake kept his voice on a note of light banter. "One should never take a car registration seriously. Now suppose I had . . ."

"It's all right, Paul," Mason interrupted. "Let her finish. What is it you want, Miss Witherspoon?"

She said, "I want things carried on fair and above board. I don't want to have you pretending this is an old friend of the family or someone who brought you down some papers. Let's be adult and civilized about this. My father thinks he should dig into the past. I know just exactly how the bugs in my biology class must have felt when they were dissected under a microscope. But if we're going to be bugs, let's be frank about it."

Marvin Adams hastily interposed, "I *want* to know something about my parents. And I don't want to marry Lois, if . . ."

"That's just it," Lois Witherspoon interrupted. "All this is making Marvin conscious of a possibility that . . . that I don't like. If you uncover evidence that his father was a millionaire who was sent to jail for rigging the stock market, or that one of his distant ancestors was hung in chains from the Tower of London for being a pirate, he'll go noble on me, and I'll have to lasso him and hog-tie him in order to get my brand on him. In case you don't know it, it's an embarrassing experience for all of us. It's making me feel like doing something rash. . . . Now that we all understand each other, can we please dispense with all subterfuge?"

Mason nodded prompt agreement. "Except when it's necessary to humor your father. After all, Miss Witherspoon, this is giving him an opportunity to discharge what he considers a family duty, and get something off his mind. It may relieve the pressure somewhat."

She said, "Yes. It's his toy. I suppose I should let him play with it."

"How's Mr. Burr getting along?" Mason asked, changing the subject.

"Apparently all right. They filled him full of dope. He's sleeping. His wife . . . *isn't* sleeping."

Marvin said, "She's out there pacing the corridor. I presume she feels rather helpless."

Lois Witherspoon flashed him a swift glance. "Helpless! In that gown?"

"You know what I mean, Lois."

"I do, and I know what *she* means. That woman is altogether too man-conscious to suit me."

Marvin Adams said reproachfully, "Now, youngster!"

Lois turned abruptly, gave Mason her hand. "Thanks for understanding," she said. "I thought we'd—break the ice all around."

Paul Drake gave a low whistle as the door closed on the pair. "That," he announced, "is personality. Sort of puts you on the spot, doesn't it, Perry? Is *she* in on this old murder case—affected by it?"

Mason pushed his hands down into his pockets. "Naturally," he said, "it looks like a lot of foolish and wasted effort to her. She thinks Marvin Adams was kidnaped when he was a child of three, and that her father's concern is all caused by his desire to investigate the family of his future son-in-law."

"Well," Drake asked curiously, "where *does* the murder came come in?"

Mason said, "Marvin Adams doesn't suspect it, but he's the son of the man who was executed for that murder seventeen years ago, and if either one of those high-strung, nervous kids had any idea of what we're investigating, it would turn loose some emotional dynamite that would blast the Witherspoon family wide open."

Drake slid down on the davenport, surrendering to a characteristic muscular relaxation that left him limp as a piece of loose string. "Witherspoon knows all about it?" he asked.

"Yes," Mason said. "He's had a copy of the transcript of the old trial made. It's there in the desk. You're going to have to read it over tonight."

Drake said, "I'm betting that kid finds it all out before we've been working on the case for two weeks."

"No takers," Mason told him. "And we won't have two weeks. If we don't turn up something definite within about forty-eight hours, Witherspoon is going to conduct an original experiment in murder psychology. Think *that* one out!"

Drake grinned. "I'm damned if I do—not until after dinner. Jiggle that cocktail shaker, Della. I think it's full."

Chapter 5

Della Street stood by the entrance to the dining room watching Perry Mason with amused eyes as the lawyer was presented to Mrs. Roland Burr.

A woman would have placed Mrs. Burr in the thirties. A man would have made it somewhere in the twenties. Her hair was the color of reddish oat straw when the sun glints upon it at just the right angle to bring out the sheen. Her white gown, although far from conservative, was not daring in cut. It was the manner in which it clung to her body that assured her of the rapt attention of every man in the room.

As Drake was being presented to Mrs. Burr, Lois Witherspoon came in.

Compared with the lush beauty of Mrs. Burr's figure, Lois was girlishly athletic. Her dress was of a different type. Nor did she walk with the swaying, seductive rhythm which made Mrs. Burr's every action so noticeable. She moved swiftly with the natural verve of a dynamic young woman who is entirely free from self-consciousness. Her presence gave the room a wholesome freshness, and in some way flattened out the high-lights of Mrs. Burr's more seductive personality.

Della Street tried very much to keep in the background, watching what was going on with eyes which took in every move. But she was able to keep in the background only during the first part of the meal. Abruptly, Lois flung a question at her, and when Della's well-modulated voice answered that question, attention focused upon Mason's secretary, and somehow seemed to stay there.

"How's Roland coming along?" Witherspoon asked, abruptly.

That gave Mrs. Burr her opportunity to be the devoted wife. "I'd better take a peek and see," she said. "Excuse me, please," and she glided from the room, walking softly as if anxious not to interrupt their conversation—and as

30

though she were oblivious of the smooth swaying of her supple figure.

She was still out when the doorbell rang. Witherspoon summoned one of the Mexican servants. "That will be a nurse from El Templo," he said, "who's to relieve the nurse the doctor left in charge. You may take her directly to Mr. Burr's room."

The Mexican said in a low, musical voice, "Si, señor," and went to the door.

Mrs. Burr came gliding back. "Resting easily, the nurse says," she reported.

The Mexican servant returned, moved over to Witherspoon's chair, handed him a tray on which was an envelope. "For you, señor," he said.

"Wasn't that the nurse?" Witherspoon asked.

"No, señor. A man."

Witherspoon said, "Pardon me. We don't ordinarily have unexpected callers."

He slit the envelope open, read the brief note, looked across at Mason, and frowned. For a moment, he seemed on the point of saying something directly to the lawyer; then he said, "Excuse me, please. It's a man I'll have to see. Go right ahead with your coffee and brandy."

From outside the house, the barking of the dogs gradually quieted. There was a moment during which an awkward silence fell over the table; then Mrs. Burr asked Drake, "Are *you* interested in color photography, Mr. Drake?"

"He's a detective," Lois Witherspoon announced bluntly, "and *he's* here on business. So you won't have to beat around the bush."

"A detective! My, how interesting! Tell me, do you put on disguises and shadow people, or . . ."

"I live a very prosaic life," Drake said. "Most of the time I'm scared to death."

Mrs. Burr's eyes were naïvely innocent, but her face seemed carved of brittle chalk. She said, "Dear me, how interesting! First, one of the most noted attorneys in the country, and now a detective. I suppose, of course, there's some connection."

Drake glanced at Mason.

31

Mason looked directly at Mrs. Burr. "Purely financial, madam."

They all laughed, without knowing exactly what they were laughing at, but knowing that the tension had been broken and that the line of inquiry had been blocked—temporarily.

Abruptly Witherspoon appeared at the door. "Mr. Mason, I'd like very much to talk to you for a few moments, if the others will consent to spare you."

Witherspoon was a poor actor. His attempt at being casual and polite merely emphasized the apprehension of his voice and manner.

Mason pushed back his chair, made his excuses, and followed Witherspoon into a big drawing room.

A man of about fifty-five was standing with his back to them, studying a shelf of books, and quite apparently not even seeing the titles. It wasn't until Witherspoon spoke that he apparently realized they had entered the room. He turned quickly.

"Mr. Dangerfield," Witherspoon said, "this is Mr. Mason. Mr. Mason is an attorney who happens to be familiar with the matter about which you wished to talk. I'd like to have him hear what you were starting to tell me."

Dangerfield shook hands with Mason with the automatic courtesy of one acknowledging an introduction. He seemed completely preoccupied with his own worries as he mumbled, "Glad to meet you, Mr. Mason."

He was a chunky man of small stature, heavy set, but hard. There was no sag to his cheeks or his stomach. His back was straight as a board, and he kept his chin up, his head balanced alertly on a thick neck.

His eyes were dark, with a reddish brown tinge deep in the background. Worry lines were stamped on his forehead, and there was a gray look of fatigue about his skin, as though he hadn't slept the night before.

"Go right ahead," Witherspoon prompted. "Tell me what it was you wanted to see me about."

"About those detectives you hired," Dangerfield said.

Witherspoon glanced at Mason, saw only the lawyer's profile, cleared his throat, asked, "What detectives?"

"The detectives to investigate that old murder of David

Latwell. I was hoping it would be all over when they hung Horace Adams.''

"What's *your* interest in it?'' Mason asked.

Dangerfield hesitated for a perceptible instant. "I married David Latwell's widow.''

Witherspoon started to say something, but Mason interposed, quite matter-of-factly, "Indeed! I presume the murder was quite a shock to her.''

"It was. . . . Of course. Naturally.''

"But, of course,'' Mason went on, "she's entirely over it by now. How about a cigarette, Mr. Dangerfield?''

"Thank you.'' Dangerfield extended a hand to Mason's proffered cigarette case.

"We may as well all sit down,'' Mason said. "Nice of you to come out here, Dangerfield. You live in the East?''

"Yes. At the present time, we're living in St. Louis.''

"Oh, yes. Drive out?''

"Yes.''

"How did you find the roads?''

"Fine. We made a quick trip. Came through very fast. We've only been here a day or two.''

"Then you didn't get in today?''

"No.''

"Staying here in El Templo?''

"Yes. At the big hotel there.''

"Then I take it your wife's with you.''

"Yes.''

Mason held a match to Dangerfield's cigarette. He asked casually, "How did you learn that Mr. Witherspoon had hired any detectives?''

Dangerfield said, "People began to show up asking guarded questions. Some of our friends were interviewed. Well, Mrs. Dangerfield heard about it.

"The original affair was, of course, as you have pointed out, a great shock to her. Not only was there the shock of her husband's disappearance, but there was a period during which she thought he had run away with another woman; then the body was found, and then the trial took place. You know how it is with a trial of that sort. Everything is dug out and rehashed and aired, and the newspapers give it a lot of publicity.''

"And now?" Mason asked.

"By a little clever detective work on her own part, she discovered the detective who was working on the case was making reports to someone in El Templo. She didn't get that person's name."

"Do you know how she found out about the El Templo angle?"

"Generally. It was through a girl at the switchboard of a hotel where one of the detectives was stopping."

"How did you happen to come here—to this house?" Mason asked.

"I was a little more successful than my wife in getting information—because I started from a different angle."

"How is that?"

"I sat down in my armchair one night, and tried to figure out the *reason* why anyone would be making an investigation."

"And the reason?" Mason asked.

"Well, I wasn't certain, but I thought that it might be connected with Horace Adams' widow, or with his son. I knew that they had moved somewhere to California. I thought perhaps she had died, and someone wanted to straighten out property matters. There might have been an attempt to re-open the old probate of the manufacturing business."

"So you looked Mr. Witherspoon up?" Mason asked.

"Not in that way. As soon as we arrived in town, my wife tried to trace the detective. *I* started looking up Mrs. Horace Adams. Sure enough, I found just what I expected to find—that she had been living here, had died, and that her son was going with a rich El Templo girl. Then, of course, I put two and two together."

"But you didn't *know*," Mason said.

"As a matter of fact," Dangerfield admitted, "that's right. I ran a little bluff on Mr. Witherspoon here as soon as I came in. He convinced me I was on the right track."

"I didn't admit anything," Witherspoon said hastily.

Dangerfield smiled. "Perhaps not in just so many words."

"Why did you come here?" Mason asked.

"Don't you see? All my wife knows is that someone who lives in El Templo is trying to reopen the case. It worries her, and it's getting her emotionally excited. If she knows young Adams is here, she'll denounce him as a murderer's son. I don't want that, and you shouldn't. She thought hanging wasn't good enough for Horace Adams.''

"You knew her then, at the time of the trial?"

Dangerfield hesitated for only a moment, then said, "Yes."

"And I presume that you knew Horace Adams?"

"No. I'd never met him."

"Did you know David Latwell?"

"Well . . . I'd met him, yes."

"And what do you want *us* to do?" Mason asked.

"My wife will find out where the office of that detective agency is any day now. See what I'm getting at? I want you to see that she gets a runaround."

Witherspoon started to say something, but Mason silenced him with a warning glance.

"Exactly what do you want us to do?" Mason asked. "Can you be a little more specific?"

Dangerfield said, "Don't you get it? Sooner or later, she'll locate this detective agency and start making inquiries about the name of the client."

"The detective agency won't tell her," Witherspoon said positively.

"Then she'll find out the name of the detective who was working on the case, and get the information out of him, one way or another. Once she's started on this thing, she'll see it through. It's building up on her. She's getting intensely nervous. What I want you to do is to tip the detective agency off. Then, in place of refusing to give her information, they'll give her the information we both want her to have. We're really all in the same boat."

Witherspoon asked, "What information?"

"Tell her the client who employed them is an attorney. Give her his name. Let her go to him. He can give her a runaround with some likely stall, and she'll go back home and forget it."

"Think she will?" Mason asked.

"Yes."

"What's *your* interest in it?"

"I don't want my wife turned into a nervous wreck, for one thing. For another, I don't want to have a lot of publicity spread about regarding the business. My wife took over the business while it was in probate. We've slaved night and day building that business up. I've been advised by attorneys that in case fraud is present, together with duress and oppression, the statute of limitations won't begin to run until the discovery of the fraud.''

"And there was fraud?" Mason asked.

"How the hell do I know?" Dangerfield said. "Estelle made the deal in probate. I'm simply trying to forestall a bunch of lawsuits. I hope you won't take offense, but you know how it is. Some of these lawyers would do anything on earth to chisel in on a prosperous business such as we have.''

"Is it prosperous?" Mason asked.

"Very."

Mason looked at Witherspoon.

"You're the doctor," Witherspoon told him.

Mason got to his feet. "I think we understand each other perfectly," he said.

Dangerfield smiled. "I guess you understand me, but I'm not certain I understand you. I've given you information. What do I get in return?"

"Our assurance that we'll give it thoughtful consideration," Mason said.

Dangerfield got up and started for the door. "I guess that's about all I can expect," he announced, grinning.

Witherspoon said hurriedly, "Don't try to go out until I've had the night watchman secure the dogs.''

"What dogs?" Dangerfield asked.

"I have a couple of highly trained police dogs that patrol the grounds. That's why there was a delay about letting you in. The dogs have to be locked up before visitors go in or out.''

"Guess it's a good idea." Dangerfield said, "with things the way they are now. How do you take care of the dogs?''

Witherspoon pressed a button by the side of the door. He explained, "That is a signal to the watchman. When he gets this signal and sounds a buzzer, I'll know the dogs are tied up.''

They waited for not more than ten seconds; then the buzzer sounded. Witherspoon opened the door, said, "Good night, Mr. Dangerfield, and thank you very much.''

Dangerfield paused halfway to the gate, looked at Mason, and said, "I don't suppose I'm any closer to what I want to know than I was when I started, but I bet five bucks she doesn't get anything out of you."

With that he turned, walked through the heavy iron gate, and climbed in his car. The gate clanged shut. A spring lock snapped into position.

Witherspoon hurried back to press the button signalling the watchman that the dogs could be turned loose once more.

"What's the name of the detective agency?" Mason asked.

"The Allgood Detective Agency in Los Angeles, Raymond E. Allgood."

They started back toward the dining room. Mason turned abruptly to the left toward the wing of the building where his room was located.

"Aren't you going to finish your dinner?" Witherspoon asked in surprise.

"No," Mason said. "Tell Della Street and Paul Drake I want to see them. We're driving back to Los Angeles. But you *don't* need to tell Mrs. Burr."

"I'm afraid I don't understand," Witherspoon said.

Mason said, "I haven't time to explain now."

Witherspoon's face flushed. "I consider that answer unnecessarily short, Mr. Mason."

Mason's voice showed his weariness. "I didn't sleep any last night," he said. "I probably won't sleep much tonight. I haven't time to explain the obvious."

Witherspoon said with cold dignity. "May I remind you, Mr. Mason, that you are working for me?"

"May I remind you that I'm not?"

"You're not?"

"No."

"For whom are you working, then?"

Mason said, "I'm working for a blind woman. They carve her image on courthouses. She has a pair of scales in one hand and a sword in the other. They call her 'Justice,' and she's the one I'm working for, right at the moment." And Mason swung on down the left corridor, leaving Witherspoon to stand staring at him, puzzled, and more than a little angry.

He was throwing things into his suitcase when Della Street and Paul Drake joined him.

"I should have known this was too good to last," Drake complained.

"You'll probably be back," Mason told him. "Get your things together."

Della Street opened the drawer in the big writing desk, said abruptly, "Look here, Chief."

"What is it?" Mason asked.

"Someone's opened the drawer and moved the transcript."

"Taken it?" Mason asked.

"No, just moved it—must have been reading it."

"Anybody leave the dining room while I was out there with Witherspoon?" Mason asked.

"Yes," Drake said. "Young Adams."

Mason pushed the lid of his suitcase into place by simply compressing the contents until the lock would snap shut. He said, "Don't worry about it, Della. It's in Paul's department. *He's* the detective."

Drake said, "I'd only need one guess."

"It would take me *two*," Mason announced, jerking his light overcoat out of the closet.

Chapter 6

Mason paused in front of the door which contained on the frosted glass the printed legend, "ALLGOOD DETECTIVE AGENCY, RAYMOND E. ALLGOOD, MANAGER, *Connections in All Principal Cities*." Down below in the extreme right-hand corner was the word "Entrance."

Mason pushed open the door. A blonde who looked fully as dazzling off the screen as most of the picture stars do on it, looked up at him with appraising eyes and smiled. "Good morning. Whom did you wish to see?"

"Mr. Allgood."

"Did you have an appointment?"

"No."

"I'm afraid he's . . ."

"Tell him Perry Mason is here," Mason said.

Her blue eyes widened as the eyebrows lifted. "You mean Mr. Mason—the lawyer?"

"Yes."

She said, "Right away, Mr. Mason, if you'll wait just a moment please."

She whirled toward a switchboard, picked up a line, started to plug it in, hesitated a moment, thought better of it, got up from her chair, said, "Just a moment, please," and walked into an inner office. Some few moments later, she was back, holding the door open. "Right this way, Mr. Mason. Mr. Allgood will see you now."

Raymond E. Allgood was a middle-aged man with deep lines in his face and bushy eyebrows. Eyeglasses were pinched on his nose, and from them dangled a black ribbon. He was virtually bald save for a fringe of cinnamon-colored hair which circled his ears. He seemed both flattered and uneasy.

"Good morning, Counselor," he said, arising to shake

hands. "This is indeed a pleasure. I've heard a great deal about you. I am hoping that my agency can be of service."

Mason dropped into a chair, crossed his long legs, took out a cigarette, tapped it on the arm of his chair, and studied the man behind the desk.

"Wouldn't you like a cigar?" Allgood asked hospitably, opening a humidor.

"A cigarette suits me."

Allgood nervously clipped the end from a cigar, scraped a match on the underside of his desk, lit the cigar, and shifted his position in the creaking swivel chair. "Is there something I can do for you?" he asked hopefully.

Mason said, "I quite frequently use a detective agency. So far, the Drake Detective Agency has taken care of all of my work."

"Yes, yes, I understand, but there are, of course, times when you need some supplemental investigation. Is there something in particular you had in mind, Mr. Mason?"

"Yes," Mason said. "You did some work for a Mr. John L. Witherspoon of Red River Valley."

Allgood cleared his throat, raised his hand to adjust his glasses on his nose. "Ahem—of course, you understand we can't discuss our clients."

"You've been discussing this one."

"What do you mean?"

"There's been a leak."

Allgood said positively, "Not from *this* office."

Mason merely nodded, his steady eyes impaling the detective.

Allgood twitched slightly in his chair, shifted his position, and the creaking springs of the swivel chair announced his uneasiness.

"May I—may I ask what is your interest in the matter?"

"Witherspoon's my client."

"Oh."

"There's been a leak," Mason went on. "I don't want any more leaks, and I want to find out about this one."

"Are you quite certain you're not mistaken?"

"Quite."

Again the chair creaked.

Mason gave the other no respite from the accusation of his steady eyes.

Allgood cleared his throat, said, "I'll be frank with you, Mr. Mason. I had a man in my employ, a Leslie Milter. Something may have come from him."

"Where is he now?"

"I don't know. I've discharged him."

"Why did you discharge him?"

"He . . . didn't perform his work satisfactorily."

"After he'd completed the Witherspoon investigation?"

"Yes."

"He made a good job of that, didn't he?"

"So far as I know."

"And what happened afterwards?"

"He simply wasn't satisfactory, Mr. Mason."

Mason seemed to settle himself more firmly in the chair. "Why did you fire him, Allgood?"

"He talked."

"What about?"

"The Witherspoon case."

"To whom?"

"I don't know. It wasn't my fault. Witherspoon confided in him too much. A man who uses a detective agency is foolish to tell the men who are working just what he's after. It's better for him to have his dealings with the manager and let the manager pass on the instructions."

"Witherspoon didn't do that?"

"No. Witherspoon was too anxious. He wanted to get daily reports. He arranged with Milter to ring him up on long distance every night around eight o'clock, and tell him generally what had been discovered. That's characteristic of Witherspoon. He's had his own way too much. He gets too impatient. He can't wait. He wants everything right now."

"Did Milter make any money out of talking?" Mason asked.

"I'm hanged if I can tell you, Mr. Mason."

"What's your best guess?"

Allgood tried to get away from Mason's eyes, and failed. He squirmed around in the squeaking chair, said, "I think he—may be trying to. Damn him!"

"What's his address?"

"The last address *I* had was the Wiltmere Apartments."

"Married or single?"

"Single, but . . . well, in a way, attached."

"How old?"

"Thirty-two."

"Good-looking?"

"Women think so."

"Likes to play around?"

Allgood nodded.

Mason jerked his head in the outer office. "How about the girl at the desk?"

Allgood said hastily, "Oh, I'm certain there's nothing there, nothing at all."

"Can you trust her?"

"Oh, absolutely."

"She's been with you for some time?"

"A couple of years."

Mason said, "What can you do to keep Milter quiet?"

"I'd like to know myself."

Mason got up and said, "You're a hell of a detective."

"After all," Allgood said, "you can't sew a man's lips shut—not after you've fired him."

"A really clever detective could."

"Well, I . . . I'd never thought of it that way."

"Think of it that way now, then."

Allgood cleared his throat. The chair gave a final loud squeak as he pushed it back and got to his feet. "I take it Mr. Witherspoon would be willing to compensate me . . ."

"You're doing this for *your* protection," Mason told him. "It doesn't look good to have a leak come through a detective agency."

"Well, really, Mr. Mason, there's very little one can do. These things happen. You know how some of these men are. They're here today and gone tomorrow. As I say, Witherspoon shouldn't have confided in the man."

"He was in your employ," Mason said. "Witherspoon hired you. You hired Milter. It's your funeral."

"I don't see any corpse," Allgood said with a show of feeling.

"You might find one in your closet when you apply for a renewal of your license."

"I'll see what can be done, Mr. Mason."

"Right away," Mason told him.

"I'll get right at it, yes."

"Immediately," Mason pointed out.

"Well, I . . . er . . . yes."

Mason said, "A Mrs. Dangerfield is going to show up and ask you questions. Let her worm it out of you that I employed you. Don't mention Witherspoon's name."

"You can trust me absolutely on anything like that. I'll handle her personally. You want her referred to you?"

"Yes."

"And I'm to let her worm the information out of me?"

"Yes."

"Very well."

"Keep her away from Milter."

"I'll do my best."

"Do you talk business matters over with the girl in your outer office?"

"Sometimes. She keeps the books."

"Does she ever do any work for you—on cases?"

"No."

Mason said, "Don't tell her anything about me."

He picked up his hat, looked at his wrist watch, said, "Don't wait until afternoon to get Milter shut up. Start on it now."

Allgood said, "I'll try to get something on him. I know a woman . . . an Alberta Cromwell. She claims to be his wife. She might—yes, I'll try. . . . Perhaps I can . . . There's an angle there." His hand moved toward the lever of the inter-office communicating system.

Mason left the office. The girl at the desk smiled sweetly at him, said, "Good morning, Mr. Mason," in a cooing voice. Mason stopped at a phone booth in the lobby of the building, and called the Drake Detective Agency.

"Mason talking, Paul. There's a blonde working out at Allgood's Detective Agency at the desk. You won't have any trouble spotting her; about twenty-five, the sort that people tell it's a shame she isn't on the screen. A dead-pan baby with big eyes, red lips and curves. Get on her tail as she leaves the Allgood office. Stay on her. Put a man on Leslie Milter at the Wiltmere Apartments."

43

"What does Milter do?" Drake asked.

"He's a detective."

"He won't be easy to tail."

"Why not?"

"He'll get wise the minute we put a shadow on him."

"Let him get wise," Mason said. "What do we care, just so we sew him up. Put two shadows on him. As far as I'm concerned, give him the works."

"I'll get some men on it right away," Drake said.

"The blonde comes first," Mason told him, "and if she goes out to the Wiltmere Apartments, I want to know it."

"Okay, where will you be?"

"I'll keep in touch with the office. You pass any news on to Della. You've got men on that old case?"

"Yes. I put them on the job by wire from Indio."

"Okay," Mason said. "The more I think of it, the less I like the way that case was handled. All this chivalry about keeping the name of the woman out of the case and referring to her as Miss X—I want the dope on Miss X. I want everything, name, address, love life, past and present. Then I'll predict her future."

"We're working on it," Drake said.

"Here's something else, Paul."

"What?"

"Bribe some Los Angeles reporter into sending a telegraphic tip to the Winterburg papers. Think you can fix it up?"

"Okay. I think so. What's the tip?"

"Get your stenographer on an extension line to take it down as I dictate."

He heard Drake say, "Oh, Ruth, get on the extension. Take down what's said. . . . Yeah, it's Mason. You all set? . . . Okay, Perry, go ahead. Don't talk too fast."

Mason said, "It'll run something like this: 'With the employment of Leslie L. Milter, a high-priced Los Angeles detective, to investigate a murder case which centered in Winterburg some twenty years ago, an old mystery bids fair to be cleaned up. It has long been a question in the minds of some persons as to whether the guilt of Horace Legg Adams, who was executed for the murder of David Latwell, was clearly established at the time of his trial. . . . Recently new

off to company aren't apt to make good sons-in-law. Don't say we didn't tell you, Papa.

Mason studied the clipping thoughtfully, said to Della, "Run down the hallway to the Drake Detective Agency, and see if Paul Drake would know anything about what paper this came from."

Della Street took the clipping, stood for a moment, turning it over in her fingers, said, "This is plain blackmail, isn't it?"

"I don't know," Mason said.

She said suddenly, "Wait a minute. I know what paper this is."

"What?"

"It's a little Hollywood scandal sheet. I've seen some copies. There was some veiled stuff in there about some of the movie stars."

"What is it, a newspaper?"

"No, not exactly. It's handled as a quiz test. Whom does the shoe fit and can you put it on the right foot? Look over here on the reverse side of this clipping. You can see the way it's handled."

Della Street indicated a paragraph which read,

Some 240 of our subscribers put the right shoe on the right foot of the movie star to whom we referred in our last week's column, the one who thought it would be a swell idea to give a marijuana party. It just goes to show how these things get around.

Mason jerked his head toward the telephone. "Give Paul's office a ring. If he's in, ask him if he can come down here for a second or two. I want to talk with him about this, and about Miss X."

Della put through the call, said, "He'll be here in just a moment," hung up the receiver, and asked, "You think Miss X is the missing link?"

Mason pushed his hands down deep in his trousers pockets. "Of course, Della, I'm always suspicious of district attorneys."

"And they're always suspicious of you, eh?" she said.

Mason acknowledged the point by grinning. "Now, in this case," he said, "the district attorney, according to the newspapers, reached an agreement with the defendant's lawyer by which it was stipulated that the young woman whose name had been used by the defendant as the person with whom the murdered man was supposed to have run away could be referred to throughout the case as Miss X. That's the biggest single blunder the lawyer who handled that case made."

"Why?"

Mason said, "Because it was the same as a public admission on the part of the lawyer that he didn't believe in his own client. Remember, Adams told the police Latwell had said he was going to run away with this Miss X. Then when they found Latwell's body buried under the cellar floor in the factory, the police adopted the position that this must have been a lie. The stipulation entered into by Adams' attorney indicates that *he* thought so, too. At least, it looked that way to the jury."

Della Street nodded slowly.

Mason said, "Now that's one thing about the case I can't understand. The logical move would have been for the district attorney to have introduced those initial statements in evidence, then called the woman mentioned in those statements and had her deny that she'd ever had any such conversation with Latwell."

"Well," Della Street asked, "why didn't he?"

"For one thing, this stipulation made it unnecessary," Mason said. "When Adams' attorney stipulated that the woman could be kept out of the case and referred to only as Miss X, it made the jury think that both the district attorney and Adams' lawyer knew he'd been lying. Now suppose he hadn't been lying? Suppose Latwell actually had intended to run away with this girl? See what an interesting vista of possibilities *that* opens up?"

"But wouldn't she have had to admit to the district attorney that . . ."

"There's nothing to indicate she ever talked with the district attorney or that he ever talked with her," Mason said. "She . . ."

Knuckles tapped a code signal on the door of Mason's private office.

48

"That's Drake," Mason said. "Let him in."

Paul Drake was carrying half a dozen telegrams as he entered the office. "Well, we're gradually getting somewhere, Perry."

Mason said, "Give me yours first, and then I'll give you mine."

"Milter isn't at the Wiltmere Apartments. I'll give you one guess as to where he is."

Mason raised his eyebrows. "El Templo?"

"Right."

"How long's he been there?"

"Four or five days."

"Where?"

"In an apartment house at eleven sixty-two Cinder Butte Avenue. It's a frame two-story that was turned into an apartment house—on the order of a furnished flat. There are four in the building. You know the type. Two upstairs, two down, four private entrances."

"Interesting," Mason said.

"Isn't it? Now I'll tell you something else. A young woman by the name of Alberta Cromwell claims to be his wife. She followed him down to El Templo, found the apartment next to his vacant, and rented it."

"He know she's there?" Mason asked.

"I don't see why not. Her name's on the mailbox, Alberta Cromwell."

"Why didn't she go down with him?"

"Darned if I know."

Mason handed the envelope and clipping across to Drake. "This came by special-delivery mail a few minutes ago."

Drake started to read the clipping, then lowered it to say, "I haven't given it all to you yet. The blonde in Allgood's office sneaked down to a drugstore to put in a call from a telephone booth. My operative got in the booth next to her and could hear the conversation. Guess what?"

"I'll bite. What?"

"She was ringing up the Pacific Greyhound stages to make a reservation on a five-thirty stage for El Templo."

Mason's eyes sparkled. "I want her tailed, Paul."

"Don't worry. My operative got a reservation on the same bus. What *is* this?"

49

"Looks like a blackmail clipping. Read it."

Drake read it, then puckered his lips in a whistle. "That's Milter, all right."

"I don't get it," Mason said.

"What do you mean, you don't get it?"

"I just don't understand it, that's all."

Drake said, "Gosh, Perry, it's simple as A.B.C. The All-good Agency is just so-so. It hires any old tramp that knows the ropes, and will do the work. Milter had his palm out. When Witherspoon asked for daily reports by telephone, he tipped his hand. Milter decided to move in on the blackmail racket."

"Blackmailing him for what?" Mason asked.

"To keep the dope about that case from becoming public."

Mason shook his head. "Witherspoon wouldn't pay out money to keep that hushed up."

"He would if his daughter was going to marry the guy."

Mason thought that over for a few minutes, then shook his head. "He wouldn't pay to hush it up—not *before* the marriage."

"Then that's what Milter's waiting for," Drake said. "For the marriage to take place. He's down there marking time."

Mason said, "That's logical, but if that's the case, why would he have given out that information to this scandal sheet?"

Paul said, "Milter must have got paid for the tip-off."

"How much?" Mason asked.

"I don't know," Drake said. "This is an outfit that's started up in Hollywood within the last four or five months. It dishes out authentic bits of scandal. The guy who's running the thing has a good nose for news, but he isn't trying to black-mail the individual. He's trying to blackmail the industry. That's why it's impossible to get anything on him."

"You mean he wants to make them buy him out?" Mason asked.

"That's right. He goes ahead and publishes things about the big shots in Hollywood without ever giving them a tip-off or trying to make a shakedown. In that way, they can't get anything on him. He's let it be known that his paper and its good will are for sale. The price, of course, is about a thousand times what it's worth, except to put a muzzle on it."

Mason glanced at his wrist watch, said, "Ring Witherspoon in El Templo, Della, and tell him he's going to have guests tonight."

"Me too?" Drake asked.

Mason shook his head. 'You stay here and keep on the job, trying to find out something about Miss X. Hang it, I can't get the slant on Milter."

"You don't think he's simply sitting down there waiting for the wedding to take place, and then moving in on Witherspoon?"

Mason tapped the clipping. "This *must* have come from a leak from Allgood's office. That leak seems to have been traced definitely to Milter. Milter is in El Templo. If he's there to blackmail Witherspoon *after* the wedding, why should he jeopardize his entire position by selling something like this for pin money to a Hollywood blackmail sheet? That's calculated to stop the wedding."

Drake thought that over for a moment, then said, "When you put it that way, there's only one logical solution."

"What's that?"

"Milter is down there marking time, waiting for the wedding to take place so he can put the screws on Witherspoon. That accounts for Milter. This scandal-sheet business is something else. It's an entirely separate angle."

Mason said, "It's someone who's darn close to the home plate, Paul. He knows about Witherspoon having retained me. He knows about the drowning duck. That's something Witherspoon doesn't even know about."

"I don't even know about it myself," Drake said. "What is it, a gag?"

"No. A scientific experiment. Marvin Adams performed it a few nights ago in front of Witherspoon's guests. Witherspoon wasn't there."

"How did he make the duck drown?" Paul asked. "Hold him under water?"

"No. He didn't touch him."

"Are you kidding me?"

"No. It's on the level."

51

Drake said abruptly, "You're going to El Templo tonight. Are you going to bust in on Milter?"

Mason gave the question thoughtful consideration. "I think I am."

"He may be a tough customer," Drake warned.

Mason said, "I might be tough myself. If you get anything on that Miss X business, give me a ring. I'll be down at Witherspoon's."

"How late do you want me to call you?"

"Whenever you get the information," Mason said, "call me. Now matter how late it is. And tell your shadow who's following that blond from Allgood's office to call me direct at Witherspoon's house and let me know where she goes when she gets there. That'll save time. Otherwise, he'd have to call the office and report to you, and then you'd have to call me."

"It'll only mean a matter of minutes," Drake said.

"Minutes may be precious. Let your operative report directly to me."

Drake grinned. "That's the mistake Witherspoon made."

Mason picked up some papers, pushed them into a brief case, and strapped the brief case closed.

"It may turn out to have been Milter's mistake," he said. "See if you can get a line on this Hollywood scandal sheet, Paul. It's important to find out if this information came through Milter."

"Okay, I'll see what I can do and let you know. I think I know someone who can give me the real low-down on that."

Mason said, "I can promise you one thing. If Milter sold that information to the scandal sheet, the whole thing is cockeyed. It just doesn't add up to give the correct answer."

Drake stood frowning down at the special-delivery envelope. "By gosh," he admitted, "it doesn't!"

Chapter 8

Mason jingled the bell on the huge iron gate. The deep-throated barking of big dogs drowned out the sound of the bell. A moment later, the dogs were at the gate, fangs bared, eyes gleaming yellow reflections of car headlights.

A light clicked on the porch. A Mexican came hurrying across the flagged walk, said, "Who is it, please?" and then recognized Mason and Della Street.

"Oh, yes. Uno momento. Wait, please."

He turned and darted back into the house.

The dogs withdrew some four or five feet, watchful yellow eyes staring at the pair.

Witherspoon himself came hurrying out of the house. "Well, well, I'm glad to see you. I certainly am! Get back, King. Get back, Prince. Tie them up, Manuel."

"We haven't time for that," Mason said. "Just open the gate. They know we're all right."

Witherspoon looked at the dogs dubiously.

"They won't hurt us," Mason insisted. "Open up."

Witherspoon nodded to the Mexican, who fitted a big key to the huge iron lock in the gate, shot back the bolt, and pulled the gate open.

The dogs came rushing forward.

Mason pushed through the gate, calmly ignoring the dogs, and shook hands with Witherspoon.

The dogs meanwhile moved back to sniff stiffly at Della Street. She extended the tips of her fingers with careless unconcern.

Witherspoon was nervously apprehensive. "Come on," he said. "Come on in. Let's not stay out here. These dogs are savage."

They started toward the house, the dogs falling in behind.

Witherspoon held the door open. "Damnedest thing I ever saw," he said.

53

"What?"

"The dogs. They should have chewed you up. They don't make friends that quickly."

"They have sense," Mason said. "Let's go where we can talk—privately."

Witherspoon led the way into the house.

"Our suitcases are in the car," Mason said.

"Manuel will bring them in. You'll have the same rooms you had yesterday."

Witherspoon led the way into the northeast wing, opened the door of Mason's sitting room, and stood to one side.

Mason followed Della Street in. Witherspoon came in after them, and Mason kicked the door shut.

Witherspoon said, "I'm certainly glad you showed up. There's an important . . ."

Mason said, "Forget it. Sit down in that chair and give me the low-down on this detective. Talk fast."

"What detective?"

"Leslie Milter, the one who's been blackmailing you."

"Milter blackmailing *me*!" Witherspoon exclaimed incredulously. "Mason, you're crazy!"

"You know him, don't you?"

"Why, yes. He's the detective who made the investigation of the murder. He works for Allgood."

"You've seen him?"

"Yes. He made a report to me in person once; but that was after he had completed his investigations in the East."

"You were in touch with him by long distance during the time he was making that investigation?"

"Yes. He telephoned me every night."

Mason stared down at Witherspoon and said, "Either you're lying to me, or everything is cockeyed."

"I'm not lying," Witherspoon said with cold dignity, "and I'm not accustomed to be accused of lying."

Mason said, "Milter is in El Templo."

"Is that so? I haven't seen him since that one time when he made his report."

"And haven't heard from him?" Mason asked.

"Not within the last ten days. Not since he completed his investigations."

Mason took from his pocket the special-delivery envelope

54

which he had received that afternoon. "Does this mean anything to you?" he asked.

Witherspoon regarded the envelope with an air of detached curiosity. "No."

Mason said, "Open it and read what's inside."

Witherspoon pressed the edges of the envelope together and looked inside. "Seems to be nothing in it except a newspaper clipping," he said.

"Read it," Mason ordered.

Witherspoon scissored two fingers of his right hand so as to draw out the clipping. He held it so the light struck it, but before starting to read, said, "I think we can dispense with a lot of this, Mr. Mason. Something developed this evening that . . ."

"Read it," Mason interrupted.

Witherspoon flushed. For a moment he seemed on the point of throwing both envelope and clipping to the floor; then under the steady pressure of Mason's eyes, he started reading.

Mason watched his face.

Apparently it took the first few lines to get Witherspoon's interest sufficiently aroused so that he was conscious of what he was reading. A few words more and the full import of the words struck him. His face twisted into a black scowl. His eyes, moving rapidly back and forth, finished the printed words. He looked up at Mason with a face gone grim and hard. "The swine! The *dirty* swine! To think that any man could stoop so low as to publish a thing like that. How did you get it?"

"In that envelope," Mason said. "Sent special delivery. Do you know anything about it?"

"What do you mean by that?"

"Have you any idea who sent it?"

"Certainly not."

"Know where it was published?"

"No. Where?"

"In a Hollywood scandal sheet."

Witherspoon said, "I've tried to be fair. That's where I've made my biggest mistake. I should have stopped this thing instantly. As soon as I found out about that murder."

"Do you mean," Mason asked, "that you wish now you

had gone to your daughter with all this? Do you mean you would have wrecked her happiness and stirred up all this old scandal, without first making any investigation to find out whether Horace Adams' conviction was justified?''

''That's exactly what I mean,'' Witherspoon said. ''I should have realized that the verdict of that jury was conclusive.''

''You have more confidence in juries than I have,'' Mason retorted. ''And I have a lot more confidence in juries than I have in judges. Human beings are always fallible. However, let's forget that for the moment and talk about blackmail.''

Witherspoon said solemnly, ''No man on earth could blackmail me.''

''Not even if he had something on you?''

Witherspoon shook his head. ''I wouldn't ever place myself in such a position. Can't you see? That's one reason why this whole proposed marriage is absolutely impossible.''

Mason seemed trying to control a growing impatience. ''Let's get this straight,'' he said. ''You employed the All-good Detective Agency to check up on this murder case. Leslie L. Milter was their representative. Apparently he's in El Templo right at this moment, living at eleven sixty-two Cinder Butte Avenue. He's logically the one who gave the information to the columnist who spewed out this scandal column. The Allgood Agency kicked him out for talking. That means he must have talked to someone. The columnist sounds like the most logical bet.''

''I'm distressed and annoyed to find that he wasn't trustworthy,'' Witherspoon said with dignity. ''He seemed very efficient.''

''Distressed!'' Mason all but shouted. ''Annoyed! Dammit, the man's a blackmailer! He's down here for the purposes of blackmail! Who's he blackmailing? Who *would* he be blackmailing, if not you?''

''I don't know.''

Mason said, ''Witherspoon, if you're holding out on me, I'll walk out on this case so fast . . .''

''But I'm *not* holding out on you. I'm telling you the absolute truth.''

Mason said to Della Street, ''Rush through a call to Paul

56

Drake. Tell him we've arrived. He may have something new. This thing's all cockeyed."

Mason started pacing the floor.

Witherspoon said, "I've been trying, ever since you arrived, to tell you about a most significant development. We've caught young Marvin Adams red-handed."

"Doing what?" Mason asked, continuing to pace the floor and flinging the question over his shoulder as though it had to do with a matter of minor importance.

"Being cruel to animals—at least, that's a fair inference . . . and it explains something in that newspaper clipping."

"What did he do?" Mason asked.

"He's going to Los Angeles tonight."

"I know that. I understand he's returning to college."

"He took Lois out to dinner tonight. He didn't want to eat at the house."

"So what?"

Witherspoon said irritably, "Let *me* tell it."

"Go ahead and tell it then."

Witherspoon went on, a mantle of injured dignity wrapped around him. "Marvin was out in the compound this afternoon where we keep the livestock, rabbits, chickens, and ducks. There was a mother duck and a brood of ducklings. As I get the story from the Mexican attendant, Marvin said he wanted one of the young ducks for an experiment. He said he wanted to drown him."

Mason stopped pacing the floor. "Was Lois with him?"

"That's my understanding."

"What did Lois say?"

"That's the absolutely incredible thing about the whole business. In place of being revolted, Lois helped him catch one of the ducklings and told him to take it along with him."

"You've talked to Lois about it?"

"No, I haven't. I made up my mind that she'd have to know. It's time to tell her the whole thing."

"Why don't you tell her then?"

Witherspoon said, "I've been putting it off."

"Why?"

"I think you can understand why."

Mason said, "Probably because your judgment is better than your emotions. You go to your daughter with the story the way you have it now, and she'll either sympathize with Marvin or become violently partisan, and turn against you. The girl's in love. You can't run Marvin down to her unless you have some absolute proof.''

''His father was convicted of murder.''

''I don't think *she'll* care a hoot about that,'' Mason said. ''She'll simply take the position that his father was innocent. But what will happen to Marvin when he finds out?''

''I don't care what happens to him,'' Witherspoon said.

''You might feel differently about it if he committed suicide.''

Witherspoon's face changed expression as he turned that idea over in his mind. Abruptly he said, ''I think the only thing to do is make my daughter see him in his true light.''

''When did you see him last?'' Mason asked.

''He drove away from here not over half an hour before you came.''

''Where was the duckling?''

''Apparently in the car with him.''

''Does young Adams own this car?'' Mason asked, looking at his watch.

''No. It's one that belongs to a friend of his—a boy who's attending junior college here. They shouldn't permit junk like that on the roads. It's completely disreputable.''

''Does Lois ride with him?''

''Yes. That's another thing I can't understand. She seems to think it's fun. The windshield is cracked. The springs in the seat cushions are broken. . . . Damn it, he's got her hypnotized!''

''Not hypnotized,'' Mason said. ''She's in love. That's worse—or better.''

Della Street said, ''Here's Paul Drake on the phone.''

Mason scooped the receiver to his ear. ''Hello. . . . Hello, Paul. This is Perry. We're here at Witherspoon's. What's new?''

Drake said, ''Things are coming along. You'll probably hear from my operative in El Templo in a few minutes. He called me from one of the stage stops about an hour ago, and said that the blonde had put through a call to Milter. He's expecting her. We're still working on that case in the East. I think we've found out who Miss X is. That is, we have her

58

name and identity, but haven't located her as yet. She was a cashier in a sweet shop when the murder was committed. Sure you don't want me to shut off calls after midnight?''

Mason said, ''Call me just as soon as you get information. I don't care what time it is.''

''Okay, stick around and you'll be hearing from that El Templo operative.''

''You're sure about Milter, Paul—that he's here in El Templo?''

''Positive. We've checked on him.''

''Let's get that address straight. He's living at eleven sixty-two Cinder Butte Avenue?''

''That's right. It's a big frame house that's been turned into four apartments. Milter has the one in the upper right-hand corner.''

''Okay. Call me if anything turns up.''

Mason hung up, turned to Witherspoon, and said, ''Milter's living here in El Templo, has been for days—and is here now.''

''He hasn't even tried to get in touch with me. He most certainly hasn't tried to blackmail me.''

Mason's eyes narrowed. ''How about Lois? That kid have any money in her own name?''

''Not until she's . . . wait a minute. Yes, she has, too. She's twenty-one now. Her birthday was a week ago. Yes, she has the money that was left in her mother's estate.''

''How much?''

''Rather a considerable sum.''

''How much?''

''Fifty thousand dollars.''

''All right,'' Mason said grimly, ''*that's* your answer.''

''You mean that he's blackmailing Lois?''

''Yes.''

''But Lois doesn't know anything about that murder case.''

''The kid's a damn good little actress,'' Mason said. ''Don't you ever kid yourself that a man of Leslie Milter's caliber is going to pass up a chance of that sort. Come to think of it, he wouldn't tackle you, except as a last resort, anyway. You're a tough bird, and you don't give a damn whether the scandal in connection with that murder case comes out—not until after Marvin Adams becomes your son-in-law; then, and only then, would you pay money to hush it up. Wait a minute. Marvin and your daughter weren't planning on doing anything sudden, were they?"

"What do you mean?"

"Running away and getting married?"

"She wants to announce her engagement and be married next month. I believe I told you he's going into the Army when he graduates in June, and . . ."

"I know," Mason said, "but next month is three weeks away. If Milter were planning blackmail for next month, he wouldn't be waiting around here now, where you might run into him on the street. No, that bird has sunk his fangs into someone right now, and is bleeding him white—or getting ready to."

Witherspoon said angrily, "If Lois is taking the money her mother left her, and paying it to some blackmailer in order to keep the facts about this young cad from . . ."

"Wait a minute," Mason interrupted. "You've put your finger on something. To keep the facts from being what?"

"Made public," Witherspoon said.

Mason shook his head. "I don't think so. She'd pay money to keep *you* from finding out the facts, but . . . wait a minute. *That* must be the angle. Milter must have given her the low-down, without letting her know that you know anything about it. He's threatening to go to you with the facts, unless she kicks through with some dough to buy his silence."

"Do you mean she's paid him money to . . ."

"Not yet," Mason said. "He's still here. Once he gets the dough, he'll get out. He may be closing the deal but he hasn't got it completely closed—not yet. I presume there was some legal red tape to unwind before Lois got that inheritance. Where is she?"

"I don't know. She went out."

"I want to talk to her just as soon as she comes in."

Witherspoon said, "If that man tries to blackmail Lois, I'll . . ."

Mason interrupted him. "Take a lawyer's advice, Witherspoon, and quit that habit of mentioning the things you'll do. . . . It looks as though Milter were the key to the whole business. I'm going to have an interview with Mr. Milter.

When I get done with him, he'll be sneaking out of town with his tail between his legs.''

''I'll go along with you,'' Witherspoon said. ''When I think of Lois getting into the clutches of a blackmailer . . . *I'm* going to see him.''

''Not with me, you aren't. There won't be any witnesses to *this* interview. You don't wear kid gloves when you're dealing with a blackmailer. Della, stay here and hold the fort. If Paul Drake telephones any information, make a note of it.''

''How about that girl from the detective agency?'' Della Street asked. ''She was on her way down here on the bus, and . . .''

Mason looked at his watch. ''She should have arrived— unless the bus was late. That's fine! I'll have a chance to talk to both of them together.''

Witherspoon darted out of the door. ''The dogs,'' he said. ''Wait here a few seconds, until I can get those damn dogs tied up.''

Mason looked at his watch. ''That bus should be here by now—won't that blonde be glad to see *me* come walking in!''

Chapter 9

Mason sent his car skimming along the desert highway. The lights of El Templo showed as a halo beneath steady, unwinking stars. The speedometer needle quivered around the seventy mark.

An irregularity in the road sent the car into a slight sway. Mason straightened it out and slowed his speed. Again a slight dip in the road swung the rear end over. This time, after Mason straightened the car out, he slowed to thirty miles an hour, deliberately twisted the wheel.

The rear of the car gave a wide swing.

Mason took his foot off the throttle, was careful not to use the brakes, swung over to the side of the road. Just before he reached the shoulder, he heard the unmistakable *thump-ker-thumpety-thump, thump-ker-thumpety-thump* of a flat tire.

It was the right rear tire. Mason looked at it ruefully, took off his coat, folded it, and tossed it on the back of the front seat. He rolled up his sleeves, removed the ignition key from the lock, took a flashlight from the glove compartment, and walked to the rear of the car, where he unlocked and opened the trunk. His suitcases, as well as those of Della Street, were in the trunk. He had to remove them, and then rummage around, finding the tools with which to make the tire change. With the aid of his flashlight, he assembled the bumper jack, got it into place, and started jacking the car up.

He saw headlights in the distance behind him, headlights that came swooping down the long, straight stretch of road at high speed.

As Mason raised the car so the flat tire was clearing the ground, he heard the whine of the tires on the other car, the sound of the motor; then, with a roar, the car swept on past, the current of wind created by its passage causing the jacked-up car to sway slightly on its springs. Mason watched the tail

62

light vanishing into the distance at a rate of speed which he estimated must have been around eighty.

Mason got out the lug wrench, pried off the hub cap, got off the flat tire, and dragged the spare tire out from the trunk.

He rolled the wheel into position, lifted it, got it fitted on the lugs, and completed the chore of carefully tightening them and put the hub cap back into position. Then he released the jack, got the tools back into the trunk, and then had to replace the various bags and suitcases before he could get under way once more.

He found the address he wanted without much difficulty. Milter had not even bothered to assume an alias, but a printed section torn from a business card and placed in the little holder over the doorbell said simply, "Leslie L. Milter."

Mason rang the doorbell twice. There was no response. He pounded on the door.

He heard the sound of steps on the stairs to his left. The door opened. A young, attractive brunette in a rakish hat and glossy fur coat started across the porch, saw him standing there, hesitated a moment, then turned for a frankly curious appraisal.

The lawyer smiled and raised his hat.

She answered his smile. "I don't think he's in."

"You haven't any idea where I might find him?"

"No. I haven't." She laughed slightly and said, "I hardly know him. I have the apartment which adjoins his. Several people have been in to see him tonight—quite a procession. You weren't—didn't have an appointment?"

Mason reached a prompt decision. "If he isn't home," he said, "there's no use of my waiting." He peered at the name card on her doorbell. "You must be Miss Alberta Cromwell—if, as you say, you live in the adjoining apartment. I have a car here, Miss Cromwell, perhaps I can drop you somewhere?"

"No, thanks. It's only a block to the main street."

Mason said, "I rather expected Mr. Milter to be home. I understood he was expecting someone to call, that he had an appointment."

Her eyes flashed a quick glance at him. "A young lady?"

Mason said cautiously, "I wouldn't know. I only understood that he had an appointment and that I would find him at home.''

''I think there was a young woman called, and I saw a man leaving the house shortly before you came up. I thought at first the man had rung my bell. I was in the kitchen with some water running, and I certainly thought I heard my bell ring.''

She laughed, an embarrassed little laugh which showed how nervous she was.

''I pressed the buzzer for my visitor to come up. Nothing happened, and then I heard steps on the stairs which went to Mr. Milter's apartment, so I guess it wasn't my bell at all.''

''Long ago?''

''No. Within the last fifteen or twenty minutes.''

''Do you know how long this visitor stayed?''

She laughed and said, ''My, you talk as though you were a detective—or a lawyer. You don't know who this girl was, do you?''

''I just happen to be very interested in Mr. Milter.''

''Why?''

''Do you know anything about him?''

She waited for a perceptible interval before answering that question. ''Not very much.''

''I understand he used to be a detective.''

''Oh, did he?''

''I wanted to talk with him about a case on which he'd worked.''

''Oh.''

The young woman hesitated. ''Something he'd been working on recently?'' she asked.

Mason met her eyes. ''Yes.''

She laughed suddenly and said, ''Well, I've got to be getting on up to town. Sorry I can't help you. Good night.''

Mason raised his hat and watched her walk away.

From a telephone booth in a drugstore Mason called Witherspoon's house and asked for Della Street. When he had her on the line, he said, ''Anything new from Paul Drake, Della?''

''Yes. Drake's operative telephoned.''

''What did he say?''

''He said the bus had got in right on time, that the girl had

64

got off and gone directly to Milter's apartment. She had a key.''

"Oh-oh!" Mason said. "What happened then?"

"She went upstairs, and wasn't gone very long. That's one thing the detective is kicking himself about. He doesn't know just how long."

"Why not?"

"He presumed, of course, she'd be up there some time, and he went across the street, and about halfway down the block, to a restaurant to telephone. He telephoned Drake, and made his report. Drake had told him to telephone you here. He put through the call to me here, and while I was talking with him, he happened to see the blonde walking past. So he hung up and dashed out after her. About five minutes later, he called up from the depot, says she's sitting there waiting for the midnight train to Los Angeles, and that she's been crying."

"Where's the detective?"

"Still at the depot. He's keeping her shadowed. That train is a chug-chug that carries a Pullman up to the main line, where it lays over four hours, gets picked up by a main-line train, and gets into Los Angeles about eight in the morning."

"This detective can't tell exactly how long she was up in the apartment?"

"No. It couldn't have been more than ten minutes. It might have been less. According to what he says, he thought it was a good chance to put through a telephone call and report. Naturally, he expected her to be up there for some little time. . . . You know, when a girl has keys to a man's apartment . . . the detective assumed . . . that he'd have lots of time to telephone."

Mason looked at his watch, said, "I may have time to talk with her. I'll go down to the depot and see if I can accomplish anything."

"Did you see Milter?"

"Not yet."

"A car drove away right after you left—within two or three minutes. I think it was Witherspoon. He's probably trying to locate Lois."

"Try to find out definitely, will you?"

"Okay."

"I'll beat it down to the depot. G'by."

Mason drove directly to the depot. He heard a train whistle when he was three blocks away. As he parked his car, the train was just pulling into the depot.

Mason walked around the station platform just in time to see the blond girl whom he had last seen in Allgood's office stepping aboard the car. For a moment, the light from the station fell full on her face, and there was no mistaking her identity, nor that she had been crying.

Mason returned to his automobile and had proceeded three or four blocks from the depot when he heard the sound of a siren. On the cross street a block away, a police car swept past the intersection.

At the intersection, Mason found the car had turned in the direction of Milter's apartment. Mason followed along behind, saw the police car swing over to the curb, and come to an abrupt stop.

Mason parked his own car directly behind the police car. An officer jumped out and hurried across the cement walk to the door which led to Milter's apartment. Mason was right behind him.

The officer pressed a broad thumb against the bell, then turned and saw Mason.

Mason returned the officer's stare for a moment, then turned sheepishly, and started down the steps.

"Hey, you!" the officer called.

Mason stopped.

"What did *you* want?" the officer asked.

"I wanted to call on someone."

"Who?"

Mason hesitated.

"Go ahead, let's have it."

"Mr. Milter."

"You know him?"

Mason, choosing his words carefully, said, "I have never met him."

"You want in, huh?"

"Yes. I wanted to see him."

"You been here before?"

Mason waited once more for just the right interval before saying, "Yes."

66

"How long ago?"

"About ten minutes ago."

"What did you do?"

"Rang the bell."

"What happened?"

"I didn't get any answer."

The officer pressed the bell again, said, "Stick around. I think I'm going to want to talk with you."

He crossed over to an apartment marked MANAGER, and pressed the bell.

A light in one of the lower rooms came on. They could hear the sound of bare feet on the floor; then after a few moments, the shuffle of slippered feet coming down the corridor. The door opened a crack, and a woman somewhere in the forties with a dressing gown wrapped around her frowned at Mason with cold inhospitality. Then seeing the light glinting from the shield and brass buttons on the officer's uniform, she became instantly cordial.

"Was there something I could do for you?" she asked.

"You got a man here named Milter?"

"Yes. He's in the apartment over . . ."

"I know where he is. I want to get in."

"Have you tried his bell?"

"Yes."

"I . . . if he's home . . ."

"I want in," the officer repeated. "Give me a pass key."

She seemed undecided for only a moment, then said, "Just a minute."

She vanished into the dark interior of the house. The officer said to Mason, "What did *you* want to see him about?"

"I wanted to ask him a few questions."

A radio playing somewhere in the lower floor gave forth four quick bursts of static. The officer said, "Do you live here?"

Mason gave him one of his cards. "I'm a lawyer from Los Angeles."

The officer twisted around, held the card so the light from the interior of the hallway fell on it, and said, "Oh, you're Perry Mason, the lawyer, huh? I've read about some of your cases. What are you doing down here?"

"Taking a trip," Mason said.

"You come to call on Milter?"

Mason managed to give his laugh just the right shade of expression. "I hardly came all the way down here *just* to see Milter."

"Hey, you," the officer called down the corridor to the manager, "we can't wait all night for that key."

"Just a minute. I'm trying to find it."

During the short period of silence which followed, Mason heard the metallic click of a telephone receiver being dropped into its cradle. "Considering the noise made on the radio when she dialed Milter's telephone," Mason chuckled, "she's going to a lot of trouble to keep us from knowing what she's doing."

"Hey," the officer shouted, "cut out that phoning. Get me the key, or I'm coming after it."

They heard the slippered feet again, shuffling rapidly along the corridor. "I had a hard time finding it," the manager lied. "Would you let me have your name, please—just in case there's any trouble."

"Haggerty," the officer said, taking the key.

Mason walked across the porch, waiting while the officer fitted the key to the door, then said, "Well, I won't go up with you. The matter I wanted to see him about wasn't important."

He turned and started away. The officer let him take two steps before he called, "Hey, wait a minute! I'm not so certain about that."

"About what?"

"That what you wanted to see him about wasn't important."

"I don't get you?"

"Why do you suppose I'm getting this pass key?"

"I wouldn't know."

"A little while ago some jane telephoned the desk and said that something was wrong up here. Know anything about that?"

"No."

"Know who that woman might have been who telephoned?"

"No."

"You just come along, anyway," the officer said. "Stick

along with me for a minute. I want to take a gander up here, and maybe that's all there'll be to it. Maybe you'll have some questions to answer.''

He led the way up the stairs, Mason following docilely along behind.

They entered a combined living room and bedroom. A wide, mirrored section of the wall was arranged to pivot so as to conceal a wall bed. The furniture was plain, somewhat faded. A door at the far end of the room was closed. A plain table in the center of the room held some magazines. Over at the far side was a big round goldfish bowl. In the bottom of the bowl was a little castle and some sort of green water grass. Some colored shells were strewn along the bottom of the tank. A couple of goldfish swam lazily about. In the tank, so far submerged that only the top of its head and part of its beak were protruding upward, a duck was struggling feebly.

The officer followed Mason's eyes, saw the tank, turned away, then stopped.

"Hey," he said. "What's wrong with that duck?"

Mason glanced at the duck, said quickly, "I suppose this door leads to another room."

"We'll take a chance," the officer said.

He knocked on the door, received no answer, and opened the door. He turned back to look at the fish tank. "Funny about that duck," he said. "He's sick."

A peculiar odor seeped into the room which the officer had just entered, a very faint acrid odor. The room itself was evidently intended to be used as a dining room. There was a big table in the center, a pine sideboard, and chairs of the conventional dining-room type.

Mason said, "Let's open these windows. I don't like this smell. What brought you up here? Specifically, what did that woman say?"

"Said there was something wrong up here. Let's take a look in this other room."

The officer opened the door which led to a bathroom. It was empty. Mason crossed the room and flung the windows wide open while the officer opened another door which apparently led to the kitchen.

Mason, watching his chance, doubled back quickly to the

69

living room, and reached his hand down into the goldfish tank.

The little duck had quit struggling. Mason lifted him out, a soggy, almost inert bundle of wet feathers.

The lawyer whipped a handkerchief from his pocket, wiped the bird dry, squeezing the water out of the feathers. The little duck made feeble motions with his feet.

Heavy steps sounded on the floor. Mason thrust the duck into his coat pocket. The officer, his face gray, came staggering toward Mason. "Kitchen . . . dead man . . . some kind of gas. I tried . . ." The officer stumbled, then collapsed into a chair.

Mason, glancing toward the kitchen, could see a partially opened door, the sprawled figure of a man on the floor.

The lawyer held his breath, ran to the kitchen, slammed the door shut, returned to the living room, said to the officer, "Put your head out the window. Get some fresh air."

Haggerty nodded. Mason supported him to the window, left the officer leaning on the sill.

Moving swiftly, the lawyer dashed back, picked up the goldfish bowl, darted into the bathroom, and dumped the water down the washbowl. He turned on fresh water from the bathtub tap, until the goldfish that had been flapping around on the bottom of the bowl, began once more swimming around in the tank. When the tank was once more filled with water, Mason crossed the dining room, replaced the tank on the table. The officer was still leaning out of the window. The little duck which Mason took from his pocket was stronger now, able to move about. Mason again dried the feathers, put the duck back in the water, crossed over to the window. "How's it coming?" he asked the officer.

"All in—got a whiff of that—"

Mason said, "We've got the windows open. This part of the house will air out. We've got to get those kitchen windows open. It's some deadly gas. The best thing to do is to get the fire department and smash in the windows."

"Okay. . . . I'll . . . be all right in a minute. Sort of got me for a second."

"Just take it easy," Mason told him.

"What is that stuff?" the officer asked. "It isn't stove gas."

"No, apparently some sort of chemical. How about getting downstairs?"

"There's a man in there. We've got to get him out."

"That's a job for the fire department. Have they got gas masks?"

"Yes."

"Well, let's put in a call."

Mason walked over to the telephone, called Operator, and asked the policeman, "Do you feel well enough to talk to 'em?"

The officer said, "Yes," took the telephone, and explained the situation to the fire department. He hung up the phone, came back, and sat down by the window. "I'm feeling better now. What the devil was wrong with that duck?"

"What duck?"

"The one in the goldfish bowl?"

"Oh, you mean the one that was diving?"

"He looked damn funny," Haggerty said. "Guess the gas got him."

Mason motioned toward the bowl. "The one over there?"

"Yes."

The duck was sitting on the surface of the water looking rather weak and groggy, preening his feathers.

"I guess the fresh air revived him," Mason said.

"Uh huh. What did you want to see Milter about?"

"Oh, nothing in particular."

"Yeah? At this hour of the night?" the officer asked skeptically.

"I heard he was out of a job. I thought I might have some work for him."

"What's his line?"

"He was a detective."

"Oh. . . . Working on something down here?"

"I don't think so. I heard he was out of a job."

"Where's he been working?"

"Man by the name of Allgood in Hollywood," Mason said. "You might ring Allgood up and find out about him."

Sirens announced the arrival of the fire department. A fireman in a gas mask entered the kitchen, raised the windows, dragged out the inert body. Ten minutes later, a doctor pronounced that the man was stone dead, gave it as his opinion he had died of hydrocyanic poisoning.

More policemen arrived, a man from the sheriff's office. They discovered a small water pitcher half full of liquid on the back of the gas stove.

"That's it," the doctor exclaimed. "Put hydrochloric acid in that pitcher, toss in a few lumps of cyanide, and you liberate a deadly gas. It's the same kind they use to execute criminals in a gas chamber. The effect is practically instantaneous."

"We'll look that glass over for fingerprints," the officer said.

Mason stretched, yawned. "Well, I guess there's nothing more I can do to help you."

The officer said gratefully, "You just about saved my life. If you hadn't got those windows open and got me out of here, I'd have keeled over. Gosh, that stuff is powerful."

"Glad to do what I could," Mason said.

"Where are you staying down here? At the hotel?"

"No. I'm visiting a friend—a man by the name of Witherspoon who has a ranch out here . . ."

"Oh, yes, I know him," the deputy sheriff said. "I get out there every once in a while for some dove or quail shooting. Will you be there for a while?"

"No, probably not longer than tomorrow. I think you'd better telephone Allgood and let him know about this man. Allgood might have some information that would help."

"That's a good idea," the sheriff said.

"You could put through the call from this phone," Mason observed. "Allgood probably has a night number where he can be reached."

The deputy sheriff consulted for a moment with the policeman, then put through the telephone call. Mason walked over by the window and lit a cigarette. He had taken only a few puffs, when the operator, spurred on by the statement that it was a police emergency call, located Allgood in Hollywood. Mason heard the El Templo end of the conversation.

"Hello, is this Allgood? . . . You have a detective agency there. . . . Uh huh, that's right. . . . This is the sheriff's office at El Templo. Did you have a man working for you named Milter, Leslie L. Milter. . . . Uh huh. . . . He's dead.

Found dead in his room. . . . Maybe murder. Some kind of gas. . . . Who would have been interested in bumping him off? . . . Don't know anyone, eh? . . . Wasn't working on any case for you? . . . How long? . . . Why did you let him go? . . . Just no more work for him, eh? . . . How was he, a good man? . . . Know anything about his affairs? . . . How about women? . . . I see. . . . Okay, let us know if you turn up anything. Just ring El Templo—either the sheriff's office or the chief of police. Okay, g'by.''

He hung up the phone and said, ''Worked for Allgood up until four or five days ago. Allgood let him go because he didn't have any more work. Business was kinda quiet. He says Milter was a pretty good man. He can't remember what particular cases Milter had been working on lately, but he'll look them up and let us know. He thinks it was mostly routine stuff.''

Mason heaved a sigh of relief that Allgood hadn't missed his cue, carefully pinched out his cigarette, dropped it in the ash tray, said, ''Well, I'll be going. If you want me for anything, you can reach me in care of Witherspoon.''

''How did *you* happen to be here?'' the sheriff asked.

The officer said, ''He drove up right behind me. I brought him in with me.''

They wished Mason good night, and, as Mason went down the stairs, he heard them moving the body of Leslie Milter.

Mason drove his car to an all-night service station, opened the trunk, pulled out the flat tire, and said, ''Fix this just as soon as you can. I'll be back in a few minutes and see how you're coming.''

Leaving the tire in the service station, Mason walked the five blocks to the bungalow where he had been told Marvin Adams lived.

The bungalow was a simple, unpretentious stucco building. Flowers which had been planted in the yard were evidences of Mrs. Adams' desire to beautify the place. A light was on in the front of the house. Mason rang the bell.

A studious-looking young man came to the door.

''Marvin Adams in?'' Mason asked.

''No, sir, he isn't. . . . He took the night train to Los Angeles.''

Mason said, "He was driving a car, I believe—earlier in the evening?"

"Yes."

"Your car?"

"Yes."

"He had a package I gave him to deliver. Apparently he forgot to deliver it. He must have left it in his room or in the car. It's a square package wrapped in green paper, with my name written on it. Suppose we could look in his room and see if he left it there. He might have, you know—while he was packing."

"Why, yes, sir. If you'll step this way."

The boy led the way down a corridor, past an open bathroom door, then paused, tapped on the door of the bedroom, and opened it.

It was a typical boy's room with ice skates, tennis rackets, a couple of pennants, some pictures on the walls, a rack of neckties, a bed covered with a dark woolen blanket and no spread, a pair of white tennis shoes by the side of the bed, and a couple of white sport socks lying on the floor by the tennis shoes.

Mason prowled superficially about the room. "It doesn't seem to be here. He keeps this room?"

"Yes. Another boy and I have rooms here, and Marvin keeps this one. He may rent it later."

"Well, the package doesn't seem to be here. How about the car? Where is it?"

"Outside, at the curb."

"Isn't locked, is it?"

The boy grinned. "No. You couldn't hire anyone to steal it."

Mason said, "I'll take a look on the way out. I have a flashlight."

Mason thanked the boy, said good night, and when the door had closed, slipped a small flashlight from his overcoat pocket and gave the battered sedan at the curb the benefit of a quick appraisal. It was empty.

Mason walked thoughtfully toward the service station where he had left his car, his steps pounding along the cement sidewalk. The street was dark and all but deserted so far as traffic was concerned. Mason met no pedestrians. A

74

chill had edged the desert night. Overhead, the stars were frosty, brilliant, and steady. The sidewalk was lined with smoke trees, those weird trees of the desert which branch out into lacy, leafless tendrils, looking from a distance so much like smoke that many a tenderfoot has been deceived into thinking he is seeing a welcome wisp of blue smoke silhouetted against the sky, when he is in reality looking only at a most unusual bit of desert vegetation.

The man at the service station said to Mason, "Your tire's all ready."

"So soon?" Mason asked.

The man grinned. "Uh huh. There wasn't anything wrong with it except that the cap was gone and the valve stem had worked loose. That was letting the air leak out."

"How could the valve stem have worked loose?" Mason asked.

"Well, it *might* have jiggled loose. The cap was gone. . . . Perhaps someone was playing a prank—some kid, you know."

Mason paid the man, jumped in the car, fed it gas, was going fifty miles an hour by the time he left the city limits, and was hitting eighty as he skimmed along the desert road through the silence of the star-studded night.

Chapter 10

Lois Witherspoon came to the door of the big house as Mason rang the bell at the outer gate. The dogs, setting up an uproar at the sound of the bell, came running into the oblong shaft of brilliance which was thrown out from the hallway and against which the slim figure of the girl was silhouetted.

A moment later she turned on the switch which flooded the area in front of the iron gate with brilliance.

"Oh, it's you, Mr. Mason. King—Prince—Be quiet! I haven't a key. I don't know where the watchman is. . . . Oh, here he is. Pedro, open the gate for Mr. Mason."

A somewhat sleepy-eyed Mexican servant fitted a key in the huge lock, and said, "Wait one moment, señor, until I fasten the dogs."

"It won't be necessary," Mason said, opening the door.

The dogs rushed toward him, the circled as Mason walked calmly toward the house. The younger dog jumped up and placed his forepaws on Mason's arm. The older dog trotted along quietly at the lawyer's side. Both had upright wagging tails.

Lois Witherspoon said, "Eventually, they get acquainted with the guests, but you're breaking all speed records."

"They're nice dogs," Mason said. "Peculiar thing about canine psychology. They hurl a challenge at you, and you stand still and look at them, and, as we lawyers say, 'the issue is joined.' You keep right on going about your business, and show absolutely no fear, and almost any dog is inclined to give you the benefit of the doubt. Your father in?"

"Why, no. Didn't you see him?"

"No."

"I understood from the servants he left just a few minutes after you did. I believe he said there was something he wanted to see you about, and that he'd catch you before you got to town. I wasn't here."

Mason circled her slender waist, pulled her to one side, kicked the door shut. While she was still startled, he asked, "Do you know a Leslie L. Milter?"

"Why, no."

"Anyone been trying to blackmail you?"

"Me? Good heavens, no!"

"You've been out. Where were you?"

"What business is it of yours?"

"Lots. Don't stall. We haven't time. Seconds are precious. Where were you?"

"I went into town—wanted to do an errand—and to see Marvin before he left."

"Did you?"

"Yes. I caught him at the depot."

"I didn't see you there."

"You wouldn't. We were around by the express shed on the far side."

"How long before the train came in?"

"I got there about ten minutes before train time. Marvin came about a minute or two after I got there."

"You were in the dark there, saying good-by?"

"Yes."

"And what else?"

"What do you mean?"

"What was the reason you said good-by to him here, and then went rushing into town?"

She met his eyes. He could feel her muscles stiffen under his arm. "I wanted him to drive me to Yuma—and marry me."

"When?"

"Tonight—now—at once."

"He wouldn't do it?"

"No."

Mason said, "That's better. He had a little duck when he left here. Talk fast and keep your voice low."

"Yes, he did."

"What did he do with it?"

She said nervously, "Why, he . . . he picked the duck up and asked if he could borrow it for a day or two. He promised to return it. Said he wanted to perform that experiment for a friend."

77

"Where did he get it?"

"From out in the compound. There's a mother duck and a brood of young ones. . . . I don't know what he finally did with it. He didn't have it with him at the train . . . I had forgotten about it."

Mason said, "Now listen, get this straight. Get out into the compound with a flashlight. I don't care what excuse you make. Pretend you're looking for one of the servants, or that you saw someone prowling around the place. Take one of the dogs with you on a leash. Get another young duck out of that same batch."

"I . . . ." she broke off as the dogs started barking once more.

Mason glanced out through the diamond-shaped window in the door. "Another car," he said.

"Father!" she exclaimed as Witherspoon called to the dogs and they ceased barking.

"Get out through the patio," Mason said. "Get that duck. Get into town. You'll find the car Marvin was driving parked at the curb in front of the house where he has his room. It's unlocked. Slip the duck into the back of the car—under the footrail. Mind you now, not in the front. In the back, under the footrail—and get back here as soon as you can make it."

She sucked in a quick breath. "Can you tell me what . . ."

"No," Mason said. "There isn't time, and don't tell anyone, including your father, about that drowning business. Now, get busy."

She turned wordlessly, running lightly as Witherspoon's steps came pounding down the corridor.

Mason turned and said casually, "Hello. Understand you were out looking for me."

Witherspoon said, "My God, Mason, did you hear what happened?"

"About Milter?"

"Yes."

Mason said, "I was there when the officers got in the place."

"It's terrible. . . . I want to talk with you. Come on down to my study. Mason, we're in a terrible predicament."

"What do you mean?"

"I . . . hang it, you know as well as I do what I mean."

78

"I'm afraid I don't get you."

Witherspoon said, "You remember I told you that Marvin Adams had a duck with him when he left here."

"Yes."

"That duck was in Milter's living room in a goldfish bowl."

"Same duck?" Mason asked.

"Absolutely. I identified it."

"What's his name?" the lawyer inquired as Witherspoon led the way down the corridor.

Witherspoon turned with a quick, jerking motion. "The detective?" he asked. "Milter, Leslie L. Milter."

"No, the duck."

Witherspoon stopped walking. "What the devil are you talking about?"

"The duck's name," Mason said, taking a cigarette calmly from his cigarette case.

"Good God, the duck doesn't have a name! He's a young duck. Duck. D-u-c-k. A young bird. A little duckling."

"I understand," Mason said.

Witherspoon, apparently under terrific nervous tension, knitted his brows together. There was an angry glint in his eye. "Then what the hell do you mean by asking what the duck's name was? Ducks don't have names."

"You identified him as being the same duck that Marvin Adams took away with him," Mason pointed out.

Witherspoon thought that over for a moment, then completed his journey down the corridor, and unlocked the door of his den and clicked on the light. Mason snapped a match into flame with a quick motion of his thumb, lit the cigarette, and shook out the flame.

Witherspoon said, "This is a hell of a time to be funny."

"Isn't it?" Mason agreed.

Witherspoon's den was a huge room, furnished with mission-type furniture. There were paintings of bucking horses in action, of cowboys galloping after steers. There were mounted heads on the wall, rifles suspended from pegs, six-shooters in worn, shiny holsters hanging from well-filled cartridge belts. A pottery bowl was filled with rattles cut from rattlesnakes. The walls of the room were knotty pine; and over and around the big fireplace at the far end of the room some of the more famous brands of Western history had been burnt into the wooden wall.

Worried as he was, the old pride of ownership asserted itself. Witherspoon said, "This is where I come when I want to get away from everything. I even have a bunk over there where I can sleep. I'm the only person who has a key to this room. Not even Lois—or the servants—can unlock that door, except when I have someone in here to clean. Those are some very nice Navajo rugs there on the floor. Now sit down, and tell me what the devil you were trying to do about that duck— kid me?"

Witherspoon flung open a cabinet, disclosing a shelf of bottles and glasses. Below the shelf, cunningly concealed behind a door, was an electric icebox.

"Scotch and soda?" he asked.

"Not now," Mason said.

Witherspoon poured a huge shot of Scotch into a glass, dropped in ice cubes, hissed in soda, and gulped down a good half of the mixture. He sat down heavily in one of the big, rawhide-backed chairs, opened a humidor, took out a cigar, bit the end off nervously, and scraped a match on the underside of the table. His hand was steady enough as he held the flame to the end of the cigar, but the ruddy glow of the match emphasized the network of worry lines about his forehead and eyes.

Mason asked, "Still want to talk about the duck?"

Witherspoon demanded irritably, "What are you getting at?"

Mason said, "Simply that when you identify a duck, you have to know that duck when you see him. There must be something about the duck to enable you to recognize it. There must be something which gives it a personality, something which distinguishes him from all other ducks."

Witherspoon said, "Don't be silly. I warned you this thing might happen. That damn kid is a rotter. He's no good. This is going to be a bitter pill for Lois, but she'll have to take it. It's better for her to have it happen this way than after he had become one of the family."

"The duck?" Mason asked.

"Adams," Witherspoon shouted at him. "I'm talking about Adams. Lois has no intention of marrying a duck!"

"Did you make any comments to the police about the duck?" Mason inquired.

"Yes."

"What did you say?"

"I told them it was my duck."

"Did you tell them how it got there?"

"I told them that young Adams took it off the place with him when he left this evening," Witherspoon said in surly defiance. "Damn it, Mason, I'm willing to go just so far to protect my daughter's happiness, but there comes a time when you have to quit kidding yourself. As it is, there hasn't even been an announcement of an engagement."

"You think that Marvin Adams murdered this detective?"

"Of course he did."

"And just what gives you that idea?"

"Do you know what killed him?" Witherspoon asked, his voice rising in excitement. "A neat little experiment in chemistry," he rushed on, answering his own question. "Milter was out in the kitchen, apparently fixing up a drink of hot buttered rum for himself and his guest. The murderer took a small water pitcher from the cupboard, slipped it on the back of the stove, poured in some hydrochloric acid, said, 'Well, so long, Leslie, I've got to be going now,' dropped in some cyanide lumps and walked out. The gas burner was going on the stove, heating the water with sugar in it. There were two cups on the cupboard with rum and a chunk of butter in each cup. The sound of the gas jet on the stove prevented Milter from hearing any hissing noise which might have been made by the cyanide dissolving in the hydrochloric acid. The deadly gas filled the room. By the time Milter knew something was wrong, it was too late. He started for the door, and fell over dead. The gas kept burning beneath the aluminum pan in which the sugar and water were being boiled. When the water boiled away, the sugar burned, filled the room with smoke and with a peculiar odor. That's about all that saved the officer's life when he looked into the room. The first thing he got was a whiff of the burnt sugar and the burning pan."

Mason said, "Very, very interesting, as far as it goes."

"What do you mean by that?"

Mason settled back in the rawhide chair, elevated his feet

81

to a stool, and smiled at Witherspoon. "*Two* cups," he said, "with rum and butter in each."

"Yes, that's right."

"And at the very moment he fell over dead, Milter was heating the water to pour into this mixture."

"That's right."

"Your idea is that the murderer simply placed the pitcher of water on the back of the stove, said, 'So long, Leslie,' and dropped in some cyanide."

"Well, something like that."

"Don't you get it?" Mason asked. "If Milter was preparing a drink for two people, the person who dropped the cyanide in the hydrochloric acid must have been the person for whom the second drink was intended. Therefore, he would hardly have said, 'So long, Leslie,' and walked out—not while his drink was cooking on the stove. He must have had some excuse other than that."

Witherspoon frowned through his blue cigar smoke, at the lawyer. "By George, that's so."

"And that brings us back to the duck," Mason said. "Why did you jump at the conclusion this was your particular duck?"

"Because it is my duck. It *has* to be. You remember I told you young Adams had taken a duck from the ranch when he left—a bit of damned impertinence. I'm going to have to ask Lois about that. She's got to learn the whole story sooner or later, and she may as well begin now."

Witherspoon reached for the telephone.

Mason held up his hand. "Just a minute. Before you get Lois," he said, "let's talk about the duck. Now, as I understand it, you've already told the police that the duck came from your ranch."

"Yes."

"How did you know? Where was he branded?"

Witherspoon said, "Dammit, Mason, you and I can have trouble over that duck. Every time I start talking about it, you make these nasty, sneering wisecracks. You don't brand ducks."

"Why?" Mason asked.

"Hang it! Because you don't need to."

82

"You brand cattle, don't you?" Mason inquired, indicating the wall back of the fireplace with a gesture of his hand.

"Yes, of course."

"Why?"

"So you can tell them from your neighbor's cattle."

"Very interesting," Mason said. "In China, where the families live on houseboats and raise ducks, I understand they dye the ducks different colors so they can be told apart."

"What's that got to do with this duck?"

"Simply this," Mason said. "You yourself admit you have to put a brand on your steers so you can tell the difference between those and the steers of your neighbors. How, then, are you going to identify this duck as being yours, instead of one belonging to someone else?"

"You know damn well this was my duck."

Mason said, "*I'm* thinking of when you get up in front of a jury. It's going to be rather embarrassing for you personally. You've stuck your neck out now. You'll say, 'Yes, this is my duck.' The lawyer for the prosecution will say, 'Cross-examine,' and the lawyer for the defense will start asking questions. What is there about this duck that you identify?"

"Well, his color and size for one thing."

"Oh," Mason said. "And the lawyer for the defense will ask, 'What's distinctive about his color and size?' "

"Well, it's that yellowish color which young ducklings have. And he's just the same size as the other ducklings in the brood."

"How many in the batch?"

"Eight or nine—I'm not certain which."

"Which one of the eight or nine is this?"

"Don't be silly. You can't tell that."

"So," Mason said, smiling, "you yourself are admitting this duck looks exactly like eight or nine other ducks of similar size and color, which you have on your place."

"Well, what of it?"

"And that you can't tell which of the eight or nine it is."

"Certainly not. We don't give them names, or baptize them."

"And, doubtless," Mason went on smoothly, "in other parts of the valley there are other ranches that have ducks, and it is quite possible that there are several other ranches where the young ducklings are of exactly this size, age, color, and appearance?''

"I suppose so."

"And, if those ducklings were all brought into your compound and mixed up with your ducklings, in the absence of some brand or other marking, you couldn't tell which were yours?''

Witherspoon puffed away on his cigar silently, but the rapidity with which the puffs of smoke were being emitted indicated the nerve tension under which he was laboring.

"So you see," Mason went on, "you'd cut rather a sorry figure when you endeavored to identify this duck."

"The officer said there was something wrong with the duck when he came in," Witherspoon said. "*You* should know something about that."

"Yes," Mason said, "the duck was partially submerged. But that's not unusual. Ducks dive, you know."

"The officer said it looked as though—looked as though—well, it looked as though the duck were drowning."

Mason raised his eyebrows incredulously.

"Drowning?"

"That's what the officer said."

"Oh, well," Mason said, his voice showing infinite and exaggerated relief, "there's nothing to it then. You don't need to worry in the least."

"What are you getting at?"

"Then you can identify your duck. You won't have any trouble," Mason said.

"How?"

"Why," Mason said, his smile patronizingly superior, "your duck is distinctive. If this is your duck, you have the only duck in the entire Red River Valley, probably the only duck in the world, that can't swim."

Witherspoon glowered at him. "Damn it. You know what I mean. Marvin is a chemist. He'd put something in the water."

Mason raised his eyebrows. "There was something in the water, then?"

"Yes, of course, The duck was drowning."

"Did it drown?"

"No. It recovered—and, I believe, started to swim."

"Then it couldn't have been something in the *water* that was making the duck drown."

"Well, then it was something about the gas that disabled him. With the room cleared out, he started to swim."

"I see—most interesting. By the way, you have a lot of guns here, Witherspoon. I take it you do quite a bit of hunting."

Witherspoon said, "Yes," in the voice of a man who doesn't care particularly about having the subject of conversation changed.

"These heads are some that you've bagged?"

"Yes."

"Some nice rifles there."

"Yes."

"I see you have some shotguns."

"Yes."

"And there are other shotguns, I take it, in those cases?"

"Yes."

"Do some trapshooting occasionally?"

"Yes."

"There are doves down here. You shoot those?"

"Well, not doves."

"Do some duck hunting occasionally?"

"Quite frequently."

"Good duck hunting around here?"

"Yes."

"When you hit a duck in the air with the center part of the charge of shot, I presume it kills him instantly."

For a moment, the glint of enthusiasm lighted Witherspoon's eyes. "I'll say it does! There's nothing that gives you more satisfaction than to make a good clean kill. You take one of these twenty-gauge guns with a good heavy load, and when you hit the duck with the center of the string of shot, he never knows what struck him. One minute, he's flying along, and the next minute, he's crumpled—absolutely dead."

"Falls down in the water quite frequently?" Mason asked.

"Yes."

"And how do you get them off the bottom?" Mason asked. "Do you have some sort of a drag that you drag along the bottom?"

Witherspoon's smile was exceedingly patronizing. "For a lawyer who is supposed to be so brilliant, Mr. Mason, you certainly are ignorant about things which are more or less common knowledge.''

Mason raised his eyebrows. ''Indeed!''

''Ducks don't sink. When they're shot, they float on the surface of the water,'' Witherspoon said.

''Is that so?''

''Yes.''

''Then, the fact that this duck was being overcome by gas wouldn't make him sink,'' Mason said. ''That drowning condition which the officer referred to must have been something else.''

Witherspoon, realizing the trap into which he had been led, moved forward in his chair as though preparing to get to his feet. His face turned a dark shade of reddish-purple. ''Dammit, Mason,'' he said, ''you . . .'' He checked himself.

''Of course,'' Mason went on suavely, ''I was merely trying to point out to you the position in which you have placed yourself. Rather an embarrassing position, I should say. You identified a duck to the police. Doubtless, you've started the police on the trail of young Adams. Have you?''

''Well, I told them about the duck and told them Adams had had it last. Well, you can draw your own conclusions. Adams went up there, and he's pretty apt to have been the person for whom Milter was fixing the hot buttered rum.''

Mason shook his head sadly. ''Too bad you've turned the officers loose on Adams. They're going to arrest him for murder on no evidence other than that of the duck. The officer has said that the duck was drowning. Poor little chap. He had doubtless become very much attached to Marvin Adams, and when Adams went away and left him in the fish bowl up there at Milter's place, the duck decided to commit suicide by drowning. I suppose all the excitement incident to the discovery of Milter's body made him change his mind. He decided that life was, after all, worth living. He . . .''

''Stop it!'' Witherspoon yelled. ''I don't give a damn what my arrangement is with you. I'm not going to have you sit there and treat me as though I were—as though I were—''

Mason took a deep drag at his cigarette and announced, ''That is a mere foretaste of what you've let yourself in for. A good attorney for the defense will rip you wide open in front of a jury. If there was something in the water to have made the duck drown, he'd have gone ahead and drowned. Evidently the duck changed its mind. The lawyer who tries this case is going to get you in rather a hot spot."

"We don't have lawyers like that down here,"Witherspoon said, with an ugly look, "and I have some position in the community. When I say that's my duck, my word will be taken for it. There won't be all of this cross-examination."

"And when the officer says the duck was drowning, the lawyers down here won't question that statement?"

"Well," Witherspoon said, and hesitated, then added, "Well, the officer said the duck *looked* as though it were drowning."

"But no local attorney will give you a cross-examination such as I have just outlined?"

"Definitely not."

"Why?"

"In the first place, an attorney wouldn't think of it, and in the second place, I wouldn't stand for it."

"But if young Adams is charged with crime," Mason said, "he might not be defended by a local lawyer. He might be defended by a Los Angeles lawyer."

"What Los Angeles lawyer would take the case of a young kid of that sort who has no money, no friends, no . . ."

Mason took the cigarette from his mouth, locked his eyes with those of Witherspoon, and said, "*I* would."

It took three or four seconds for the full effect of Mason's remark to soak into Witherspoon's consciousness. "You would! But you are employed by me!"

"To solve the mystery of that old murder case. Nothing was said about any other case. Could I quote you, to your daughter, for instance, as saying you have any objections?"

Witherspoon smoked nervously. "I guess I have no objection, but . . . well, of course, you'll understand that *I* can't be placed in an undignified position. All this business about the identification of a duck."

Mason got to this feet. "There's just one way to avoid that."

"How?"

"By not identifying the duck."

"But I already have."

87

Mason said, "Call up the police and tell them, now that you've thought it over, you realize one duck looks very much like another, that all you can say is this duck is similar in size, color, and appearance to one which you were advised Marvin Adams took with him when he left your ranch this evening."

Witherspoon rubbed his fingers along the angle of his jaw while he considered that suggestion. "Hang it, Mason, it's the *same* duck. You can quibble as much as you want to, but you know as well as I do it's the same duck."

Mason smiled down at his host. "Do you want to go over all that again?" he asked.

"Good Lord, no! We don't get anywhere with that."

"You'd better get in touch with the police, then, and change your mind about the identification on that duck."

Witherspoon shook his head obstinately.

Mason regarded him thoughtfully for a moment, then said, "They told me you left here shortly after I did."

"Yes. I chased you all the way into town, but couldn't catch you."

"You probably passed me on the road," Mason said. "I had a flat tire."

Witherspoon frowned as though trying to recall some event, then said, "I don't remember having seen any car by the side of the road. I was going pretty fast."

"A car went past me," Mason said, "doing about eighty."

"That must have been where I missed you."

"Where did you go?" Mason asked.

"To town."

"Looking for me?"

"Yes."

"And that's how you happened to go to Milter's place?"

"Yes."

"The only reason?"

"Yes."

"You must have been in town about thirty minutes before you went there."

"I doubt if it was that long."

"You didn't go there first?"

"No."

"Why not?"

Witherspoon hesitated perceptibly, then said, "I *did* drive past that address as soon as I got to town. I didn't see your car parked there, so I cruised around town for a while looking for you. I thought I saw . . . someone I knew. I tried to find her . . . I doubt if it was as much as thirty minutes."

"Wait a minute. Let's get this straight. You thought you saw someone you knew—a woman, but you couldn't find her?"

"It was a case of mistaken identity. I was driving down the main street cruising around, looking for you, when I caught a glimpse of this woman, just as she was turning a corner. I'd already gone past the intersection, so I turned the corner at the next block and tried to find her by running around the block."

"Who was this woman?"

"I don't know."

"You said she was a friend."

"No. I only *thought* she was a friend."

"Who?"

He hesitated a moment, then said, "Mrs. Burr."

"It wasn't she?"

"No."

"How do you know?"

"Because I asked the night nurse if Mrs. Burr was out. She said Mrs. Burr had gone to bed early."

"She and her husband have separate rooms?"

"They do now—after the accident. Before that, they occupied the same room."

"A nurse is with Burr all the time?"

"Yes, for the present—until after he gets back to a normal state of mind."

"What's the matter with his mind?"

"Oh, the usual irresponsibility which follows the use of morphia in some cases. The doctor says it isn't unusual. He got pretty flighty for a while. His leg's tied up to a weight though a pulley in the ceiling. They caught him trying to untie the rope. He said he had to get out of there because someone was trying to kill him. The doctor says it's a postnarcotic reaction, and that it's all right, but he has to be watched. If he'd managed to get out of bed, he'd have got

89

that fracture out of position and it would have had to be set all over again.''

Mason looked at his watch. ''Well, I've got work to do.''

''Aren't you going to stay here tonight?''

Mason shook his head, started for the door, then paused to say, ''I'm telling you for the last time—ring up the police and change your identification of that duck.''

Chapter 11

Driving toward town, Della Street said, "You whisked me out of there so fast I didn't have an opportunity to get it all straight. What happened?"

"Milter was murdered."

"By whom?"

"The police are going to nominate Marvin Adams within about twelve hours unless we do some fast work."

"Is that why Lois went running out?"

Mason grinned. "*I* wouldn't know."

"Why didn't you let me do it, Chief?"

"Do what?"

"Whatever had to be done."

"I wanted to keep it all in the family."

"You can't trust her, as far as that boy is concerned. She's simply crazy about him. If you let her in on anything that might hurt you, she'd betray you if she ever thought it would help him."

"I know. But I had to rely on her because, in the first place, the dogs knew her, and in the second place, she knew her way around the ranch. You'd have got into trouble. I realize the risk of using her. It's a big risk."

"Where are we going now?"

Mason said, "We've got an errand to do in town. Then we're going to overtake that midnight train. It hauls a sleeper up to the main line, and switches it off to wait for the through train to Los Angeles. I understand the car's hooked up about three o'clock in the morning. That gives us less than an hour."

"Did that blonde girl from the detective agency take the train?"

"Uh huh."

"Anyone else?"

"Marvin Adams."

"They're on the train together?"

"Well, they're both on the train."

"Is that just a coincidence?"

"I don't know."

"What's the errand in town?"

"I want to see Alberta Cromwell. She has the apartment that adjoins Milter's."

"His common-law wife?"

"Widow."

"Do you think she knows of the murder?"

"She must if she's home."

"Suppose she isn't home?"

"That's one of the things I want to find out."

"Won't the police still be in possession of Milter's apartment?"

"Probably."

"Will you take a chance on running into them?"

"No."

"But won't you have to, to find out if she's home?"

Mason grinned. "There are two ways of finding out if a young lady isn't home. One of them is to look in her home."

"What's the other?"

"To find her away from home."

"Come on," Della said. "Quit holding out. Where?"

Mason said, "There are also just two ways of leaving town, for a young woman who has no automobile. One is by the train. The other is by bus. The last train has gone. We'll look in the bus station first."

"Would you know her if you saw her?"

"I think so. In any event, I met a young woman who claims to occupy the apartment next to Milter and who gave her name as Cromwell."

Della Street settled back in the seat. "Pumping you for information when you don't want to loosen up is like trying to get water out of a dry well."

Mason grinned. "I can't very well give something I haven't got."

"No, but if you had, you wouldn't. *I'm* going to snatch forty winks. I don't suppose you want me to go into the Greyhound depot with you?"

"Definitely not."

"Okay, just wake me up when you come out."

She twisted her shoulders until she got her head in a comfortable position, and closed her eyes. Mason drove on at high speed until he reached the main street of El Templo. Then he slowed and drove to within half a block of the Greyhound bus depot. Apparently Della Street was still asleep as he slipped quietly out of the car, gently closed the door, and walked rapidly down the sidewalk.

There were four persons sitting on the wide benches, waiting for the three o'clock bus to Los Angeles. Alberta Cromwell was occupying an isolated corner, her elbow resting on the arm of the bench, her chin propped on the palm of her hand. She was staring with fixed, unseeing eyes at a rack of magazines in front of her.

As Mason sat down almost beside her, she turned her head just far enough to take in his feet and legs, then swung her eyes back toward the magazine rack.

Lurid covers, featuring various so-called authentic detective cases, were stacked in rows, one above the other. These covers for the most part showing well-curved young women engaged in a desperate struggle for life and, one would gather from the state of their clothing, for honor.

After several seconds had elapsed during which Alberta Cromwell remained motionless, Mason said calmly, "Rather depressing thinking about a murder against *that* background, isn't it?"

She jerked her head around at the sound of his voice. As she recognized him, an involuntary nervous start betrayed her emotion, but after a moment, when she spoke, her voice was calm. "Are you, too, going to Los Angeles?" she asked.

Mason held his eyes steadily on her profile. "No."

She turned once more to look at him then, and her eyes faltered. She turned quickly away.

Mason said, "Don't you think it would be better to tell me about it?"

"There's nothing to tell. About what?"

"Your reason for going to Los Angeles so suddenly."

"I don't think it's sudden. I've been planning to go for some little time."

"Let's see," Mason said. "You don't seem to be carrying a suitcase. Not even an overnight bag."

"Is that any business of yours?" she asked. "After all, I think you're presuming entirely too much upon what was, merely a—a—"

"Yes," Mason prompted. "Merely a what?"

"An attempt to be neighborly."

"You told me that you only knew Leslie Milter slightly."

"Well?"

"I suppose any wife could say as much of her husband," Mason observed.

She tilted her chin upward, dropped her lashes, and made it quite plain that she didn't care to continue the conversation.

Mason got up, walked over to the newsstand, and bought four or five of the magazines. He came back to the bench, seated himself beside her, and casually started turning pages. Abruptly he said, "Interesting thought here, that the criminal really does more to bring about his own capture than the police. Trying to cover up nearly always gives the police something definite on which to work—regardless of what clues might connect a person with the original crime."

She said nothing.

"Now take your case, for instance," Mason said, quite calmly, as though discussing the matter from a completely detached viewpoint. "Your absence won't mean so much to the police tonight, but in the morning they'll begin making investigations. At least, by noon, they'll be *looking* for you. By afternoon, they'll be *searching* for you. By midnight, you'll be the prime suspect."

"Of what?"

"Of murder."

She whirled to stare with widening eyes and an expression which mirrored horror. "You mean . . . somebody . . . was killed?"

Mason said, "As though you didn't know."

"I don't know."

"You seemed in rather a hurry to leave the house about the time I was ringing the bell."

"Did I?"

"Yes."

94

"Well, what of it?"

"Nothing. Just a coincidence, that's all. However, when the police start checking up on Milter, they . . ."

"Exactly *what* has Leslie Milter done now?" she asked.

Mason said, "He didn't do it. It was done to him. He's dead. Someone killed him."

Mason could feel the bench move at her sudden start.

"Not so good," the lawyer said.

"What?"

"The convulsive start. The first time when you saw me here, you did it naturally. This was rehearsed. There's quite a difference between the two. You *might* have fooled me if I hadn't seen that first jump."

"Say," she demanded, "who are you?"

"The name's Mason. I'm a lawyer, from Los Angeles."

"*Perry* Mason?"

"Yes."

"Oh," she said in a tone which was faint with dismay.

"How about a little talk?"

"I—I don't think I have anything to say."

"Oh, yes, you have. People sometimes underestimate their own powers of conversation. Think things over a little."

Mason gave his attention once more to the magazines. After a few minutes, he said, "Here's a young woman who ran away. If it hadn't been for that, the police never would have had anything on her. Strange thing about that desire to get away from something. A person wants to run and doesn't stop to realize that it's the worst thing he could possibly do. Let me see what they did with this woman."

Mason turned the pages of the magazine, said, "She went to Tehachapi for life. That must be rather a terrible thing, a young, good-looking woman suddenly plunged behind the walls. Year after year, she watches herself getting older. When she eventually gets out, her skin is harsh, her hair is gray, her figure is gone. The lightness has left her step. The sparkle isn't in her eyes. She's just a dejected, middle-aged . . ."

"Stop it!" Alberta Cromwell all but screamed at him.

"Pardon me," Mason said. "I was just talking about the magazine." He looked at his wrist watch. "Another thirty minutes before the bus is due. I suppose the back door of your apartment opens onto a porch—place for garbage and perhaps a screen cooler. Is there a partition between that and the porch on the adjoining apartment, or is it just a railing?"

"A wooden railing."

Mason nodded. "Was he perhaps fixing a hot buttered rum for you, and then you—Well, suppose *you* tell me what happened?"

She compressed her lips in a thin, tight line.

Mason said, "He was expecting this blonde girl from the detective agency when the Los Angeles bus came in. She had a key to the apartment. Probably he didn't want you to know that."

"But I *did* know it," she blurted. "It was just a matter of business. I knew she was coming."

"Oh, so he convinced you it was just a matter of business, did he?"

She made no answer.

Mason said, "You mean he *tried* to convince you, and you pretended that you'd let him."

She turned, and he could see the torment in her eyes. "I tell you it was business. I knew she was coming down there. Her name's Sally Elberton. She works for the detective agency where Leslie was employed. Their relationship is purely business."

"Did you know she had a key?"

"Yes."

"She must have come sooner than he expected," Mason said.

She said nothing.

"Did Miss Elberton know about you?"

She started to say something, then checked herself.

"Quite apparently," Mason said, "she did not. So she came, and you slipped out of the back door, climbed over the rail, and went into your own apartment. I wonder how long it was before you went back."

She said, "It wasn't Sally Elberton."

"How do you know?"

"Because I—I was curious. After a while, I went to the window and watched."

"And what did you see?"

"I saw him when he left the apartment."

"Oh, it was a man?"

"Yes."

"Who?"

"I don't know his name. I've never seen him before."

"What did he look like?"

She said, "I jotted down the license number of his automobile."

"What is it?"

"I'm not giving out that information."

"A young man?" Mason asked.

Once more she refused to answer.

Mason said, almost musingly, "Then after he left, you went back to ask Leslie what it was all about. You looked through the little glass window in the back door. Or did you open the door and get a whiff of the gas? You wondered whether to leave the door open, whether—no, wait a minute. That back door must have been locked and the key turned in the lock. He would have done that, so that you wouldn't have interrupted his tête-à-tête. That's an interesting thought. If he'd trusted you a little more implicitly, if he'd left the back door unlocked, you *might* have got it open in time to have saved his life. So then you rushed back to your apartment and came downstairs to try the front door. You found me ringing the doorbell and knew the door was closed and locked. That, I guess, just about covers it."

She said nothing.

Mason started thumbing through the magazine again. "Well," he said, "if you can't talk about crime, we can at least read about it. Here's a photograph showing . . ."

With a quick motion of her arm, she knocked the magazine from his hand to the floor, jumped to her feet, and started out of the bus depot. She was almost running by the time she reached the door.

Mason waited until the door of the bus depot had swung shut before he moved; then he picked up the magazines from the floor, placed them in a neat pile on the wooden bench in the waiting room, and walked out.

Della Street wakened as he opened the door of the car. "See her?" she asked.

"Yes."

"Where is she?"

"Gone."

"Where?"

"Home."

Della smiled, a sleep-drugged, wistful little smile. "You *do* have a way with women, don't you, Chief?"

Chapter 12

The train, having stopped briefly to pick up a lone passenger, gathered momentum. Early morning sunlight was touching the snow-capped crests of high mountain ranges on the right. The locomotive, speeding past orange groves laden with golden fruit, whistled intermittently for grade crossings. In the sleepers, Pullman porters were beginning to haul out baggage and pile it in vestibules. In the diner, passengers were thinning out as the train approached the suburbs of Los Angeles.

Mason entered the dining car. Sally Elberton was seated alone at a table for two.

"One, sir?" the dining steward asked, holding up a finger at Mason. "We'll have just time to serve you."

Mason said, "Thank you. I'll sit here," and walked calmly over to seat himself opposite the young woman.

She kept her eyes on her plate for a moment, then elevated a cup of coffee to her lips, casually glanced at Mason, dropped her eyes back to the plate, then suddenly snapped her eyes back into a startled glance at the lawyer, the coffee cup held motionless in her hand.

"Good morning," Mason said.

"Why—were you on this train? I didn't know . . . You've been . . . south?"

"Just got on a little while ago," Mason said.

"Oh." She smiled. "I got on early, myself—been visiting a friend."

A waiter bent solicitously over Mason's shoulder. "If you'll put your order in right away, sir . . ."

"Just a pot of coffee," Mason said.

He opened his cigarette case, took out a cigarette, lit it, settled back in the chair with one arm resting lightly on the edge of the table. "Did you get to see him?" he asked.

"Who?"

"Your friend."

She studied him for a moment as though debating whether to be angry or facetious, then smiled and said, "As it happened, my friend was not a him, but a her."

"The name wouldn't by any chance have been Milter?" Mason asked.

This time she decided to freeze him with cold indignation. "I don't know what gave you that idea in the first place," she said, "or who gave you the right to inquire into my private affairs."

"I was just preparing you," Mason said, "sort of giving you a dress rehearsal."

"Rehearsal for what?"

"For the questions that are coming later."

"I can assure you," she said, her voice coldly formal, "that if anyone has the slightest right to ask me questions I will be able to answer without any assistance, Mr. Mason."

Mason moved back slightly so that the waiter could bring his coffee. He handed the waiter a dollar bill, said, "Get the check, pay it, keep the change," shifted his position slightly, waited until the grinning waiter had retired, and then asked quite casually, "Was Milter alive or dead when you called?"

She didn't so much as bat an eyelash. Her face was a mask of cold disdain. "I don't know to what you are referring," she said.

Mason put sugar and cream in his coffee, stirred it, and drank the coffee slowly, enjoying his cigarette while he looked out at the scenery. The blonde who sat across from him continued to keep that cool stare of an annoyed young woman who is keeping herself very much aloof.

Mason finished his coffee, pushed back his chair, and got to his feet.

Surprise showed in the young woman's eyes. "Is . . . is that all?" she asked, the words slipping in an unguarded moment through the wall of her reserve.

Mason smiled down at her. "You answered my question when I first asked it," he said.

"How?"

"By that look of stiff surprise, by that dead pan, and the studied calmness of your reply. You'd been rehearsing your

100

answer to it all night. You knew *someone* was going to ask it.''

With which he calmly strode from the diner, leaving a very disconcerted young woman craning her neck to stare at his back as he jerked open the door, crossed the vestibule, and went into the sleeper.

Mason found Marvin Adams in the last car. Adams stared up at him incredulously, got to his feet. "Mr. Mason!" he exclaimed. "I didn't know you were taking *this* train."

"I didn't either," Mason said. "Sit down, Marvin. I want to have a quick talk with you."

Adams moved over so that Mason could sit down beside him.

Mason crossed his knees, made himself as comfortable as possible, leaning an elbow on the cushioned arm of the Pullman seat. "You took a duck from Witherspoon's place last night," he said.

Marvin's face broke into a grin. "Cutest little cuss you ever saw. I got to feeding him flies, and he was just like a pet."

"What happened to him?"

"I don't know what *did* happen to him. He disappeared."

"How?" Mason asked.

"I took him into town in the car I was driving."

"Your car?"

"No, one that I'd borrowed from one of the boys there in El Templo. It was the sort of car a junior-college kid would drive. You know, it has seen a lot better days, but it gets you there and gets you back."

"You drove it out to the Witherspoon ranch?"

Marvin Adams grinned. "Took the old junk heap out and parked it right in front of the family mansion," he said. "I always thought it made Witherspoon sore when he saw that heap parked out in front of the place. Two and three times he told me whenever I wanted to come out, if I'd just telephone in, he'd have a chauffeur drive one of his cars in and pick me up."

"You didn't do that?"

"I'll say I didn't. The old heap didn't look like much, but it was my sort. You know the feeling."

Mason nodded. "Lois didn't mind?" he asked.

The gleeful grin on the young man's face faded into a tender smile. He said quietly, "She loved it."

"All right," Mason said, "you took the duck into town in that car, and what happened?"

"I'd said good-by to Lois. I had a quick job of packing a suitcase on my hands, and then a train to catch—and I suddenly realized I was hungry. I wanted a hamburger. There wasn't any parking place on the main street. I knew a nice little restaurant down on Cinder Butte Avenue. I took the car down there and parked it. . . ."

"Directly in front of the restaurant?" Mason interrupted.

"No. The place was pretty well cluttered up with cars. I had to drive about a block before I found a parking place. Why?"

"Nothing," Mason said. "Just getting the picture straight is all. Guess that's the lawyer in me. Go on."

"Why all the commotion about the duck? Is old man Witherspoon sore at losing one of his prize ducks?"

Mason avoided that question, countered with another. He said, "That time when I first met you, you were mentioning something about sinking ducks with some new type of chemical. What's it all about?"

"They're known as detergents," Adams said.

"What's a detergent?"

The young man's face showed the enthusiasm a person feels when he's discussing a favorite subject. "The molecules of a detergent are built up on a complex structure. One end of each of the long molecules is hydrophobic, or, in other words, it tends to be repelled by water. The other end is hydrophilic, or has an affinity for water. When a detergent is mixed with water and applied to an oily surface, the end of the molecule which doesn't affiliate with the water adheres to the oil. The other end affiliates with the water. Everyone knows there's a certain natural antipathy between oil and water. They don't mix. But a detergent does more than mix them. It really marries them."

"You mentioned something about a sinking duck," Mason said.

"Yes, you can accomplish things with a detergent that seem physically impossible. Quite frequently, nature uses the repellent properties of oil and water to give animals or plants

102

a certain protection. Take the duck, for instance. The duck's feathers ordinarily repel water, and therefore enclose within a good-sized volume a mass of air. If a small amount of this detergent or wetting agent is put on the water, the detergent immediately wets the oily feathers. Then, by capillary attraction, the water soaks into the feathers in the same way it would soak up into a sponge. If you're interested, I can send you some material on it.''

"No, thanks. That won't be necessary. I just wanted to find out something about it. I suppose you intended to use this duck in connection with a similar experiment.''

"Yes, I did. Gee, he was a cute little cuss. I thought I'd keep him as a pet. The experiment doesn't hurt him any. You can have a lot of fun with it; particularly when some guy doesn't like you and wants to call you on every slip you make, you can throw out a remark about a drowning duck and . . .''

"The way you did with Burr?'' Mason asked.

Adams grinned, nodded his head, then after a moment added, ''I was showing off in front of Lois. But Burr had it coming. He's always had a chip on his shoulder as far as I was concerned.''

"Any reason?'' Mason asked.

"None that I can see. Of course, Mr. Mason, I'm going to be frank with you. Witherspoon doesn't like the idea of my marrying into the family. I know that—but that's not going to stop me. I'm going to do what will make Lois happy. And I have a right to consider my own happiness. In the next few months, I'm going into the Army. I don't know what's going to happen after that. No one does. I know it's going to be a tough job. I . . . gee, I'm talking too much.''

"No, you aren't,'' Mason said. "Go on. Let's have the rest of it.''

"Well,'' Adams said, ''I feel that I'm going to be risking my life, and a lot of fellows just like me are going to be risking their lives, so that birds like Witherspoon can enjoy the things they have. I suppose I shouldn't feel that way, but—well, anyway, I feel that if I'm good enough to go out and fight for John L. Witherspoon, I'm good enough to marry into his family. I know it doesn't make sense in a way, but—oh, hang it, I love Lois and she loves me, and why should we get silly and store up a lot of tragedy for ourselves. We may have only a few weeks together.''

"Why wouldn't you consent to go to Yuma and marry her last night?" Mason asked.

Adams let his face show surprise; then his eyes narrowed slightly. "Who told you about that?" he asked in a coldly formal voice.

"Lois."

Adams remained silent for several seconds, then said, "Because it was a sneaky way to go about it. I wrote her a letter after I got on the train, and told her if she still felt the same way about it next week, to go ahead and tell her dad what we were going to do, and then we'd do it."

Mason nodded. "About this duck. Did you have any particular reason for taking him?"

"Yes, I did." Adams fished in his pocket and pulled out a letter. "This speaks for itself," he said.

Mason shook the folded sheet of paper from the envelope and read:

Dear Mr. Adams:

Talking with some friends of yours, I understand you have a chemical you can put in water and make a duck sink without touching it.

Some men at my club have been riding me pretty hard, and it would be worth an even hundred bucks to me to be able to take them on something of this sort. Your friends tell me you're going to be in Los Angeles on Monday morning. If you'll telephone Lakeview two-three-seven-seven-one, and make an appointment, I'll have five nice new crisp twenty-dollar bills waiting for you.

Sincerely yours,

Gridley P. Lahey

Mason studied the letter for almost a minute, then abruptly folded it, put it in his pocket, and said, "Let me keep this. I'll phone Mr. Lahey. Let me know where I can get in touch with you after I've arranged an appointment. I'd like to be there when you perform the experiment."

Adams seemed puzzled.

"It's quite all right," Mason said. "Let me handle it, and will you do me a favor?"

"What?"

"Don't mention this letter to *anyone*. Don't mention about ducks drowning, unless you are asked some specific question along those lines by someone who is entitled to expect an answer."

"I'm afraid I don't follow you, Mr. Mason."

"Suppose I should tell you this was primarily for Lois?"

"Then I'd do it."

"Then do it," Mason said.

The train slowed to a stop. The porter yelled, "Los Angeles. Los Angeles. All out for Los Angeles."

Mason got to his feet. "How much of this detergent would it take to sink a duck?"

"A very small amount of the right kind. A few thousandths of one per cent."

"It floats on the surface of the water then?"

"Well, not exactly, although it amounts to the same thing. The water repellent end of the molecules is trying to get away from the water. That makes the molecules tend to congregate in larger numbers around the surface of the water, and any surfaces which are wet with water."

Mason said, "I see, and these molecules dissolve the oil. . . ."

"Strictly speaking, they don't dissolve the oil. They simply keep the oil from repelling the water. Once the detergent is removed from water and the feathers, the duck swims along the same as ever."

"I see," Mason said as the line of passengers started shuffling down the aisle of the train. "I'm interested in that duck. You say you left it in the machine?"

"Yes."

"Where?"

"In the front seat."

"Couldn't it have flopped over the back of the front seat down into the rear of the car?"

"No. It was too young to do any flying. It might have dropped down to the floor in the front of the car, but I looked the floor over pretty carefully."

Mason said, "Say nothing whatever about this detergent,

105

or the experiment of sinking the duck. If anyone asks you, tell them you wanted the duck simply as a pet. And don't, for the moment, mention this letter which you received from Los Angeles.''

''All right, I'll do it if you say so, Mr. Mason. But look here, I want that hundred dollars. That looks as big as the United States mint to me right now. A man who's working his way through college and wanting to get married—well, you can see how it is.''

''I see no reason why I can't take care of that,'' Mason said, reaching for his wallet.

''No, no. I only meant that I didn't want you to let this chap get away. Be sure you get in touch with him.''

Mason took out five twenty-dollar bills. ''Don't worry. I'll describe the experiment to him and collect the hundred.''

Adams seemed dubious.

Mason shoved the currency into his hand. ''Don't be silly. This is just to save me getting in touch with you again. Where can I tell this man to get his detergent?''

''Oh, there are lots of places. The Central Scientific Company, the country's foremost makers of laboratory equipment, in Chicago, for one—or the National Chemical Company in New Orleans. Or, of course, the American Cyanamid and Chemical Corporation in New York. He won't have any trouble getting a detergent, just so he knows what to ask for.''

Mason asked, ''Where can I get in touch with you, in case I need any more information?''

Adams took a card case from his pocket, withdrew a card, scribbled a number on it, and handed it to the lawyer.

''All right,'' Mason said. ''I'll call you if I need you. I have to see about some baggage, so don't wait for me. Go right ahead.''

Mason watched Marvin Adams walk rapidly down the runway which led to the underground crossing below the tracks.

The boy had gone but twenty or thirty steps when a quiet, unobtrusive individual who had been standing with his back against the wall, looking the passengers over, stepped out so as to block the way.

''Your name Adams?'' he asked.

Marvin Adams, looking somewhat surprised, nodded.

The man flipped back the lapel of his coat far enough to show a badge. "The boys down at headquarters want to ask you a few questions," he said. "It won't take long."

Mason marched on past with no sign of recognition as Adams, his eyes wide and startled, stared in astonishment at the detective from headquarters.

"You mean . . . they want to ask questions . . . of me?"

Mason didn't hear the man's answer.

Chapter 13

Della Street was waiting in Mason's car outside the depot. The lawyer slid in behind the wheel.

"Everything okay?" she asked.

"Yes."

"Talk with the girl on the train?"

"Uh huh."

"Get anything out of her?"

"More than she wanted to give—not as much as I wanted to get."

"Was Marvin Adams on the train?"

"Uh huh."

"I looked around to see if I could spot any plain-clothes men hanging around," Della Street said.

Mason deftly spun the steering wheel, guiding the car out of the parking place. He flashed her an amused, sidelong glance. "Did you?" he asked.

"No."

"What made you think you could?"

"Spot a plain-clothes man?"

"Yes."

"Aren't they—well, aren't they sort of typical?"

"Only in fiction," Mason said. "Your real high-class detective is altogether too intelligent to look like a detective."

"Was one of them there?"

"Uh huh."

"Did he arrest the blonde from the detective agency?"

"No," Mason said. "He arrested Marvin Adams."

She looked at him as though she might be seeing his face for the first time. "They arrested Marvin Adams!"

"Yes."

"And you didn't . . ."

"Didn't what?" Mason asked as she paused, groping for words.

"Didn't stay to help him out?"

"How could I help him out?"

"By telling him not to talk."

Mason shook his head.

"I thought that was one of the reasons you were so anxious to get on the train."

"It was."

"Come on, loosen up, stingy," she chided. "Don't be like that!"

Mason said, "As it happens, the best thing he can do is to go ahead and tell his story in his own way. Just so he leaves out one particular thing, and I've already arranged for that."

"What's that thing?" Della Street asked.

Mason took the letter from his pocket, and handed it to her. She read it while Mason was guiding the car through the early morning city traffic.

"What does that mean?" she asked.

"Nine hundred and ninety-nine chances out of a thousand, it means Gridley P. Lahey is a purely fictitious individual. The telephone number will probably be that of some large department store or some factory which employs several hundred or more workers."

"Then it means that . . ."

"That the murder was premeditated," Mason said, "that it was worked out to a split second in its timing. Whoever did it planned things deliberately so that Marvin Adams would take the rap."

"And what does that mean?"

"Lots of things. Among others, it means that the search for the murderer can be narrowed into a very small circle."

"How?"

"In the first place," Mason said, "Marvin Adams was picked for a particular reason. That reason is that the person who picked him knew something Marvin doesn't know himself."

"You mean about his past?"

"That's right. That person must have known about Marvin's father, must have known that Milter had been working on the case."

"Anything else?" she asked.

109

"Yes. It means the person knew about the experiment of the drowning duck."

"What else?"

Mason said, "This is something that puzzles me. He knew somehow that the duck that was left in Milter's apartment was going to be identified. Now, *how* did he know that?"

"He must have known that Witherspoon was going in to El Templo."

"Witherspoon himself apparently didn't know that until after I'd started. It was something he did on impulse unless . . ."

"Unless what?" she asked.

Mason's lips tightened. "Unless the whole thing was deliberately planned in just that way by the one man who knew that the duck could and would be identified."

"You mean—that it was—"

"John L. Witherspoon," Mason finished for her.

"But, Chief, that's preposterous."

Mason said, "It might *not* be preposterous. He might have laid his plans to get Adams in a spot. He may have wanted to make Adams *think* he'd committed a murder."

"But not an actual murder?"

"Perhaps not."

"Then something must have miscarried about this man's plans."

"That's right."

"Where would that leave this man—in case he had made a mistake?"

"Right on the spot," Mason said. "Legally, he might be able to show it wasn't first-degree murder. It might be manslaughter. But he *might* have a hard time proving his point to a jury."

Della Street's voice was vibrant with feeling. "Well, why keep beating around the bush? Why not call a spade a Witherspoon?"

"Because of the laws about slander and libel. We won't say anything until we can prove it."

"When will that be?"

He said, "I don't know. Perhaps we'll sit tight, and let the district attorney at El Templo say it."

They were silent for the rest of the trip to the office. Mason

110

swung the car into the parking lot across the street from his office building. They crossed over, and Mason asked the elevator starter, "Is Paul Drake in his office?"

"Yes, he came in half an hour ago."

They rode up in the elevator. Mason paused to poke his head into Drake's office, said to the girl at the switchboard, "Tell Paul I'm on the job. Ask him to drop in and see me as soon as he gets a chance."

Mason and Della Street walked down to the lawyer's private office. Della Street was still opening mail when Drake's steps sounded outside the door. His knuckles tapped a distinctive code knock.

Mason let him in.

Drake walked across to the big overstuffed leather chair and squirmed around in it so that he was sitting sideways, his legs drooped over the arm of the chair.

"Well, Perry, you called the turn on that one."

"On what?"

"On the fact that after a case gets just so old, people begin to get careless and certain things come out in the open."

"What have you uncovered?"

"Miss X is a Corine Hassen."

"Where is she now?"

"Darned if I know, but we're on her trail and it's almost a cinch that we'll be able to find her."

"Is it a warm trail?"

"No. It's cold as a frog's belly, Perry. I can't find anyone who saw her after the time of the trial. That's a long time."

Mason nodded. "The prosecutor managed to keep her out of it by reaching an agreement with the defense, that she could be referred to as Miss X. Under the circumstances, she was almost certain to get out from under and sit tight until it had blown over."

Drake said, "Where there's so much smoke, there *must* have been a little fire."

"Meaning what?"

"Meaning that Latwell must have been playing around with her a bit. Incidentally, I can produce two witnesses who can give us something on that angle. Latwell knew her."

"Intimately?" Mason asked.

"I don't know. I do know that he'd been seen with her

111

several times. Of course, the theory of the prosecution was that Adams knew about this, and therefore had dragged her name into it."

"How old was she?" Mason asked.

"About twenty-five."

"She'd be about forty-five now."

"That's right."

"Attractive?"

"My correspondents telephone that her pictures, taken twenty years ago, indicate she was rather good-looking, not a knockout, you understand. As I understand it, her face was a little pinched around the eyes. Her figure was the distinctive thing about her. It was swell—twenty years ago. She was a cashier in a chocolate shop, candies, ice cream, light lunches, and things of that sort."

"Just how did this Hassen girl disappear?" Mason asked.

"Well, she was living with her aunt. Her father and mother were both dead. She said she had an opportunity to get a job out on the Pacific Coast, that she had a boy friend who was always hounding her to marry him, that he was intensely jealous, and she was tired of the whole business, and intended to skip out and not leave any forwarding address, that she'd get in touch with her aunt after a while—more or less the same old story."

Mason frowned. "I'm not so certain it is. When did she leave, Paul?"

Drake consulted a memorandum book. "Just about the time of the murder."

Mason said, "Start on it as a regular disappearance, Paul. Look over everything, hospital records, unidentified bodies, and all that."

"Around Winterburg City?" Drake asked.

"No," Mason said. "Around Los Angeles and San Francisco for a start . . . and try Reno, particularly."

"I don't get you," Drake said, frowning.

Mason said, "Let's look at this thing logically. The big trouble is we get hypnotized by facts and start placing a false interpretation upon those facts because of the sheer weight of circumstances.

"Now in this case the evidence looked very dark against Horace Adams. Somewhere during the trial, his attorney got

112

panic-stricken and became convinced that his client was guilty. No matter what happens, Paul, a lawyer should never become convinced of the guilt of his client.''

''Why?'' Drake asked. ''Are lawyers' consciences that brittle?''

''It isn't a question of a lawyer's conscience,'' Mason said. ''It's a question of doing justice to a client. Once you become convinced your client is guilty, you interpret all of the evidence in a false light and weigh it by false standards. You can see what happened in this case with the mysterious Miss X. Now, I'm acting on the theory that Horace Adams was innocent. In that case, the story he told about Miss X may well have been the truth. Then it's quite possible Miss X did go to Reno to join Latwell.''

Drake said, ''I can't figure that, Perry. Adams may have been innocent; but when he felt he was caught in a mesh of circumstantial evidence, he tried to lie out of it. If this gal had gone to Reno, she'd have read of Latwell's murder in the papers, and . . .''

''And what?'' Mason asked, as Drake hesitated.

''Probably taken a run-out powder,'' the detective said, after a moment's thought.

Mason smiled. ''Well, Paul, we need a point of beginning, and we haven't time to plod along on a cold trail. Have your correspondents see what they can do in Winterburg, but start some men working at Reno. That may make a good short cut. Let's cover the hospital records and do all of the routine in connection with a disappearance case. Then let's consider *your* suggestion. Suppose you were in Reno, wanted to disappear, and were running away from something in the East? Where would you go? Nine times out of ten it would be Los Angeles, or San Francisco, wouldn't it?''

''Well, yes,'' Drake admitted, after thinking the question over.

''All right, while you're covering Reno, cover Los Angeles and San Francisco. Look for a trace of Corine Hassen, either under her own or an assumed name.''

''An assumed name isn't going to be easy,'' Drake said.

''Oh, I don't know. She must have used her right name on occasion, at the post office, at banks, on her driving license. See what you can do.''

"Okay, I'll start men on it right away."

Mason pushed his thumbs in the armholes of his vest, sunk his chin on his chest, and stared moodily at the pattern in the carpet, "Hang it, Paul, I'm making a mistake somewhere—I've already made it."

"How do you know?"

"It's just the feeling I have when I get off on a wrong trail. Perhaps it's my subconscious trying to warn me."

"Where could you have made a mistake?"

"I don't know. I have a feeling it has something to do with Leslie Milter."

"What about him?"

Mason said, "When you once get the correct master pattern, every single event fits into that pattern. It dovetails with every other event which impinges upon it. When you get a master pattern which seems to accommodate *all* of the events except *one*, and you can't make that event fit in, it's pretty apt to mean that your master pattern is wrong.

"Now take Milter. Milter was undoubtedly trying to get blackmail. Yet he passed the word on to that Hollywood scandal sheet. By the way, have you found out anything about that?"

"I've found out that the thing came as a leak. I can't get Milter's name in connection with it, but it's a cinch that's who it was."

Mason said, "Yes, even without any information from the scandal sheet, it stands to reason Allgood fired Milter for talking. Therefore, Milter must have talked to someone. To whom? Apparently not to Lois. Not to Marvin Adams. He could have talked to Witherspoon all he wanted. No, he must have talked to that Hollywood scandal sheet.

"Now put yourself in Milter's position. He was a blackmailer. He was carefully stalking his prey. He was in the position of a submarine that has one torpedo and is lying in wait for a dangerous destroyer. He must be certain to make a hit with that one shot in a vital spot. Under those circumstances, you can't imagine him frittering away his ammunition. Yet that's what the tip-off in the scandal sheet amounted to. If he got anything at all for it, it was only pin money and . . ."

114

"They never pay for tips," Drake said. "They sometimes grant favors, but they don't pay."

For several seconds, Mason was thoughtfully silent; then he said, "Also note that he must have been the one who sent this special-delivery letter to me. He wouldn't have done that if he'd been blackmailing Witherspoon or getting ready to blackmail Lois or Marvin or . . . by George!"

"What?" Drake asked.

Mason regarded him thoughtfully. His brows pulled together in a level line over his eyes. "Hang it, Paul, there's one solution that would make things hang together. It's a weird, bizarre solution when you look at it in one way, and when you look at it in another, it's the *only* logical solution."

"What are you holding out on me?" Drake asked.

"Not a thing," Mason said. "It's all there right in front of us. Only we haven't seen it."

"What?" Drake asked.

"Mr. and Mrs. Roland Burr!"

"I don't get you."

"Get this," Mason said. "Burr met Witherspoon. Apparently that meeting was fortuitous. Actually, it could have been arranged very nicely.

"Apparently all you have to do is to run across Witherspoon in El Templo, be interested in fly-fishing or color photography, and Witherspoon starts talking. A clever man could make a very favorable impression and . . . yes, by George, that's it. That *must* be it. Burr, or his wife, must have picked up something. *They* could have tipped off the scandal sheet— or they *may* be planning to shake Witherspoon down, and this column was the means they used to soften him up."

Drake pursed his lips, gave a low whistle.

Mason said, "Make a note, Paul, to find out something about Mr. and Mrs. Roland Burr."

Chapter 14

It was shortly before noon when Della Street came hurrying into the office. She said, "Mrs. George L. Dangerfield is waiting out there, says she simply has to see you on a matter which she can't even discuss with anyone else."

Mason frowned. "I thought Allgood was going to telephone and tip me off before she came down here."

"Want me to get him on the phone?" Della asked.

Mason nodded.

A few moments later, when Allgood came on the line, his voice sounded distinctly worried. "Your secretary said you wanted to talk with me, Mr. Mason."

"Yes, about that leak out of your office. You've heard about Milter?"

"Yes. Most unfortunate. . . . When the police telephoned me, they tipped me off that he was dead, so I could cover up a lot of stuff."

"I was there," Mason said. "It was a swell job. Did you know that your secretary listened in on our conversation and went down to see Milter last night?"

"Yes. She finally told me everything. I could see something was on her mind this morning. She kept worrying about it, and about half an hour ago she came in and said she wanted to talk with me. She told me the whole story. I was just on the point of ringing up to ask you if I could get in touch with you. I didn't want to call you from the office."

Mason said, "You were going to let me know before Mrs. Dangerfield came down."

"Yes, I will."

"She's here now."

"What? The devil she is!"

"Waiting in my outer office."

"I don't know how she got any information about you. It certainly didn't come through *my* office."

"Nor through your receptionist?" Mason asked.

"No. I feel quite certain. That young woman made rather a complete confession. I don't want to tell you the details over the phone. I'd like to come down to your office."

"Come ahead," Mason said. "Can you start right away?"

"Yes. It will take me about twenty-five or thirty minutes to get there."

"All right, come along."

Mason hung up the phone, said to Della Street, "Allgood says she didn't get the tip through him. Let's get her in here and see what she has to say. What does she look like, Della?"

"Well, she's pretty well preserved. She's taken care of herself. As I remember it, she was about thirty-three at the time of the trial. That would make her over fifty now. She doesn't look it by ten years."

"Heavy? Dumpy?" Mason asked.

"No. She's slender and—flexible. Her skin's in good shape. She's taken good care of herself. I'm giving you the points a woman would notice. The externals, the style."

"Blonde or brunette?"

"Decidedly brunette. She has large, dark eyes."

"Glasses?"

"I think she has to wear them in order to see well, but she carries them in her purse. She was just putting the spectacle case away when I went out to talk with her. She uses her eyes to advantage."

Mason said, "Tell me something about women, Della. Could she have let herself go to seed, and then brought herself back this way?"

"Definitely not," Della Street said. "Not at the age of fifty-odd. She's a woman who has taken care of herself all her life. She has eyes, and legs and hips, and she knows it—and uses them."

"Interesting," Mason said. "Let's have a look at her."

Della Street nodded, withdrew to escort Mrs. Dangerfield into the office.

The woman came directly toward Mason, walking with smooth, even rhythm. When she gave the lawyer her hand, it was with warmth and friendliness, and she raised long, dark lashes, and let him have the full benefit of her eyes. "I can't begin to tell you how much I thank you for seeing me.

117

I know you're a very busy lawyer and that you see people by appointment only, but my business is particularly important, and,'' she said, glancing at Della Street, ''highly confidential.''

Mason said casually, ''Sit down, Mrs. Dangerfield. I have no secrets from my secretary. She takes notes on conversations and keeps my records straight for me. I seldom trust anything to memory that can be put in writing. Make notes of what Mrs. Dangerfield has to say, Della.''

Mrs. Dangerfield took the rebuff with good grace. For a moment she stiffened; then she was smiling at Mason once more. ''Of course! How stupid of me,'' she said. ''I should have known that a lawyer who handles as much work as you do, must systematize these matters. The reason I was concerned is because what I have to say is so very, *very* confidential. The happiness of others depends on it.''

Mason asked, ''Did you wish to retain me to do something for you, Mrs. Dangerfield? Because if you did . . .''

''No, not at all. I wanted to talk with you about something you're handling for someone else.''

''Sit down,'' Mason invited. ''A cigarette?''

''Thank you, I will.''

Mason gave her a cigarette, took one himself, and lit first one, then the other.

Mrs. Dangerfield sat down in the big chair, studied Mason for a moment in sidelong appraisal through the first puffs of her cigarette smoke, then said abruptly, ''Mr. Mason, you're doing some work for Mr. John L. Witherspoon.''

''What leads you to make that statement?'' Mason asked.

''Aren't you?''

Mason smiled. ''You made an assertion. I'm asking a question.''

She laughed. ''Well, I'll change my assertion into a question.''

''Then I'll still answer it with a question.''

She moved her long, well-manicured fingers in a nervous, drumming motion on the arm of the chair, took a deep drag from the cigarette, looked at Mason, and laughed. ''I see I'm not going to get anywhere sparring with a lawyer,'' she said. ''I'll put my cards on the table.''

Mason bowed.

She said, "My name is Mrs. George L. Dangerfield, just as I told your secretary. But my name has not *always* been Mrs. Dangerfield."

Mason's silence was a courteous invitation to proceed.

With the manner of one dropping an unexpected bit of information which will have explosive repercussions, she said, "I was formerly Mrs. David Latwell."

Mason didn't change expression. "Go ahead," he said.

"That information doesn't seem to surprise you," she announced, her voice showing disappointment.

"A lawyer can seldom seem to be surprised—even when he is surprised," Mason announced.

"You're a very baffling individual," she said, with just a trace of irritation in her voice.

"I'm sorry, but you said you wanted to put cards on the table." Mason made a little gesture at the desk. "There's the table."

"Very well," she surrendered. "I was Mrs. David Latwell. My husband was murdered by Horace Adams. Horace and David were in partnership in Winterburg City."

"When did the murder take place?" Mason asked.

"In January of 1924."

"And what happened to Adams?"

"As though you didn't know!"

"Did you come to give information, or to try and get some?" Mason asked.

She thought that over for a moment, then turned to him frankly, and said, "A little of both."

"Suppose you change the purpose of your visit and simply try to give me information."

She smiled, "The murder was committed in the early part of 1924. Horace Adams was hanged in May of the year following.

"Horace had a wife—Sarah. Sarah and Horace, David and I, made a foursome on occasions. Horace and Sarah had a boy, Marvin. He was about two years old at the time of the murder, about three when his father was executed. I don't think Sarah ever liked me or fully trusted me. Sarah was a mother. She devoted her entire life to her husband and to her child. I couldn't see things that way. I was childless and—I was attractive. I liked to step around and see the night life a

119

bit. Sarah didn't approve of that. She thought a married woman should settle down in a rut.

"That was some twenty years ago. Ideas of marriage have changed some since then. I'm mentioning this to show that Sarah and I didn't always get along too well, although, because our husbands were partners, we made things seem very smooth and harmonious on the surface."

"Did the men know you didn't get along?" Mason asked.

"Good heavens, no! It was too subtle for men to get, just the little things that women can do. The raising of an eyebrow at a proper time, or just the way she happened to look at the length of some skirt I'd be wearing; or when her husband would compliment me on my appearance and turn to her to ask her if she didn't think I was getting younger every day, she'd agree with him, with just that cooing touch of sweetness which is entirely lost on a man but means so much to a woman."

"All right," Mason said, "you didn't like each other. So what happened?"

"I'm not saying that," she said. "I'm saying that Sarah didn't approve of me. I don't think Sarah ever liked me. I didn't dislike her. I pitied her. Well, then the murder took place, and I could never forgive Horace Adams for the things that he said in trying to cover up that murder."

"What were they?" Mason asked.

"He had killed David, and, as it turned out, had buried the body in the cellar of the manufacturing plant, and then cemented over the floor again. All I knew was that David had disappeared rather abruptly. Horace telephoned me there had been some trouble in connection with one of the patents, and David had had to go to Reno very hurriedly on business, that he'd write me just as soon as he got located there and found out how long he was going to have to stay."

"Did the fact that he was going to Reno make you at all suspicious?" Mason asked.

"To tell you the truth, it did."

"Why? Because he had been interested in some other woman?"

"Well, no—not exactly. But you know how it is. We were childless, and—I loved my husband, Mr. Mason. I loved him a lot. As I've grown older, I realize that love isn't everything
120

in life, but at that age things seemed different to me. I made myself attractive because I knew we were never going to have any children and because I wanted to hang onto my husband. I tried to give him everything that any other woman could possibly offer. I tried to be just as attractive as the girls he'd meet who might want to flirt with him. I tried to keep his attention centered on me. I—oh, in my way, I lived my life for my husband just as well as Sarah lived her life for her husband, only Sarah had a child. That made things a lot different somehow.''

"Go ahead," Mason said.

She said, "I'll be absolutely frank with you, Mr. Mason. I think perhaps there was a little jealousy on my part—of Sarah Adams. She could afford to let her hands get rough and harsh. When we'd go to a nightclub on a foursome, she'd look out of place. She looked just like what she was, a house-wife who had spent the afternoon with her child and then, at the last minute, fixed herself up and put on her best bib and tucker to go out. She didn't look like—like a part of the scheme of things, like a part of the night life, like she was really fitting the clothes she was wearing. But she was holding Horace Adams' love. You could see that.''

"Despite his comments on how nice *you* looked?" Mason asked.

"Oh, that!" and she snapped her fingers. "He saw me just as he saw every other woman, as so much scenery. He'd appreciate a good-looking woman just as he'd appreciate a good-looking painting or something; but his eyes were always coming back to his wife. He'd keep looking at her with that expression of being settled and comfortable and secure and happy.''

"And your husband didn't look at you that way?" Mason asked.

"No."

"Why not?"

"He was built differently. He—I'm not kidding myself a bit, Mr. Mason. My husband would have stepped out on me if someone had come along who was physically more attractive than I was. I made it my business to see that I led the procession, that's all.''

"I see."

121

"I'm not certain that you do. You'd have to know how a woman feels about those things in order to understand. It was an effort, and somewhere in the background was a fear, a fear that my foot might slip and I wouldn't head the procession any more."

"So when you thought your husband had gone to Reno, you . . ."

"I was scared stiff," she admitted, "and then when I didn't hear from him, I became frantic. I happened to have a friend in Reno. I wired that friend to check over all the hotels and find out where David was staying and find out—well, find out if he was alone."

"And then what?" Mason asked.

"When I found David wasn't registered in any hotel in Reno, I went up to have a showdown with Horace; and then Horace acted so evasive and so completely uncomfortable that I knew he was lying or trying to cover something up; and *then* he told me that David had run away with another girl."

"Who?" Mason asked.

"I don't think her name needs to enter into it."

"Why?"

"Because, of course, David hadn't run away with her. He hadn't had anything to do with her. It was just something Horace had made up to try and cover up the murder."

"Where is this woman now?" Mason asked.

"Good heavens, I don't know. I've entirely lost track of her. I don't think I ever even knew her. She was just a name to me. I would, of course, have found out more about her if it hadn't been for the way Horace acted. I called in the police, and it wasn't long before the police found out that he was lying and that David had been murdered. I don't know. I suppose that if Horace had told the truth, he could have escaped the death penalty."

"What was the truth?"

"They must have had some terrible quarrel over something there in the plant, and Horace struck my husband down in a fit of anger. Then he was panic-stricken and knew he had to do something with the body. In place of calling in the police and confessing, he waited until night, broke a hole in the cement, dug a grave, buried David, covered the place over with cement, put a lot of rubbish and shavings over the new cement until it could harden, and, of course, had me thinking all the time that David had gone to Reno very unexpectedly on business."

"How long before you began to get suspicious?" Mason asked.

"It must have been three or four days. I guess it must have been five days before Horace told this story about David having run away with the woman . . . after my friend reported David wasn't in Reno."

Mason leaned back in his swivel chair and closed his eyes as though trying to reconstruct something from the past. "Go right ahead. Keep on talking, Mrs. Dangerfield."

"It's a terrible thing to be in love with somebody and have that person killed. It comes first as a numbing shock, and then—well, I had an overpowering, terrific hatred for Horace Adams, for his wife, and I guess if I'd thought of it, even for the little boy. There wasn't a particle of sympathy or charity in my make-up. When the jury brought in a verdict against Horace that meant he would hang, I was wild with joy. I went out and celebrated all by myself."

"You didn't feel any sympathy for Mrs. Adams?" he asked, still keeping his eyes closed.

"None whatever. I tell you, I hated her. I didn't feel any sympathy for anyone. I could have pulled the rope that hung Horace Adams, and been glad to do it. I tried to get them to let me be present at the execution, but they wouldn't."

"Why did you want to?"

"I just wanted to scream, 'You murderer!' at him when the trap opened, so that he could have my words ringing in his ears as his neck broke. I—I tell you I was savage. I'm rather an emotional animal, Mr. Mason."

The lawyer opened his eyes, looked at her, and said, "Yes, I can appreciate that."

"I'm telling you all this so you'll understand my present position."

"What *is* your present position?" Mason asked.

"I realize something of how terribly wrong I was."

"You're sorry?"

"Not for the way I felt toward Horace," she said hastily. "I could have killed *him* with my bare hands. I'm glad that

123

his lawyer bungled his defense all up so that they hung him. As I say, if he'd told the truth, he'd probably have gotten off with manslaughter or second-degree murder, but the way he tried to cover up and everything—well, we won't talk about that, because I want to talk about Sarah.''

"What about Sarah?''

"I suppose that I persecuted Sarah. I tried to keep her from getting her share of the money out of the business. I was nasty in every way I could be. Sarah took what cash she could get, and disappeared. It was, of course, the only thing for her to do, on account of the boy. She didn't have much money, just a little. I never knew where she went. No one did. She covered her tracks pretty carefully. The boy was too young to remember, and she felt that she could bring him up so he would never know his father was executed for murder.''

"Do you know where she went?'' Mason asked.

She laughed at him and said, "Don't be so cagey, Mr. Mason. Of course, I do, now. She went to California. She worked and worked hard—too hard. She gave the boy a pretty good education. He always thought his father had been killed in an automobile accident, that they didn't have any other relatives. She carefully kept him from knowing anything at all about his past life or having any contacts which would reveal it to him. It was a splendid thing. She sacrificed her entire life for that.

"Well, she worked too hard. She got run down and got tuberculosis. Four or five years ago she went to the Red River Valley. She was well thought of there. She kept on working even when she should have been resting. If she'd gone to a hospital and had absolute quiet, she might have cured herself, but she was putting her boy through school, so she worked until—until she couldn't work any more.''

"And then?'' Mason asked.

"Then she died.''

"How do you know all this?'' Mason asked.

"Because I made it my business to find out.''

"Why?''

"Because—believe it or not, I developed a conscience.''

"When?''

124

"Quite a while ago. But it didn't really hit me until someone employed a detective who started investigating the case."

"Who employed him?"

"I don't know. I thought it was Sarah at first. It was someone living in El Templo. I couldn't find out who."

"Why did you come to me?"

"Because I think you know who was back of it all and why."

"What makes you think that?"

"Because I've located Marvin Adams. I find that he's unofficially engaged to the Witherspoon girl and that you were seen out at Witherspoon's house."

"How did you know that?" Mason asked.

"By accident. To tell you the truth, Mr. Mason, I was in El Templo because I thought the detective agency was located there. This detective was telephoning reports to El Templo. I found that out through the girl at the switchboard in the Winterburg City Hotel. They were station-to-station calls. I didn't get the number."

"And how did you find out about me?"

She said, "By a chance remark that was dropped by Mrs. Burr."

"Mrs. Burr?" Mason asked.

"Don't be so mysterious. You've met her out there at Witherspoon's."

"And you know her?" Mason asked.

"Yes. I've known her for years."

"Where did you meet her?"

"In Winterburg City."

"Indeed?"

"She used to live there."

Mason picked up a pencil from his desk, slid his thumb and forefinger up and down the polished sides, slowly and thoughtfully. *"That,"* he said, "is very interesting. She must have been rather a little girl at the time of the murder."

"What are you getting at?"

"Wasn't she?"

Mrs. Dangerfield averted her eyes and frowned as she made an effort at concentration. "No," she said, "she wasn't. She was at least seventeen or eighteen—perhaps nineteen. How old do you think she is now, Mr. Mason?"

Mason said, "I'm afraid I'm not much of a judge of ages. I thought she was in the late twenties or early thirties—and I would have said that *you* couldn't possibly have been more than thirty-eight or thirty-nine."

"Flatterer!"

"No, I really mean it," Mason said. "I'm not trying to flatter you. I'm really interested in seeing how a woman can continue to be young, regardless of the actual number of birthdays she may have had."

She said, "I'm not going to tell you how old I am, but Diana Burr is—let me see—she was . . . yes, she's between thirty-eight and thirty-nine."

"And you recognized her after all these years?" Mason asked.

"What do you mean, after all these years?"

"When did you see her last?"

"Oh, about three years ago."

"Then you know her husband?"

Mrs. Dangerfield shook her head. "I don't think so. Diana's name originally was Diana Perkins. She was quite a problem to her mother. Mrs. Perkins used to talk with me. They lived in our block. Then Diana ran away with a married man. She came back after four or five years, and claimed the man had divorced his wife and married her."

"What did the wife have to say about it?"

"Oh, she'd left. People had lost track of her. Perhaps Diana was telling the truth. Perhaps not. Well then, Diana left town again for a while and showed up with a brand-new husband."

"Burr?" Mason asked.

"No," she said, smiling. "Not Burr. Diana, I am afraid, is inclined to trade the old ones in on the new models as fast as they come out. Let's see. What *was* her husband's name? Radcliff, I think it was, but I'm not certain about that. I think he divorced her. She was back in Winterburg City for a little while, and then left for California. She married Mr. Burr in California."

"So you met her on the street and talked with her?"

"Yes."

"Did she mention anything about that old murder case?"

"No. She was very tactful."

"Does she know that Marvin Adams is the son of the man who was hanged for murder?"

"I'm almost certain she doesn't. At least, she didn't say anything about it. Of course, Sarah died before Mrs. Burr came to El Templo. She's only been there two or three weeks. I don't think the name Adams meant a thing to her."

"And you didn't tell her?"

"No, of course not."

"All right," Mason said, "that explains how you found out about me. Now go ahead and tell me what you wanted to see me about."

She said, "I—I wanted to get something off my mind."

"Wait a minute. One more question. Did you know Milter, the detective who was investigating this thing?"

"I have seen him a couple of times, although he didn't know it. I never met him, in the sense that you mean. I never actually talked with him."

"What time did you leave El Templo, Mrs. Dangerfield?"

"Early this morning."

"Where's Mr. Dangerfield?"

"He's staying on in El Templo. I left a note telling him I was going to take the car and be away for the day. He was snoring peacefully when I left. He likes to stay up late at night and sleep late in the morning. I'm just the opposite. I've trained myself so I can go to bed and go to sleep. He can come in without disturbing me. Quite frequently I get up in the morning and go out, long before he's wakened. I like to take walks in the early morning. I find that exercise before breakfast helps a lot."

Mason leaned back once more in the swivel chair and again closed his eyes as though trying to reconstruct mentally some event from the past. "So you made an investigation to make certain that your husband wasn't in Reno?"

"My husband. Oh, you mean David. Yes."

"Who made the investigation?"

"A friend."

Mason said, "Every time you've referred to that investigation, you've used the expression 'a friend.' Don't you think that's rather indefinite? You have never used a pronoun in referring to this friend. Is that because you are afraid to do so?"

"Why, Mr. Mason, what are you getting at? I don't understand you. Why should I be afraid to use a pronoun?"

"Because it would have had to be either him or her, and that would have indicated the sex of this friend," Mason said.

"Well, what difference does that make?"

"I was just wondering if this 'friend' might not have been your present husband, George L. Dangerfield."

"Why . . . why . . ."

"Was it?" Mason asked.

She said angrily, "You have the most unpleasant manner of trying to . . ."

"Was it?" Mason repeated.

Abruptly she laughed and said, "Yes. I can realize now, Mr. Mason, how you've made such a reputation as a cross-examiner. Perhaps I *was* trying to cover that up a little bit, because of the fact that it might sound—well, a little—well, a person might have drawn an erroneous conclusion from it."

"The conclusion would have been erroneous?" Mason asked.

She was in complete possession of her faculties now. She laughed at him and said, "I've told you, Mr. Mason, how much I cared about my husband, and how afraid I was that I might lose him. Do you think a woman who felt that way would take chances with some other man?"

"I was merely interested in uncovering something which you seemed to be trying to cover up. Perhaps it's merely the instinct of a cross-examiner," Mason said.

She said, "I had known George L. Dangerfield before our marriage. He had been—rather crazy about me; but he hadn't been in Winterburg City for more than two years prior to the time I wired him. I had only seen him once after my marriage, and that was to tell him definitely and positively that my marriage terminated everything between us."

Mason repeated her words slowly. *"Terminated everything between us."*

Once again she was angry; then she caught herself and said, "You do have the most unpleasant manner of prying into a person's mind. All right, if you want it that way, the answer is yes."

128

Mason said, "You left El Templo before the papers came out this morning?"

"Yes. Why?"

"Just why did you come *here*?"

"I told you it was my conscience that sent me here. I know something that I didn't ever tell anyone about."

"What?"

"I wasn't a witness at that old trial, so nobody asked me. I didn't volunteer this information."

"And what was the information?"

"Horace Adams and David had a fight."

"You mean an argument?"

"No, I mean a fist fight."

"What was it about?"

"I don't know."

"When?"

"The day David was murdered."

"Go ahead," Mason said. "Let's have it all."

She said, "David and Horace had a fight. I think David got the worst of it. He came home and was terribly angry. He went to the bathroom and put some cold towels on his face; then he fooled around in the bedroom for a while and went out. It wasn't until sometime afterwards that I began to wonder what he'd been doing in the bedroom. I remember having heard a bureau drawer open and close. As soon as I thought of that, I ran to the bureau and opened the drawer where David always kept his gun. The gun was gone."

"Whom have you told about this?" Mason asked.

"Not a soul on earth except you. Not even my husband."

There was a long silence in the office while Mason turned her statement over in his mind; then he glanced over at Della Street to make certain Della had taken it all down in shorthand.

Della nodded almost imperceptibly.

The silence made Mrs. Dangerfield uneasy. She started pointing out the obvious. "You see, Mr. Mason, what that would mean. If Horace's lawyer had said frankly that they'd been fighting, if it had appeared that David had pulled a gun and Horace had struck him over the head—who knows? It might have been self-defense, and he'd have gone free. In any event, it wasn't the kind of murder they hang men for."

129

"And what did you intend to do?" Mason asked.

She said, "Understand one thing, Mr. Mason. I'm not going to make a howling spectacle of myself. I'm not going to have people pointing the finger of shame at me. But I thought that I might sign an affidavit, and give it to you, to hold in strict confidence. Then, if this business about the old case should begin to ruin Marvin Adams' life, you could go to the girl's father—in strict confidence, of course—and show him this affidavit, tell him of your talk with me, and Marvin could—well, you know, live happily ever after."

She laughed nervously.

Mason said, "That's very interesting. Twenty-four hours ago it would have been a simple solution. Now it may not be such a simple solution."

"Why?"

"Because now the record of that old case may come out in public, in spite of anything we can do."

"Why? What's happened within the last twenty-four hours? Has Mr. Witherspoon . . ."

"It was something that happened to this detective, Leslie L. Milter."

"What?"

"He was murdered."

For a moment she didn't grasp the full significance of Mason's words. She said mechanically, "But I'm telling you that if his lawyer had . . ." She caught herself in the middle of the sentence, straightened in her chair. "*Who* was murdered?"

"Milter."

"You mean someone killed *him*?"

"Yes."

"Who—who did it?"

Mason once more picked up a pencil from his desk, slowly slid his fingers up and down the polished shaft of wood. He said, "That is quite apt to be a question which will become increasingly important as time goes on—a question which will have very important bearing upon the lives of several persons."

130

Chapter 15

Mrs. Dangerfield seemed for a moment almost dazed, then abruptly she said, "I must call my husband at once."

Mason glanced at Della Street. "You can put through a call from here."

Mrs. Dangerfield got to her feet, said, "No. I—I have some other things I want to do."

Mason said, "There are one or two more questions I'd like to ask you, Mrs. Dangerfield."

She shook her head with sudden firm decision. "No. I've said everything I care to, Mr. Mason. My husband didn't know I was coming. I left a note for him that I was going to be away today. I didn't tell him where I was going I . . . I took the car. . . . I think I'd better let him know where I am immediately."

"You can use this phone," Mason said. "We can get a call through in just a few minutes."

"No," she announced definitely, and looked around the office somewhat as an animal might look at some new cage. "This the way out?" she asked, pointing toward the door into the hall.

"Yes," Mason said, "but . . ."

"I'll talk with you later, Mr. Mason. I'm leaving right now."

She swept out through the door.

Mason said to Della Street, "Quick, Della. Drake!"

But Della Street's fingers were already whirring the dial on the telephone. She said, "Drake's office? A woman just left this office, a Mrs. Dangerfield. Fifty, looks forty, brunette, dark eyes, dark blue coat. She's at the elevator. Get a tail on her right away. Follow her. See where she goes and what she does. Quick!. . . That's right."

She hung up and said, "They'll pick her up right away."

"Good work, Della."

131

Della said, "I'd give a hundred dollars to know what she says over the wire to her husband."

Mason's eyes narrowed. "What she's most interested in is finding out where he was last night—when Milter was murdered. Rush me through a call to the chief of police at El Templo."

Della Street put through the call, explaining to the operator that it was an emergency, and within less than a minute, Mason had the police officer at El Templo on the line.

Mason said, "This is Perry Mason, the lawyer, in Los Angeles. A Mrs. Dangerfield has just left my office. Her husband is there in El Templo. She's going to put through a telephone call to him. If you can listen in on that telephone call, I think you'll get some interesting information that . . ."

"You're Mason?" the voice interrupted.

"Yes."

"What's this woman's name?"

"Dangerfield."

"Spell it."

Mason spelled it.

"She's putting through that call?"

"Yes. Right away."

The voice said, "Hold the line a minute. There's someone here wants to talk with you, but I'll get busy on this first."

Mason held the line, said to Della Street, holding his palm cupped over the transmitter, "At least we're getting some intelligent co-operation down there. They'll probably never tell us what's said, and they may not admit they listened in on the conversation, but I'll bet they manipulate things so they're put in on the call."

The man's voice came over the wire again. "Hello. Hello. This Mr. Perry Mason?"

"Yes."

"All right. Mr. Witherspoon wants to talk with you."

Witherspoon's voice was no longer the carefully controlled voice of a man who is accustomed to issuing orders and dominating every situation in which he finds himself placed. There was something almost pathetic in the eagerness of his voice as he said, "Is this you, Mason?"

"Yes."

"Come down here. Come down at once!"

"What is the matter?" Mason asked.

Witherspoon said, "There's been another one."

"Another what?" Mason asked.

"Another murder."

"You mean someone in addition to Leslie L. Milter has . . ."

"Yes, yes. Good God, it's preposterous! The damnedest thing you ever heard! They've *all* gone crazy. They . . ."

"Who was murdered?" Mason asked.

"The man who was staying in my house, Roland Burr."

"How?" Mason inquired.

"Same way. Somebody left a vase of acid in his room, dropped some cyanide in it, and walked out. The poor guy was laid up in bed with this broken leg. He couldn't have got out even if he'd wanted to. He just had to stay there and take it."

"When?"

"Just an hour or so ago."

"Who did it?" Mason asked.

Witherspoon almost shouted into the telephone. "That's why you have to come down here at once!"

"Who did it?" Mason repeated.

"These damn fool police claim that *I* did," Witherspoon shouted.

"Are you under arrest?"

"I guess it amounts to that."

Mason said, "Say nothing. Sit tight. I'm on my way down."

He hung up the telephone, motioned to Della Street, said, "Get your things, Della. We're headed for El Templo."

Della Street said, "You're forgetting Allgood. He's on his way down."

Mason had pushed back his chair, and was starting for the coat closet. He stopped abruptly, standing by the corner of the desk. "That's right. I'd forgotten all about Allgood."

The telephone rang. Della Street, picking up the receiver, said, "Just a moment," held her hand over the mouthpiece, and said, "He's in the office now."

Mason settled back in his swivel chair. "Bring him in, Della."

Allgood tried to look frowningly impressive as he fol-

133

lowed Della Street into the office. His glasses were pinched on his nose. The black ribbon, hanging down until it merged in the lapel of his coat, gave his face a certain stern severity.

A smile twinkled at the corners of Mason's mouth. "Sit down, Allgood," he said.

Allgood made something of a ceremony of seating himself. "Thank you, Counselor."

"What about this visit your secretary made to Milter?" Mason asked.

"I am most distressed by it, Counselor. I wanted to explain to you."

"Explain what?"

"How it happened."

Mason said, "I have only a few minutes. Go ahead."

Allgood's index finger twisted itself nervously around the narrow silk ribbon which dangled down from his glasses. "I want you to understand that Miss Elberton is an exceedingly loyal young woman," he said.

"Loyal to whom?"

"To me—to the business."

"Go ahead."

"It happens that Milter had kept in touch with her. Milter has the annoying habit of persistence in such matters."

"Even when he's not wanted?" Mason asked.

"Apparently."

"All right," Mason said impatiently, "she knew where Milter was. How did it happen she was listening in on our conversation?"

Allgood admitted, "That was due to an inadvertence on my part and a certain amount of natural curiosity upon hers. There's an interoffice communicating system in my office, and just before you came in I happened to have been conversing with her. I left the lever in such a position that our conversation was audible in the outer office. She took it upon herself to communicate with Milter—that is, to try to do so."

"She didn't do it?"

"No."

"Why not?"

"She says that Milter was otherwise engaged when she arrived at his apartment."

"Was he alive?"

134

"She doesn't know."

"Why not?"

"She didn't go up. Someone else was up there."

Mason said, "Baloney! She had a key to his apartment."

"Yes, I understand that. She explained how that happened. It seems that . . ."

"Never mind," Mason interrupted. "If you fall for those explanations, I don't. Let's get down to brass tacks. Milter was a blackmailer. I took your word for it when you told me that you were very much distressed at his talking and had dismissed him from your employ. In view of what's happened since, I'm not so certain."

"Not so certain about what?" Allgood asked, his eyes looking all over the office, except at that particular portion of it which was occupied by Perry Mason.

Mason said, "Your agency seems to be mixed in it right up to its necktie."

"Mr. Mason, are you intimating that I . . ."

Mason said, "I haven't time for the dramatics. I'm simply telling you that at first I took your word and your explanation. I'm not taking either, now, without checking up. There's altogether too much coincidence. I talk with you about one of your operatives who's gone in for blackmail. You 'inadvertently' leave the intercommunicating office system on so that my conversation is audible to your secretary. She goes down to El Templo. She has a key to this man's apartment. You know, Allgood, it *could* be that you were engineering a little shakedown. Having got all the money you could legitimately garner from Witherspoon, you used Milter as a stalking horse to put the finger on Witherspoon and get some more."

Allgood jumped to his feet. "I came here to make an explanation, Mr. Mason, not to be insulted!"

"All right," Mason said, "that's why you came here. You're here. You've made your explanation. Please consider the insult as a purely gratuitous interpolation which was not on the original program as planned."

"It's not a joking matter," Allgood said blusteringly.

"You're damn right it isn't."

"I've tried to be fair with you. I've put all of my cards on the table."

135

"You put a deuce spot on the table," Mason said. "The picture cards didn't get there until I shook them out of your sleeve. When I entered your office, your secretary went in to your office to tell you I was there. I couldn't hear your conversation because *at that time the interoffice communicating lever wasn't thrown over*. You must have done that after she went out and while I was on my way in. That means you did it deliberately. How about this column in the Hollywood scandal sheet?"

"I'm sure I don't know what you're talking about."

"You don't?"

"No."

Mason nodded to Della Street. "Get me Paul Drake on the line."

There was a moment of uncomfortable silence before Della broke it by saying, "He's on the line, Chief."

Mason picked up the telephone. "Paul, Allgood is here in the office. The more I think things over, the more I think that whole blackmailing business may have been thought out in advance—sort of a sequel to employment, if you know what I mean."

Drake said, "I see."

"Allgood's here in the office now. I'm wondering if that Hollywood scandal sheet didn't get its tip through Allgood. You said they didn't pay anything?"

"That's right, not in money. They pay in advertising and hot tips."

Mason said, "See if they've been boosting Allgood's agency, will you? And don't leave the office. I'm going out. I'll stop by on my way to the elevator and give you some interesting news. Check up on that scandal sheet and see if it looks as though Allgood is the fair-haired boy-child."

Mason dropped the receiver into place, said to Allgood, "Well, I won't detain you. I just wanted you to understand the way I felt about it."

Allgood started for the door, paused, turned, and jerked his head toward Della Street. "Get her out of here."

Mason shook his head.

"I have something to say to you."

"Go ahead and say it then."

136

"I notice that police picked up Marvin Adams when he got off the train this morning."

"Well?"

"I also am advised that you had a highly confidential talk with Marvin Adams before the train pulled in at the depot. He handed you a letter."

"Go ahead," Mason said.

"I'm wondering if you told the police about that talk and about the letter."

Mason said, "I have lots of talks about which I don't tell the police. My talk with you, for instance. I haven't told them about that—yet."

Allgood said, "How would you like it if this Hollywood paper published a little quip to the effect that the police might do well to check up on the distinguished lawyer with whom a certain young man was talking just before the train from El Templo pulled into Los Angeles; that it might be well to ask this young man what the lawyer told him not to mention to the police—and what was in the letter he gave the lawyer. You see, Counselor, when it comes to being nasty, two people can play at that game very nicely."

Mason motioned to Della Street. "Get Paul Drake on the phone," he said.

Once more there was a silence while Della Street got the detective on the wire. This time, however, Allgood's eyes were not shifting around the office. Hard and glittering, they stared defiantly at Perry Mason.

"Here's Drake," Della Street said.

Mason said, "Hello, Paul. I'm countermanding that order about having you look up Allgood's connection with that scandal sheet."

A triumphant smile twisted Allgood's face. "I thought you'd see the light, Counselor. After all, we may as well be reasonable. We're both businessmen."

Mason waited until Allgood had finished, then said into the telephone, to Paul Drake. "The reason I'm telling you that is because there's no use wasting time on that angle. Allgood didn't tip off the man who writes that column. . . . He writes it himself. He owns the damn paper. He's just given himself away."

Once more Mason dropped the receiver into place.

137

Allgood looked as though someone had punched him in the stomach.

Mason said, "You're not dealing with a tyro now, Allgood. I know my way around. You gave yourself away with that last threat. It's rather a neat racket. You publish these little innuendoes and hint at scandal. The persons who are affected come running to the office of the publication to find out what can be done about it, and wind up in the hands of the Allgood Detective Agency. In the meantime, some of the big Hollywood moguls are considering buying the paper out so as to put a muzzle on it, and your price is one that will give you about ninety-nine per cent clear profit."

"You can't prove one word of that," Allgood said.

Mason indicated Della Street. "I'm making the statement in the presence of a witness," he said. "Go ahead and sue me for slander, and *give me a chance to prove it*! I dare you."

Allgood paused for a moment uncertainly, then turned and stormed out of the room.

Mason looked at Della Street, smiled. "Well," he said, "that clears up one angle."

"What?"

"Where that tip-off came from in the paper. Allgood thought he was going to put the squeeze on Witherspoon. He thought he'd pull the wool completely over my eyes."

"But you were onto him?"

"Not entirely. I *did* notice that he'd left the lever depressed on that interoffice communicating system, so the girl in the outer office could hear everything we said. That's why I told Drake to shadow her. Come on. Let's beat it for El Templo."

Della grabbed up her shorthand notebook. "Well," she said, "our suitcases are still in the car. We might well be commuting. Don't forget to stop in and see Paul Drake."

"I won't. Did you get the gist of that telephone conversation?"

"There's been another murder?" she asked.

"That's right."

"Who?"

"Roland Burr."

"Have the police made an arrest?"

"Yes."

"Adams?"

"No. Our esteemed contemporary, John L. Witherspoon. Think that one over."

They stopped in at Drake's office. Mason talked, while he kept his eye on the minute hand of his wrist watch. "Get this straight, Paul, and get it fast. There's been another murder. Roland Burr. The police have arrested John L. Witherspoon. Looks as though they have something of a case."

"Know what the evidence is?" Drake asked.

"Not yet. Here's the angle that interests me. Diana Burr, Roland Burr's wife, originally came from Winterburg City. She was eighteen or nineteen years old at the time of the murder. Latwell and Horace Legg Adams had a fist fight the day Latwell was murdered. Latwell went home, got a gun, and disappeared. That was the last his wife ever saw of him. Looks as though it may have been self-defense."

"Fight over a woman?" Drake asked.

"Mrs. Dangerfield gave me the information. She wouldn't say. She's going to play her cards close to her chest, won't let me use that statement except privately. But it's something to work on."

"Only that we can't prove it except through her."

Mason nodded impatiently, said, "All this is preliminary to the point I'm making."

"What's that?"

"Diana Burr was a local product. She kept going away and getting married and coming back in between marriages. Roland Burr was her third venture, perhaps her fourth. Now then, *if* she'd been playing around, there's just a chance she might have come back to one of her first lovers for her final marriage. Just on the off-chance, Paul, look up Roland Burr. See if he doesn't have a Winterburg City background."

"What would it mean if he does?"

"Then see if he knew Corine Hassen," Mason said.

"Isn't that all pretty much of a coincidence?" Drake asked.

"Coincidence, hell! If it's what I think it is, it was careful, deliberate planning. Witherspoon was wide open. Anyone could have laid the foundation to play him for a sucker. His pride in the things he owns, his desire to show them, his enthusiasm for fly-fishing and color photography. Hell's bells, Paul, it all checks."

"Checks with what?" Drake asked.

"A design for deliberate, premeditated murder."

Drake said, "I don't get you."

"I haven't time to explain," Mason said, starting for the door. "You'll get it as you dig out the facts."

"What were you doing with Allgood?"

Mason grinned. "Putting a little pressure on him. The guy gave himself away. Bet you a hundred to one, he's running that Hollywood scandal sheet. It feeds him business, gives him a chance to utilize the information he gets in his business, and is laying the foundation for a big chunk of money when he gets ready to let go."

"Then this blonde was acting under his instructions?"

"Darned if I know. They all may have been working on an individual double-cross, but you can bet one thing. *He's* the one who published that dope in the scandal sheet. I called on him and gave him something to think about, so he handed it right back to me by cutting out the portion of the column relating to Witherspoon and sending it on to me. If it hadn't been for my call, he'd probably have sent it on to Witherspoon direct. Witherspoon would have called Allgood to find out about it, and Allgood would have sold him on another investigation at some fabulous price."

Drake said, "I've heard talk about Allgood playing both ends against the middle, but you went pretty far with him, didn't you, Perry? You can't prove any of that stuff and . . ."

"The hell I can't," Mason said. "Let him sue me. I'll start taking depositions, looking at books, and I'll prove it fast enough."

"If you're right," Drake said, "he won't sue."

"He won't sue," Mason remarked positively. "Come on, Della. We're headed for El Templo."

Chapter 16

John L. Witherspoon, held temporarily in custody at the sheriff's office, was permitted to talk with his lawyer privately in a witness room which opened off from the courtroom.

"The damnedest, most absurd thing you ever heard," Witherspoon stormed. "And it all started with my identification of that damned duck."

"Suppose you tell me about it," Mason said.

"Well, I told the police about the duck. And I told them about Marvin having taken that duck from the ranch. The whole thing was as plain to me as the nose on my face. Hang it, it still is."

"What did you tell the police?" Mason insisted.

"I told them that Marvin Adams had taken a duck from my place. I identified it as being my duck—the one that Marvin Adams had taken. That was all the police needed. They decided to grab Marvin Adams. They caught him as he got off the train in Los Angeles."

"Go ahead," Mason said.

"Apparently Adams told a pretty straightforward story. He said he'd taken a duck and put him in his automobile and that the duck had vanished, and that was all he knew about it. He admitted that he hadn't searched the car completely, but felt sure the duck was gone. The police thought so, too. They got in touch with the police here, and they went out and searched the car Marvin was driving—and what do you think they found?"

"What did they find?" Mason asked.

"Found that damn duck over in the back of the car. The little son-of-a-gun had flopped over the back of the front seat somehow, got down on the floor and crawled under the foot rest." Witherspoon cleared his throat, shifted his position uncomfortably in the chair. "A damnable combination of peculiar coincidences put me in something of a spot," he said.

"How so?" Mason asked.

"Well, after you left the house last night, I wanted to catch up with you, just as I told you, but I didn't tell you exactly what happened after that—that is, I told you but I didn't tell it in its proper sequence."

"Go ahead," Mason said noncommittally.

"I chased in after you. I missed you when you were off by the side of the road changing a tire. I told you that I looked around uptown to try and find you, and thought I saw Mrs. Burr and went off on a tangent trying to find her. Well, that's true. The thing that I didn't tell you about was something that I thought might embarrass me personally."

"What was it?"

"Immediately on reaching town, I drove to Milter's apartment. I told you that I didn't see your car parked near there, so I kept on going. That isn't true. I didn't pay any attention to cars. I was too steamed up. I slid my car into a parking place at the curb, got out, and went directly to Milter's apartment, and rang the doorbell. Naturally, I thought you were up there. Not having overtaken you on the road, I thought you'd kept ahead of me."

"You went to Milter's apartment then?"

"Yes."

"Immediately on reaching town?"

"Yes."

"And what did you do?"

"I rang the doorbell."

"Then what?"

"No one answered, but I saw the door hadn't been closed all the way. I pushed against it impatiently, and the door came open. The spring lock hadn't clicked into place."

"What did you do?" Mason asked.

"I walked part way up the stairs and someone heard me coming—a woman."

"You saw her?"

"No, I didn't, not her face, at least. I was halfway up the stairs when this woman came to the head of the stairs. I could see a leg and some underthings—felt embarrassed as the devil. She wanted to know what I was doing, breaking into

142

the apartment. I said I wanted to see Mr. Mason, and she told me Mr. Mason wasn't there and to get out. Naturally, under the circumstances, I turned around and went downstairs."

"You didn't tell me anything about this," Mason said.

"No, I didn't. I felt rather cheap about the whole business. I realized that a man in my position couldn't afford to admit having broken in on something of that sort. I didn't see the woman's face, and she hadn't seen mine. I thought no one knew who I was."

"Did they?"

"Some woman who lived next door. She'd heard some talk, and evidently she's one of those curious people who peek out through window shades, and pry into other persons' business."

"She saw you?"

"Not when I went in, but when I came out," Witherspoon said. "She identified the car. She'd even jotted down the license number. Why, is more than I know, but she had."

"Didn't she give any reason for writing down the license number?"

"I don't know. She tells the police that she thought a woman came in with me. Probably because she heard the voice of a woman in the apartment next to hers."

"*Did* some woman go in there with you?"

"No," Witherspoon said. "Of course not. I was alone."

"Lois wasn't with you?"

"Absolutely not."

"Nor Mrs. Burr?"

Witherspoon shifted his eyes. "I want to talk with you about Mrs. Burr in a minute. That's another one of those damnable things."

"All right," Mason said. "Tell it in your own way. It's your funeral. You may as well make the oration."

"Well, that woman next door reported my license number to the police. Naturally, if that duck in the goldfish bowl was my duck, and it came from my place, and Marvin Adams *hadn't* brought it, the police thought perhaps I *had*."

"Rather a natural assumption," Mason commented dryly.

"I tell you it's the damnedest combination of coincidences," Witherspoon stormed angrily. "I get angry every time I think of it."

"Suppose you tell me about Burr."

"Well, this morning, of course, I told Mrs. Burr about the excitement in El Templo and about how Milter had been murdered. Roland Burr was feeling better, and he wanted to see me, so I went in and had a talk with him."

"And you told him about it?"

"Yes."

"What did he say?"

"Well, he was curious—the way anyone would be."

"Did you tell him anything about Milter?" Mason asked.

"Well, a little something, not much. I've grown rather fond of Roland Burr. I felt that I could trust him."

"He knew I was at the house?"

"Yes."

"Did he know why?"

"Well—well, I think some of those things were discussed in a rather general way."

"Then what?"

"This morning Roland Burr asked me to bring him his favorite fishing rod. I told him that I would as soon as I could get to it."

"Where was it?"

"He said he'd left it in my den. I believe I told you that I'm particular about that den of mine. There's a lock on the door, and I have the only key to it. I never let the servants go in there except when I unlock the door and stand around watching them. I keep quite a stock of liquor in there, and that's one thing about these Mexicans. You can't trust them around tequila."

"And Burr had left his fishing rod in there?" Mason asked.

"Apparently so—that is, he said he had. I don't remember that he did, but he must have."

"When?"

"He was in there with me, chatting. That was the day he broke his leg, and he'd had his fishing rod with him. But I can't remember that he *left* it there. I can't remember that he didn't. Well, anyway, he asked me to get it for him, said there was no particular hurry about it, but he'd like to have it to sort of play around with it. He's a regular nut about fishing rods, likes to feel them, whip them in his hands, and all that sort of thing. Plays with them the way a man will play with some favorite gun, or camera, or other toy.''

"And the police know about that rod?'' Mason asked.

"Oh, yes. Mrs. Burr and the doctor were there at the time. I promised I'd get it for him, and then the doctor left to drive into town; and Mrs. Burr said she'd like to go in with him. I told her I was going to be in town later on, and I'd pick her up and drive her back.''

"So she went in with the doctor?''

"Yes. . . . That left me there in the house alone, except for the servants.''

"And what did you do?''

"Well, I fooled around for a while with some odds and ends, and intended to go into the den to get Burr's fishing rod, as soon as I got a chance.''

"What time was this?''

"Oh, around eighty-thirty or nine o'clock I guess. I had a lot of things to do around the place, getting the men started on their work, and so forth. Burr had told me he was in no hurry for the fishing rod. Sometime in the afternoon, I think he said.''

"Go ahead,'' Mason said. "Get to the point.''

"Well, about an hour later one of the servants passed by the room. You know where his room is. It's on the ground floor, and the windows open on the patio. The servant looked through the window and saw Burr sitting in bed, and from the position in which he was sitting—well, dammit, the Mexican saw he was dead.''

"Go ahead,'' Mason said.

"The servant came and called me. I dashed to the door, opened it, saw Burr there on the bed, and immediately saw a vase sitting on the table about ten feet from the bed. I got a whiff of some peculiar gas, and it keeled me over. The Mexican dragged me out into the corridor, slammed the door shut, and called the police.

"The sheriff came out, took a look through the window, came to the conclusion the man had been killed in the same way that Milter had been killed, and smashed in the windows and let the place air out. Then the officers went in. There's no question about it. He'd been killed in the same way—

cyanide of potassium dropped into the vase of acid. The poor devil had never stood a chance. He was there on the bed with his leg in a cast and a weight on the leg suspended from a pulley. He couldn't possibly move out of bed.''

"Where was the nurse?" Mason asked.

"That's just it," Witherspoon said. "That damn nurse was at the bottom of the whole business."

"In what way?"

"Oh, she got temperamental—or Burr did. I don't know which. The nurse is telling an absolutely preposterous story."

"Well, where *was* she?" Mason asked. "I thought Burr was to have someone in constant attendance."

Witherspoon said, "I told you that they caught Burr trying to get out of bed, that Burr said someone was trying to kill him. The doctor said it was a plain case of nervous reaction after the administration of narcotics. No one paid very much attention to it—not then. Of course, later on, when this thing happened, his words had the effect of a prophecy. So the police got in touch with the nurse. The nurse said that Burr had told her in confidence that *I* was the someone he expected to try and kill him."

"The nurse hadn't said anything about that to the authorities?"

"No. She also thought it might have been a reaction from the narcotics. The doctor was certain of it. You know how a nurse has to defer to the doctor on a case. Under the circumstances, if she'd said anything to anyone, she'd have been guilty of all sorts of professional misconduct. She had to keep her mouth shut—so *she* says—now."

Mason said, "That still isn't answering my question as to where the nurse was when all this happened."

"She was in town."

"And Burr was there alone?"

"Yes. You see, Burr absolutely couldn't move out of that bed. He could, however, use his arms and hands, and there was a telephone right by the bed. As a matter of fact, he really didn't need a nurse in attendance all the time. He could have got action whenever he wanted to pick up the telephone receiver. I have an inter-room telephone communication in the house. You can press a key on the switchboard and hook your telephone in on one of the outside trunk lines, or you can switch it over to any one of half a dozen rooms in the house, simply by pressing the proper button. Burr could have called the kitchen any time he wanted anything.''

''Tell me about the nurse,'' Mason insisted.

''Well, when Burr was first put to bed and the leg set, he had his wife take a bag out of the closet and bring it to him. That bag had some of his fishing flies, a couple of his favorite books, a little flashlight, five or six books of the pocket series, and various odds and ends. He could keep that bag by the side of his bed, reach down in it, and tie flies, look over his reels, or get a book.

''After this nurse came on the job, she told him that she thought it would be better for him to tell her whenever he wanted anything, so she was going to unpack the bag and put the contents over on the dresser. She told him to ask her for whatever he wanted. She said she wasn't going to have the bag there where she'd stumble over it every time she walked around the bed.

''That infuriated Burr. He said no woman was going to mix his fly-tying stuff all up, that he'd keep his things by the side of his bed, and whenever he wanted them, he'd get them.

''The nurse tried to show her authority, and grabbed the bag. He managed to catch her wrist, and all but twisted her arm off. Then he told her to get out and stay out. He said he'd start throwing things at her if she so much as stuck her head in the door. The nurse telephoned the doctor. The doctor came out, and the nurse, Mrs. Burr, the doctor, and I all had a talk with Burr. The upshot of it was that the doctor and the nurse went back to town. Mrs. Burr went with them to pick up a new nurse. The telephone was left switched on to the kitchen, and the women in the kitchen were told to pay particular attention to see that Burr's telephone was answered just as soon as he picked up the receiver in his room. It certainly seemed as though it would be safe enough to leave him alone under those circumstances. At least the doctor thought so.''

''And you?'' Mason asked.

''Emphatically,'' Witherspoon said. ''To tell you the truth, I was just a bit fed up with Burr's going temperamental. I told him, somewhat forcefully, that I thought it would be better for him to go to a hospital. Of course, I had to make allowances for the man. He'd been suffering a great deal of pain. He was still very weak and very sick. The danger of complications had not yet passed. He was nervous and irritable. The after effect of the drugs was distorting his mental perspective. Undoubtedly, he was hard to get along with.

"However, I think his actions were very unreasonable, and his treatment of the nurse decidedly boorish."

"And what connects you with his death?" Mason asked.

"The damn fishing rod. There he was on the bed with the fishing rod in his hands. He'd just started to put it together. He had two joints in his right hand, and the other joint in his left hand. Well, you can see where that leaves me. I'm the only one who could have got the fishing rod, the only one who could have given it to him. I was alone in the house. The dogs were loose. No stranger could have got in. The servants swear they hadn't gone near the room. The poor devil never stood a chance. There he was, held motionless in bed, and this vase of poison stuck on the table about seven or eight feet from the bed, where he couldn't possibly have reached it to have knocked it off, or done anything about it."

"But he could have picked up the telephone?"

"Yes. Evidently the gas took effect too quickly for that. He didn't even know what was happening. Someone—some friend of his had walked in the room, handed him that fishing rod, probably said, 'Look, Roland, I happened to find your fishing rod. It wasn't in Witherspoon's study at all. You left it somewhere else,' and Burr had taken the fishing rod and started to put it together. The friend had said, 'Well, so long. If there's anything you want, just let me know,' and dropped some cyanide of potassium into the acid, and walked out. A few seconds later, Burr was dead. It had to be some intimate friend. Well, there you are."

"From the police viewpoint," Mason said, "it's a perfect case. You were about the only one who had the opportunity. How about motive?"

Witherspoon became embarrassed.

"Go ahead," Mason told him. "Let's have the bad news. What about the motive?"

"Well," Witherspoon blurted, "Mrs. Burr is a very peculiar woman. She's as natural as a child. She's affectionate and impulsive and—well, lots of things. You'd have to know her to understand.''

''Never mind beating around the bush,'' Mason said. ''Specifically what's the motive?''

''The police think I was in love with Mrs. Burr and wanted to get her husband out of the way.''

''What makes them think that?''

''I've told you. Mrs. Burr is natural and demonstrative and affectionate, and—well, she's kissed me a couple of times right in front of her husband.''

''And sometimes not in front of her husband?'' Mason asked.

''That is the hell of it,'' Witherspoon admitted. ''No one has been present when she's kissed me in front of her husband except the three of us. But a couple of servants have seen her kiss me when her husband *wasn't* there. Most natural thing in the world, Mason. I can't explain it to you. Some women are just naturally affectionate and want to be fondled and kissed. I wasn't making any passionate love to her, the way it sounds when the servants tell it. Mexicans don't understand anything except passion in lovemaking. I simply slipped my arm around her in a fatherly sort of way—and, well, she put her face up to be kissed, and I kissed her.''

''Can the police trace any of the poison to you?''

''That's another bad thing,'' Witherspoon admitted. ''The acid is stuff I keep on the ranch, and I always use cyanide for poisoning ground squirrels and coyotes. Ground squirrels are a terrific pest. Once they get into a field of grain, they eat the grain off. They hang around the stable and eat the horses' hay. The only way you can get rid of them is to poison them. It's customary all over California to poison ground squirrels, and cyanide is one of the things that's used. They use quite a bit of strychnine and other stuff. I've got poisoned barley on the ranch, keep it there all the time. I also have a stock of cyanide. Well, there you are. Just a plain damn case of circumstantial evidence, without a thing on earth for the police to go on except those circumstances. It puts me in a hell of a spot.''

''Doesn't it,'' Mason said.

Witherspoon flashed him an angry glance.

''You might turn back the hands of the clock eighteen

years," Mason went on dryly, "and think about how Horace Adams must have felt when the police put him in jail, charged him with murder, and he realized that circumstances had conspired to weave a web of evidence around him. I remember when I told you that circumstantial evidence could be the greatest perjurer on earth, not because the circumstances lied, but because men's interpretation of the circumstances lied. You were inclined to be rather skeptical then."

"I tell you," Witherspoon said, "this is something unique. Dammit, this couldn't happen again in a hundred years."

"Well, make it eighteen," Mason said.

Witherspoon glowered in impotent rage.

"Do you want me to represent you?" Mason asked.

"Hell, no!" Witherspoon roared angrily. "I'm sorry I ever sent for you. I'll get myself a lawyer who isn't trying to teach me some moral lesson. I'll get myself a *good* lawyer. I'll get the best money can buy. I'll beat this case hands down."

"Go ahead," Mason said, and walked out.

Chapter 17

Lois Witherspoon regarded Mason with flashing eyes. "You can't do that to my dad," she said.

"Do what?"

"You know very well what I mean. If it hadn't been for me planting that second duck, Dad wouldn't have been in this."

"How did I know that your father was going to get a fishing rod for Burr and then claim he hadn't done it?"

"Don't you *dare* say my father is lying."

Mason shrugged his shoulders. "The force of circumstantial evidence is against him."

"I don't care how much circumstantial evidence is against him. I guess I'd believe my own father. He has his faults, but they don't include lying."

"It would be nice if you could convince the police of that," Mason pointed out.

"You listen to me, Mr. Perry Mason. I'm not going to stand here and bandy words with you. I want some results. You know just as well as I do that my father never killed Roland Burr."

"The problem is to convince twelve men in a jury box," Mason said.

"All right, I'm going to start convincing them right now. I'm going to the police and tell them about planting that duck in Marvin's car and about the fact that you got me to do it."

"What good will that do?"

"That will explain how the duck got in Marvin's car and . . . and . . ."

"And that it was the duck that Marvin had taken in his car that was found in Milter's apartment," Mason said.

"Well . . . even supposing . . ."

"And that, of course, would point straight at Marvin."

"Well, Marvin has a complete alibi."

151

"For what?"

"For the murders."

"What's his alibi for Milter's murder?"

"Well . . . well, I'm not certain he has an alibi on *that*, but he was in Los Angeles in custody of the police when Burr was murdered. So," she finished triumphantly, "the evidence on that duck isn't gong to hurt him in the least."

"It may not hurt him," Mason said, "in the way that you mean, but it will hurt him in another way."

"How?"

"Don't you see? The minute the police begin to investigate him, they'll start asking questions about his past. They'll want to find out about his background. The newspapers will go to town on that."

"In what way? You mean about his being kidnaped?"

Mason said, "Don't you know the truth back of that kidnaping story?"

"I . . . the kidnaping story is all I ever heard."

Mason smiled at her. "Your father gave me some typewritten transcripts, some old newspapers. I took them out to the house with me so I could work on them. While we were at dinner, someone got in my room and went through them."

"Mr. Mason, are you accusing me of being a snoop like that?"

"I'm not making any accusation at all. I'm merely making a statement."

"Well, I had nothing whatever to do with it. I never saw any transcripts, as you call them."

"And you don't know the true facts back of that kidnaping story?"

"No. All I know is what Marvin's mother told him on her deathbed."

"That was a lie," Mason said. "It was a lie which she told to insure her son's happiness. She knew he was in love with you. She knew that your father was the sort who would want to know all about Marvin's family. She knew that once your father started investigating, he'd find something which was rather unsavory."

"What?"

"Marvin's father was convicted of murder in 1924. He was executed in 1925."

152

Her face froze into lines of horror. "Mr. Mason!" she exclaimed. "That can't be!"

"That's the truth," Mason said. "That's why your father employed me. He wanted me to investigate the record and see whether I could find some proof in it of Horace Adams' innocence."

"Could you? Did you?"

"No."

She looked at him as though he had hit her.

"Your father wasn't going to tell you until he handed it to you all at once," Mason went on.

"What do you mean by that?"

"Forbid you to have anything to do with Marvin Adams, to see him, write to him, or talk with him on the telephone."

"I don't care what Marvin's father did. I don't care *who* he was. I love *him*. Do you understand, Mr. Mason? I love *him*!"

"I understand," Mason said. "I don't think your father does."

"But," she said, "this is—this is— Mr. Mason, are you certain? Are you absolutely certain that what Mrs. Adams said about the kidnaping wasn't true?"

"Apparently there's no question about it."

"And his father was convicted of murder and—and hanged?"

"Yes."

"And you say his father was guilty?"

"No."

"I thought that was what you said."

"No. I said that, from an examination of the record, I couldn't find any proof that he was innocent."

"Well, doesn't that amount to the same thing?"

"No."

"Why not?"

"In the first place, my examination was limited to the record. In the second place, I found some things which indicated his innocence, but that wasn't proof. However, I am *hoping to prove* that he was innocent, from things which didn't appear in the record, but which are beginning to come out now."

"Oh, Mr. Mason, if you could only do that!"

"But," Mason went on, "in case the police should start investigating Marvin's background, find out about this old murder case, and air it in the newspapers, my work would be exceedingly difficult. Even after I had accomplished it, it wouldn't be effective. Once people get the idea that Marvin's father was a murderer, I can come along a few days, or perhaps a few weeks, later, and prove that he wasn't. People will always think it was some sort of hocus-pocus that was worked out by a high-priced attorney who was hired by a millionaire father-in-law so that Marvin could be whitewashed. They'll be whispering stories about him behind his back as long as he lives."

"I don't care," she said. "I'll marry him anyway."

"Sure," Mason said. "*You* don't care. You can take it. But how about Marvin? How about your children?"

Her silence showed how forcefully that thought had struck her.

Mason went on, "Marvin is sensitive. He's enthusiastic. He's keen to get along. He didn't have much when he went to school, didn't have much in the way of clothes, didn't have much in the way of spending money; but he had personality. He had something which made him a leader. He was president of his class in high school. He was the editor of the high-school paper. Now, in college, he's popular and successful. People like him and he responds to their liking. Take that away from him. Let him be placed in such a position that people are whispering behind his back, and conversation stops whenever he comes into a room. That . . ."

"Stop it!" she cried.

Mason said, "I'm talking facts."

"Well, you can't let my father be convicted on account of a duck . . ."

Mason said, "That duck will have absolutely nothing to do with your father's conviction or acquittal *so far as the murder of Roland Burr is concerned*. It was simply a statement he made about the duck which caused the police to become suspicious of him in the first place. The only way to acquit your father is to find out who gave Roland Burr that fishing rod."

"How are we going to do that?" she asked. "The servants all say they didn't. There was no one else in the house. Mrs.

154

Burr had gone to town with the doctor, and according to the testimony of both the doctor and Mrs. Burr, the fishing rod was one of the last things Roland Burr asked for before they went out. It was while all three of them were in the room together, and they all went out at the same time."

"That makes it look very bad indeed," Mason admitted.

"Mr. Mason, can't you do *something*?"

"Your father doesn't want me to represent him as his lawyer."

"Why not?"

"Because I insisted on pointing out to him the similarity of the predicament in which he now finds himself, and that in which Horace Adams found himself some eighteen years ago. Your father doesn't like that. His position was that the Witherspoon family couldn't afford to have an affiliation with the family of someone who had even been *charged* with murder."

"Poor Dad. I know just how he feels. Family means so much to him. He's always been so proud of our family."

"It might be a good plan for him to get jolted out of that," Mason said. "It might be a good thing for all of us to get jolted out of it."

"I'm afraid I don't follow you."

"We've been taking too much for granted simply because of our ancestors. We've hypnotized ourselves. We keep saying proudly that other nations should be afraid of us because we never have lost a war. We should put it the other way. It might be a good thing for us all to learn that we have to stand on our *own* two feet—beginning with your father."

She said, "I love my father, and I love Marvin."

"Of course, you do," Mason said.

"I'm not going to sacrifice one for the other."

Mason shrugged his shoulders.

"Mr. Mason, *can't* you understand? I'm not going to let my father's position become jeopardized because I planted that duck in Marvin's car."

"I understand."

"You don't seem to be of very much help."

"I don't think anyone can help you, Lois. It's something you've got to decide for yourself."

"Well, it makes a difference to you, doesn't it?"

155

"Probably."

"Can't you think of some way out?"

Mason said, "If you tell the authorities about having planted that duck in Marvin's car, you're going to get yourself out of a very hot frying pan into a very hot fire. It won't get your father out of it—not now. It will simply get Marvin in."

"If it hadn't been for the duck, they never would have started suspecting Father."

"That's all right, but they've started now. They've uncovered enough evidence so they're not going to back up. You *might* find yourself facing the situation of having your father tried for the murder of Roland Burr, and Marvin on trial for the murder of Leslie Milter. Wouldn't *that* be something?"

She said, "I don't like the idea of temporizing with my conscience because of results. I think it's better to do what you think is right, and let the results take care of themselves."

"And what do you think is the right thing to do?"

"Tell the authorities about that duck."

"Would you promise to wait a few days?" Mason asked.

"No. I won't promise. But I—well, I'll think it over."

"All right," Mason said, "do that."

She looked as though she would have liked to cry on his shoulder, but she summoned her pride, and walked out of the room with her chin held very high.

Mason went down to Della Street's room, tapped on the door.

Della Street, her eyes anxious, flung the door open. "What did she want, Chief?"

Mason smiled. "She wanted to get squared with her conscience."

"About that duck?"

"Yes."

"What's she going to do?"

"Eventually she's going to tell all about it."

"What will that do—to you?"

"It will leave me in something of a spot down here," Mason said.

"And I suppose that's looking at it optimistically?"

His smile became a grin. "I always look at things optimistically."

"How long will she give you to work out some solution?"

"She doesn't know herself."

"A day or two?"

"Perhaps."

"And where does that leave you?"

Mason said, "Sitting right in the middle of a volcano that's due to blow up at any minute. Suppose, Della, you see if you can't be the perfect hostess and dig up a drink."

Chapter 18

Excitement ran high in El Templo. That John L. Witherspoon had been charged with murder and was having a preliminary hearing before Justice Meehan, was sufficient to bring men into town in large numbers. The case was discussed in restaurants, hotel lobbies, pool halls, and barber shops. There were about as many different theories as there were men discussing the murders.

Lawrence Dormer, the attorney representing Witherspoon, was considered the best trial lawyer in the valley, and Dormer was quite frankly not only puzzled by the evidence, but was taking advantage of every technicality which the law afforded. It was being noised around the streets that Dormer had decided the evidence was sufficient to warrant the judge holding Witherspoon over for trial; that he would, therefore, not disclose his own hand by putting on any witnesses, but would force the district attorney to put as many cards as possible on the table.

Lois Witherspoon, torn between her love for her father and for Marvin Adams, still remained silent concerning her connection with the case; but it was the silence of a tension within which was building up to the bursting point.

Della Street said, "You're going to have to watch that girl, Chief. She'll stand up publicly somewhere and spill her story all at once. She isn't accustomed to concealing things. She's never bothered to resort to deceit. She likes the truth—and she's an all-at-once sort of girl."

Mason nodded.

"Don't you understand what that means?" Della Street asked.

"What?"

"Down here you're in foreign territory. You're in a county where you're an outsider, where the local people all hang together. Something which might be overlooked in Los Angeles won't be overlooked here. What would pass as a good trick in the city, will be considered particularly reprehensible down here. Good grief, they may even charge you with being an accessory to the murder before they get done.''

Again Mason smiled.

Knuckles sounded on the door of the hotel suite.

"See who that is, Della."

Della Street opened the door.

George L. Dangerfield stood on the threshold. "May I come in?" he asked.

"Certainly," Mason said. "Come on in."

Dangerfield said, "My wife and I have been subpoenaed as witnesses."

Mason raised his eyebrows.

"I found out something about the theory on which the district attorney is going to try this case tomorrow, and I thought you should know, because—well, it may have an effect on . . . on lots of things."

"What?" Mason asked.

"He's going to reopen that old case."

"You mean the Adams case?"

"Yes."

"Why?"

"Do you remember," Dangerfield said, "when Witherspoon was talking with you in the hotel there in Palm Springs? He's reported to have said that if it became necessary, he'd put young Marvin Adams in a position where it would look as though murder was the only way out, and force the boy to show his true character that way."

Mason smiled. "I never remember anything a client says to me, Dangerfield."

"Well, the point is," Dangerfield went on, "that you explained to him what a dangerous idea that was, and there was a little more conversation back and forth along those lines. Well, one of the bar boys, a college lad working at the Springs on his vacation, happened to overhear that conversation. There was a screen behind the table where you were sitting, and this boy was standing back of that screen polishing a window."

Mason said, "Very interesting. I take it the boy knew Witherspoon?"

"Yes, he recognized him."

"Very, very interesting, and how did *you* learn all this?"

"From the district attorney. The district attorney found out that my wife and I were in town, and subpoenaed us as witnesses. He's been talking with me about that old case."

"What did you tell him?" Mason asked.

Dangerfield said, "That's just the point. I kept telling him that I didn't see why that should enter into the present case and that there was no use digging up old memories."

"He's talked with both you and your wife?"

"No. So far, he's talked only with me. He's going to call my wife this evening. I . . . well, I wanted to see what could be done. I thought perhaps we could take the position that it was making her too nervous—get a doctor to give his certificate or something of that sort. You're a lawyer. You'll know how those things are arranged."

"They aren't supposed to be arranged," Mason said.

"I know, but they are just the same."

"Why doesn't your wife want to give a statement?"

"We can't see any use in reopening that old case."

"Why?"

"Hang it," Dangerfield blurted, "you know why. My wife told you. She knew that David Latwell had a gun in his pocket when he went to the factory the day he was murdered. . . . And she kept silent about it—all through the case."

"Did she ever lie about that?"

"No. No one ever asked her. She simply didn't volunteer the information."

"So she told you about that?"

"Yes."

"When?"

"Last night."

"Highly interesting," Mason said. "Won't it be peculiar if, as a result of trying Witherspoon for murder in 1942, we clear up a murder that was committed in 1924?"

"You can't clear it up," Dangerfield said. "You *might* make it appear that a verdict of manslaughter *could* have been returned. That won't clear anything up."

"Or make it appear justifiable self-defense."

"You can't bring Adams back to life," Dangerfield said. "And you might make my wife commit perjury."

160

"How?"

"She'll never admit knowing about that gun when she gets on the witness stand," Dangerfield said. "She says that if she can meet with you, Witherspoon and Marvin Adams, she'll tell exactly what happened, but that she's not going to be held up to public scorn as a woman whose, well, you know."

"And so?" Mason asked.

"So she sent me to tell you that if you want that old case cleared up, it will have to be done in a private conference. That if she ever takes the stand, she'll deny the whole business. It's up to you to keep her from being called."

Mason pursed his lips. "Will she tell the district attorney anything about the gun?"

"No, of course not."

Mason pushed his hands down deep in his pockets. "I'll think it over," he promised.

Chapter 19

It was a new experience for Perry Mason to sit in a courtroom as a spectator—and it was a trying experience.

The expert bronco-buster who sits in the grandstand at a rodeo instinctively sways his body as he watches another rider trying to stay on a bucking horse. The expert pinball-machine player, standing as a spectator, watching another send the metal balls rolling down the inclined plane, will instinctively push with his own body as the balls hit the cushioned bumpers.

Perry Mason, sitting in the front row of the spectators' chairs in the crowded courtroom at El Templo, listening to the preliminary hearing of the case of The People of the State of California versus John L. Witherspoon, at times would lean forward in his chair as though about to ask a question. When some objection was made, he would grip the arms of the chair as though about to get up and argue the matter.

However, he managed to sit silently through the course of the long day's trial while the evidence presented by the district attorney piled up against the defendant.

Witnesses testified that Roland Burr had been a guest at the defendant's house. It was made to appear that the defendant had invited Burr to his house after a casual conversation during which it had developed that they shared a number of hobbies, among which were fly-casting and photography. It was also made to appear that when they had first met in the lobby of the hotel, Witherspoon had not issued his invitation until after Mrs. Burr had appeared, and been introduced.

The figure of Mrs. Burr began, bit by bit, to assume a more important place in the trial.

Servants testified that Roland Burr made frequent trips to town. Upon most of these trips, his wife would accompany him. But there were times when Burr was in his room that Mrs. Burr would meet Witherspoon in the corridors, or in the patio. Witherspoon's Mexican servants testified with obvious reluctance, but the story which they told built up a damning case of motivation, indicating a growing intimacy between the defendant, Witherspoon, and Mrs. Burr, the wife of the man who had been killed.

Then came more evidence of stolen kisses, little intimacies, which, under the questioning of the district attorney, began to assume sinister proportions—figures entwined in hallways, low voices at night by the swimming pool, beneath the stars. Bit by bit, he brought out every "clandestine caress," every "surreptitious sexual advance."

With cold, deadly precision, the district attorney, having proved motivation, began to prove opportunity. The doctor who had been attending Burr testified to the condition of the patient, that it was obviously impossible for the patient to have left the bed, that not only was his leg in a cast, but it was elevated and held in place by a weight which was suspended from a pulley in the ceiling, one end of a rope being on this weight, the other fastened securely to the patient's leg. Photographs were introduced showing the position of the deadly glass of acid from which the cyanide fumes had been generated. It had been placed some ten feet from the bed, on a table which had originally been designed as a stand for a typewriter but which had been introduced into the room as a medicine table at the suggestion of John L. Witherspoon himself when the deceased had broken his leg.

The doctor also testified that when he and Mrs. Burr had left the house, the last request of the decedent had been that Witherspoon get his fishing rod, which the deceased said he had left in Witherspoon's study.

Servants testified that no one but Witherspoon had a key to that study, that, at the time the murder must have been committed, Witherspoon, the servants, and the decedent were alone in the house. The district attorney introduced evidence about the dogs, showing that it would have been impossible for any stranger to have entered the house while the trained police dogs were patrolling the grounds.

The fishing rod which the deceased was holding in his hand when the body was discovered was conclusively identified as being the particular fishing rod which Burr had asked Witherspoon to get for him. Photographs were introduced

163

showing the body as it had been discovered. Two joints of the fishing rod had been put together. The decedent was holding the tip of the rod in his left hand. The right hand was gripped about the ferrule of the second joint. The entire position of the body indicated that the man had been in the act of placing the last joint in the rod when he had been overcome by the fumes of the gas.

"The Court will observe," the district attorney said, indicating the photograph, "that quite evidently the decedent had just received the fishing rod when the gas fumes were released."

"Objected to," Lawrence Dormer, the attorney for the defendant, shouted, getting to his feet. "I object to that statement, Your Honor," he went on, with the vehemence of indignation. "That is plainly a conclusion. It's something . . ."

"I'll withdraw the statement," the district attorney smirked. "After all, Your Honor, the photograph speaks for itself."

Dormer resumed his seat at the counsel table.

The district attorney went calmly on, building up his case. Medical testimony showed approximately the time of death. Medical testimony also showed the manner of death.

The district attorney called James Haggerty, the officer who had entered Milter's apartment with Mason when the body was discovered. The district attorney asked him his name, his occupation, while Lawrence Dormer sat tense in his chair, ready to object to the first question by which the district attorney would attempt to open the door to prove that other murder.

The district attorney said, "Now then, Officer Haggerty, I will ask you if, when you entered the apartment of Leslie L. Milter on the night prior to the murder of Roland Burr, you noticed anything which would indicate that hydrochloric acid or cyanide of potassium were present in that apartment."

"Objected to," Dormer shouted, getting to his feet. "Your Honor, this is not only incompetent, irrelevant, and immaterial, but the asking of that question constitutes prejudicial misconduct on the part of the district attorney, and I assign it as such. The defendant in this case is being tried for one

164

crime, and for one crime alone. That crime is the murder of Roland Burr. There is no point of law which is better established than that when a defendant is being tried for one crime, the Court or jury cannot be prejudiced against him by having evidence introduced of another crime. Apparently, it is the contention of the district attorney that he can introduce this extraneous evidence . . .''

"I am inclined to agree with Counsel for the defendant," the Court ruled, "but I'll listen to the district attorney's argument."

District Attorney Copeland was fully prepared, not only with argument, but with a bristling list of authorities.

"If the Court please," he said, in the calm manner of one who is very sure of his ground and who is making an argument upon which he is thoroughly prepared, "there is no question as to the general rule stated by Counsel for the defense. There are, however, certain exceptions.

"I will state at the outset that where exceptions to the rule exist, the evidence is permitted only for the purpose of showing opportunity, only for the purpose of showing some fact in connection with the crime for which the defendant is on trial, and not for the purpose of proving him guilty of any other crime.

"Under that rule, evidence of prior forgeries has been admitted for the purpose of showing that the defendant has practiced the signature of a certain individual. In connection with certain sexual crimes, previous acts have been admitted in order to show that the natural barriers of restraint have been broken down. And so in this case, Your Honor, I wish to introduce this evidence, not for the purpose of proving that the defendant murdered Leslie L. Milter, but only for the purpose of proving that, first, he was familiar with that method of murder, second, that he had a quantity of hydrochloric acid, third, that he had a quantity of cyanide of potassium, fourth that he knew full well the deadly gases which were liberated by these chemicals when placed in solution.

"Now then, if the Court please, I have a long list of authorities covering the rule of law. I would like to cite these authorities to the Court and would like to read from some of them.

"For instance, Your Honor, quoting from volume sixteen

165

Corpus Juris, at page 589, I read, quote, Where the nature of the crime is such that guilty knowledge must be proved, evidence is admissible to prove that at another time and place not too remote, accused committed or attempted to commit a crime similar to that charged—end of quotation.

"In order to show that the defendant knew of the deadly gas which would be liberated by . . ."

Judge Meehan glanced at the clock and interrupted the district attorney to say, "It's approaching the hour of the afternoon adjournment. The Court would like very much to have an opportunity to make some independent investigations upon this point. It is, quite apparently, a crucial point in the case, one which will be argued at some length. The Court will, therefore, adjourn this case until tomorrow morning at ten o'clock. The defendant is remanded to the custody of the sheriff. Court will take a recess until tomorrow morning at ten o'clock."

Deputy sheriffs escorted Witherspoon from the courtroom. The judge retired from the bench. Spectators began talking among themselves excitedly. It was quite apparent that the wall of evidence which the district attorney was beginning to erect so remorselessly around the figure of a man who had been so prominent in the life of the community was impressing the spectators.

Lois Witherspoon, her chin held high, her eyes hard and dry, swept out of the courtroom, disdaining both the looks of pity which were bestowed upon her by some, and the stares of contempt which she encountered from others.

Back in his suite at the hotel, Mason stretched out in a comfortable chair, said to Della Street, "This feels good after those hard chairs in a courtroom."

Della said, "You kept looking as though you wanted to get on your feet and charge into the fray."

"I did," Mason admitted.

"From all I can hear, he's making a pretty good case against Witherspoon."

Mason smiled. "Perhaps Witherspoon will suffer enough to learn a little charitable compassion. He'll know now how Horace Adams felt eighteen years ago. Heard anything from Paul Drake yet?"

"No."

"You transmitted my message to him?"

"Yes. I told him you wanted that girl from the Allgood Detective Agency shadowed, that you wanted to know, as far as possible, everything Roland Burr had done the day we arrived, as well as the day before."

"Prior to being kicked by the horse," Mason said, smiling. "After that, he stayed put."

She said, "Drake's working on it. He's been in and out all day, sending telegrams and talking over the telephone. He has a couple of detectives down here working. He said he'd be here in time for a cocktail before dinner."

Mason said, "Well, I'll go in my room and take a bath and change my clothes. I never saw humanity packed into a courtroom quite so closely. They exude moisture, odor, and interest. I feel sticky all over."

He went to his own room and was halfway through a bath when Paul Drake came in. "My gosh, Perry, I don't know whether it's mind reading or how you do it, but you certainly do get the damnedest hunches!"

"What this time?" Mason asked.

"About that mysterious Miss X in the old murder case, Corine Hassen."

"What about her?"

"We've located her."

"Where?"

"In Reno, Nevada."

"Dead?" Mason asked.

"Yes."

"Murdered?"

"She jumped into Donner Lake and committed suicide. The body wasn't identified, but police had photographs on file."

"When?" Mason asked.

"Apparently just about the time David Latwell was murdered."

"The date is very, very important," Mason said.

"I have it all here for you, including photographs of the body."

"You say she wasn't identified?"

"No. The body was absolutely nude when it was found, and they never discovered any of her clothes. Apparently a

167

damned attractive young woman. The verdict was that it was suicide. You can compare these photos. It's Corine Hassen, all right."

"Do you, by any chance, know whether she could swim?" Mason asked.

"I haven't found that out, but I'll be finding it out rather shortly."

Mason said, "Things are beginning to take shape."

"I don't get you, Perry," Drake said. "Honestly, I don't."

Mason dried himself with a towel, laid out clean underwear. Once more that peculiar granite-hard look was on his face.

"How about that girl from the Allgood Detective Agency?"

"Sally Elberton. We're having her shadowed."

"You can put your finger on her any minute?"

"Yes."

Mason said, "Unless I'm very much mistaken, Lois Witherspoon is going to serve an ultimatum on me tonight. And I wouldn't doubt if I heard from her father."

Drake said, "I've got some more dope for you on Roland Burr. He came into town quite frequently, buying photographic supplies and things of that sort. The day that you came down from Palm Springs—the day he was kicked by the horse—he seems to have been particularly active. He went into town four or five times. Apparently he was getting photographic supplies, and doing errands. But he went to the post office a couple of times. On one trip his wife wasn't with him."

Mason paused in the act of putting on his shirt. He asked, "Did you inquire particularly at all of the places where parcels could be checked, to see if he had . . ."

"That's another thing you were right on," Drake said. "At the Pacific Greyhound depot, he left a parcel, received a check in return for it, and so far as I've been able to find out, never returned for that particular parcel. The girl on duty doesn't remember him doing so."

"Wait a minute," Mason said. "There were several girls on duty there."

Drake nodded. "That's where the broken-leg business comes in handy."

168

"How do you mean?"

"Well, you see that parcel was checked around noon of the day when his leg was broken. The girl who was on at the checking station goes on duty at nine o'clock in the morning and gets off at five o'clock in the afternoon. By five o'clock, his leg was broken. Obviously, he couldn't have gone down *after* he'd broken his leg."

"How about that package?" Mason asked.

Drake said, "The package is gone. Therefore, *someone* must have presented the pasteboard claim check."

"The girl doesn't remember who called for the package?"

"No. She remembers Burr, but she doesn't remember the package particularly. It was just a small package done up in brown paper. She *thinks* it was about the size of a cigar box, but she can't be certain. They have quite a few packages checked in and out."

"The girl who waits on that parcel-checking counter has other duties?" Mason asked.

"Yes. She also runs the magazine stand and acts as cashier at the soda fountain."

"No chance someone sneaked around the counter and got that package without presenting a claim check, is there?"

"None whatever," Drake said. "They'll swear to that. They keep a pretty close watch on those packages—and a person would have to raise up a section of the counter to get in and out."

Mason said, "Well, I guess that gives me an out, but I don't mind telling you, Paul, it was a close squeeze."

Drake watched the lawyer drawing on his trousers, said, "You don't need to be so darn smug about it. What are you holding out on me?"

"Nothing," Mason said. "The cards are all on the table. Find out anything about Burr having a Winterburg City background?"

Drake said, "That's another thing you were right on. Burr lived in Winterburg City."

"When?"

"I don't know exactly when, but it was several years ago. He was in the insurance business there."

"What did he do after that?" Mason asked.

"Went out to the coast and got in on a big parking-station

169

deal, getting some leases, and that stuff. He ran the parking station for a while afterwards. Since then, he's been in half a dozen things. There's a gap in his life. I can't find anything from about 1930 to 1935. I don't think he ever went back to Winterburg City, though.''

Mason said, ''Get his fingerprints, Paul. Find out if he ever did time. The coroner's office probably took his fingerprints.''

''Come on,'' Drake said. ''You were playing something more than hunch in this thing. Kick through and give me the low-down.''

Mason said, ''There isn't any low-down yet, Paul. I'll tell you though some of the things which made me get those hunches. Understand, when I start work on a case, I act on the assumption my client is innocent. Therefore, it was no trick at all to get the hunch that Corine Hassen might have gone to Reno. Now then, *if* Adams was telling the truth and Latwell *had* intended to run away with her, and if she *had* gone to Reno, then it's obvious that something must have intervened to change the entire picture. That something resulted in the murder of David Latwell. Wasn't it reasonable to suppose that that same something could have resulted in the murder of Corine Hassen?''

''There were no marks of violence on the body,'' Drake said. ''A canoeing party happened to glimpse the body in the clear waters of the lake. They sent in an alarm to the sheriff's office, and the body was recovered. There was evidence indicating she must have come from Reno. The body was taken back to Reno, photographs were made, and a coroner's jury returned a verdict of death by drowning.''

''It still could have been murder,'' Mason said.

Drake thought that over. ''Well, as I get the picture, Milter wasn't playing the blackmail angle. That must have been Burr and his wife who had moved in on Witherspoon and were planning to collect from him. But I don't see how that helps us any, Perry. It simply builds up an added motive for murder. Witherspoon's got himself in a spot, and . . .''

He broke off as knuckles tapped on the door. Della Street called, ''How about it, Chief? Are you decent?''

''Just,'' Mason said. ''Come on in.''

Della Street slipped into the bedroom, said, "She's out there."

"Lois Witherspoon?"

"Yes."

"What does she want?"

"She wants to see you immediately," Della said. "She's reached a decision. I think she's going to tell it all right now."

Mason said, "Okay, we'll have it over with."

Lois Witherspoon got to her feet as Mason entered the sitting room of his suite in the hotel. She said, "I want to talk to you alone."

"That's all right," Mason said, indicating Paul Drake and Della Street. "You can say what you have to say in front of these people."

"It's about that duck you had me plant in Marvin's car," she said. "It looks now as though they're going to be successful in dragging the Milter murder into it. That means the duck becomes important. I'm *not* going to sit by and let my father get smeared with that . . ."

"I don't blame you," Mason said.

"I'm going to tell them about the duck. You know what that will mean."

"What will it mean?"

She said, "I'm sorry I did it. I'm sorry for my sake. I'm sorry for Dad's sake. And I'm sorry for yours."

"Why for mine?"

"They won't let you get away with anything like that down here, Mr. Mason."

"Why not?"

"It was planting evidence. I don't know much law, but it certainly seems to me that it's a violation of law. If it isn't, it's a violation of legal ethics—or so I should think."

Mason lit a cigarette. "Know anything about surgery?" he asked.

"What do you mean?"

Mason said, "There are times when you have to cut, and cut deep in order to save the patient's life. This was what you might call legal surgery."

"Isn't it illegal?"

"Perhaps."

"Is it going to make trouble for you if I tell?"

"Definitely."

Her eyes softened somewhat. She said, "Mr. Mason, you've been very, very nice. I don't know why you made me do that—yes, I do, too. You sympathized very much with Marvin, and I think you're holding something back from me."

Mason said, "That's what I want to talk with you about. Sit down. Let's have a cocktail and a cigarette and talk."

"We'll dispense with the cocktail," she said. "Let's make it a cigarette, and I'd like to have you hand it to me straight from the shoulder."

"Can you take it?"

"Yes."

Mason said, "I've already told you the truth about Marvin's background and why your father employed me. And I told you that I hadn't found anything *in the record* of that murder case, but that I was working on another angle. Well, I now have the proof I need. I can clear Marvin of the stigma of his father's tragedy—but I can't do it unless I can do it *my* way. Once you say anything about the duck, I'm mixed up in the case—up to my neck. Once I'm mixed in it, I can't be free to do the things I want to clear up that old case. Once Marvin hears of that old case, he'll run out on you. You should know that.

"The district attorney would love to get me hooked with that duck business. He also wants to put on evidence about that old murder case. You're going to play right into his hands. If the district attorney tries to put on evidence concerning that old case as additional motivation for Burr's murder, the witnesses will commit perjury. I want the thing handled my way."

"How is that?" she asked, apparently hesitating about forming her decision.

"I want you to get one message to your father."

"What?"

"Tell him to make his damn fool lawyer *sit down and shut up*," Mason said, with so much feeling that his hearers were startled.

"Why? Why, what do you mean? He hasn't said very

much. He's cross-examined the witnesses and only made one or two objections."

"He's objecting to that question about what the officer found when he went up to Milter's apartment," Mason said.

"Well, good heavens, isn't that the whole thing? Doesn't the whole case hinge on that? As I told you, I don't know much law, but it seems to me that if they can drag that other murder into it, and smear Dad with a lot of suspicion in the one case and a lot of suspicion in the other, then people will think he's guilty and . . ."

"Of course they will," Mason said, "and so will the judge. But the newspapers have already commented on that stuff. Every man, woman, and child in the courtroom who's old enough to read or think knows the evidence that the district attorney is trying to bring out. If your dad manages to suppress it by a legal technicality, it will still be lurking in the back of the judge's mind. What does your father's lawyer intend to do?"

"I don't know."

Mason said, "I heard that he thinks the case is so black that the judge won't dismiss it, that therefore he's not going to try to put on any evidence at this time, but let your father be bound over for trial, and put on his evidence at the time of the trial."

"Well, isn't that good legal policy?"

Mason looked at her and said, "No."

"Why?"

"Because your father is a proud man. This thing is eating into his spirit. A little of it will do him good. Too much of it will ruin him. What's more, it will ruin him in the community. This is a small place. Your father is prominent. He's got to smash this thing right in its tracks or it will smash him. If his lawyer starts taking advantage of technicalities, and people feel that your father was acquitted on a technicality . . . oh, well, what's the use?"

She said, "Do you want me to talk with Dad?"

"No," Mason said morosely.

"Why not?"

Mason said, "Because it's not my case. It's even unethical for me to say a word about what the other attorney is doing."

She said, "But what are *we* going to do about the duck?"

"Go tell your story if you want," Mason said. "It won't help your father any at this time. It'll drag Marvin into it, bring out all of that scandal, probably cause the boy either to commit suicide, or, in any event, will send him rushing away to join the Army without finishing his education—and you know what'll happen. He'll try his darndest not to come back. If he does, he'll never see you."

She was white-faced, but steady-eyed. "What am I supposed to do?" she asked.

"Let your conscience be your guide," Mason said.

She said, "Very well, I'm going out and announce my engagement to Marvin. I'm going to get him to go over to Yuma and we'll be married tonight. Then I'm going in and tell the judge about the duck."

Mason said moodily, "About what I expected you'd do."

She looked at Della Street, saw the sympathy in Della's eyes, and said savagely, "Don't sympathize with me. I suppose I could go feminine with very little urging and start bawling, but this is something that takes action, not tears."

"Suppose he won't marry you?" Mason asked.

She said, with tight-lipped determination, "I can fix things so he will."

"And then you're going to tell about the duck?"

"Yes. I hope it won't hurt you, or spoil your plans, but I'm going to tell them, anyway. I'm tired of having a lie bottled up inside me."

"And then what?"

"Then," she said, "if we can't prove Marvin's father was innocent, what's the difference? Marvin will already be my husband. He *can't* run away then."

"There'll be a lot of smear stuff in the newspapers," Mason said.

"Let them smear. What bothers me most is what it's going to do to you—but I can't jeopardize my father's position by keeping silent any longer."

Mason said, "I'll take care of myself. Don't worry about me. Go ahead and tell 'em about the duck."

She suddenly gave him her hand. The cold fingers squeezed his palm. "I guess you've done some wonderful things in your life, Mr. Mason, but I think this is about the most wonderful—being such a good sport—and what you did for Mar-

174

vin, and being willing to have your professional career put in danger—well, thanks.''

Mason patted her on the shoulder. "Go to it," he said. "You're a fighter. You can get what you want out of life—if you fight hard enough for it.''

She said, "Well, don't think I'm not going to fight hard enough," and started for the door.

They watched in silence while she turned the knob. It was no time for conventional good-bys or the inane formulae of politeness. They simply stood, watching her.

The bell of the telephone exploded the silence. Della Street jumped as though a gun had gone off behind her. Lois Witherspoon paused, waiting.

Mason, being nearest the telephone, scooped it up, placed the receiver to his ear, and said, "Hello. . . . Yes, this is Mason. . . . When? . . . Very well, I'll be there right away.''

He dropped the receiver into place, said to Lois Witherspoon, "Go get your boy friend, drive over to Yuma, and get married.''

"I'm going to.''

"And keep quiet about that duck," Mason said.

She shook her head.

Mason grinned. "You're not going to have to say anything about it.''

"Why?''

He said, "Your dad's sent for me. He wants me to come in and act as his lawyer tomorrow.''

She said coldly, "You can't act as his lawyer, Mr. Mason.''

"Why not?''

"Because you've contributed to building up some of the evidence against him.''

"Ethically, you're probably right," Mason said, "but it's an academic question which you won't need to worry about—because tomorrow I'm going to walk into court and blow that case against your father into a million pieces of legal wreckage.''

She stood for a moment looking at the determination of his face, the gleam in his eyes. Abruptly, she came toward him. "Would you like to kiss the bride?" she asked.

Chapter 20

The courtroom buzzed with excitement as Perry Mason strode past the barrier which separated the counsel table from the spectators and took his seat beside Lawrence Dormer and the defendant.

Judge Meehan called Court to order.

Lawrence Dormer got to his feet. "If the Court please," he said, "I would like to move that Mr. Perry Mason be associated in the defense of this case."

"It is so ordered," Judge Meehan said.

Mason slowly arose. "Now then, Your Honor," he observed, "upon behalf of the defendant, John L. Witherspoon, we withdraw the objection the defendant made yesterday to the question which the district attorney asked Officer Haggerty. Let the officer go ahead and answer it."

District Attorney Copeland was more than surprised. It was a moment before he could master his astonishment. Sensing a trap, he got to his feet, and said, "Of course, the Court will understand that the question is asked only for the purpose of showing that the defendant would have had access to similar poisons, a knowledge of their use and application, and a knowledge of the fatal nature of this gas."

"That is my understanding," Judge Meehan said.

"I trust that counsel understands it," Copeland announced, looking across at Perry Mason.

Mason sat down and crossed his knees. "Counsel understands the law—or thinks he does," he said with a smile.

For a long thirty seconds, District Attorney Copeland hesitated; then he had the question read to the witness and received his answer.

Feeling his way cautiously, Copeland showed the discovery of the body of Leslie Milter, that the poison, its disposition and use were exactly the same as that which had caused the death of Roland Burr.

176

Copeland also showed that Witherspoon had appeared at the apartment some thirty or forty minutes after the discovery of Milter's body, that he had then stated to the witness, Haggerty, that he was in search of Perry Mason, who, Haggerty informed him, had just left. Witherspoon had then stated he "had been looking everywhere for Mr. Mason, and had come to Milter's apartment as a last resort." The witness stated Witherspoon not only had made no reference to an earlier visit to Milter's apartment, but had given his hearers to understand that this was the first time he had ever been there.

All of these questions went into the record and were answered without objection. From the extreme care with which Copeland phrased his questions, it was apparent that he was becoming more and more worried.

At the close of Haggerty's examination, he got to his feet, and said, "If the Court please, this evidence will be connected up by my next witness, by whom we will prove that this defendant was seen leaving Milter's apartment at just about the time the murder must have been committed. The Court will understand that this course of procedure may be somewhat unusual, that all of this line of evidence is being offered for a very limited purpose, and," he added triumphantly, *"it has been received without objection on the part of the defendant."*

"Any further questions?" Mason asked.

"No. You may cross-examine."

Mason said, "Mr. Haggerty, when you first entered that apartment, you noticed a goldfish bowl with a small duck in it?"

"Objected to as not proper cross-examination," Copeland said promptly. "The evidence concerning the murder of Milter was introduced for a very limited purpose. I have no desire to try the murder case at this time."

"It doesn't make any difference what *you* desire," Mason said. "You opened the door on direct examination far enough to serve your purpose. Under the laws of cross-examination, I have the right to throw it *all* the way open. And that's just what I'm going to do, Mr. District Attorney, *throw it wide open!*"

Copeland said, "Your Honor, I object. This is not proper cross-examination."

"Why not?" Mason asked. "You've sought to connect the defendant with the murder of Milter."

"But only for the purpose of showing familiarity with that particular method of perpetrating a murder," the district attorney said.

"I don't care what *your* purpose is or was," Mason told him. "I'm going to prove that John L. Witherspoon couldn't have had anything to do with the murder of Milter. I'm going to prove that Milter was dead before Witherspoon ever started up the stairs to that apartment. I'm going to prove it by your own witnesses as well as by some of mine. And then I'm going to hurl your argument right back into your teeth. You've walked into this and . . ."

Judge Meehan pounded with his gavel. "Counsel will refrain from personalities," he said. "Counsel will address his argument to the *Court*."

"Very well," Mason said with a smile. "Your Honor, I submit that the district attorney has sought to introduce certain evidence for a limited purpose. There was no objection on the part of the defense to that evidence. He has shown the part of it which he thought would benefit his case. We're entitled to show it all."

"So far as this specific question is concerned," Judge Meehan said, "the objection is overruled. The witness will answer it."

"That's right. There was a duck in that goldfish bowl," Haggerty said.

"And was there anything peculiar about that duck?"

"Yes."

"What?"

"Well, it seemed to be—it was sort of paddling around in the water—it looked like a duck that didn't know how to swim—looked like it was drowning."

The roar of laughter which came up from the courtroom drowned out the beating of the judge's gavel.

Haggerty shifted his position uncomfortably on the stand, but glared dogged defiance at the laughing spectators.

"This being an agricultural community," Mason conceded with a smile, when the uproar had subsided, "I take it that the idea of a duck that hasn't learned how to swim, and drowns in a goldfish bowl is rather amusing to the spec-

178

tators. Are you *certain* that the duck was drowning, Mr. Haggerty?''

Haggerty said, ''There was something wrong with that duck. I don't know what it was, but it was sunk down under the water. Just a little of it was sticking up.''

''Have you ever heard of ducks *diving*?'' Mason asked.

A titter ran around the courtroom.

Haggerty said, ''Yes,'' and then added, ''But this was the first time I ever saw one dive stern first.''

A gale of laughter swept the courtroom before it was silenced.

''But you're certain there was something wrong with the duck when you entered that room?'' Mason asked, when order had been restored.

''Yes. It wasn't sitting right. It was about two-thirds sunk.''

''What happened to the duck after that?'' Mason asked.

''Well, the duck seemed to get well. I was pretty much all in myself from getting a whiff of that gas. Then, when I got to feeling better, I looked at the duck again. That time, it was floating on the water all right.''

''Was the duck still in the fish bowl when the defendant entered the apartment?'' Mason asked.

''Yes.''

''Did the defendant make any statement about that duck?''

''Yes.''

''What?''

''He said it was his duck.''

''Anything else?''

''He said that Marvin Adams, a young man who had been calling at the house, had taken the duck away with him that evening.''

''And the defendant identified the duck positively?''

''Yes, absolutely. He said that he'd swear to it anywhere. It was his duck.''

Mason bowed and smiled. ''Thank you very much, Officer Haggerty, for having made a very good witness. I have no further questions.''

District Attorney Copeland hesitated a moment, then called, ''Alberta Cromwell.''

Alberta Cromwell marched down the aisle of the courtroom, held up her hand, took the oath, then seated herself in the witness chair. Once she glanced at Perry Mason, and her eyes were hard and defiant, the eyes of a woman who had made up her mind as to exactly what she is going to say, and has determined to deny those things she is not willing to admit.

Copeland was suave once more. This time he was on more familiar legal grounds, and his manner and the tone of his voice showed it. "Your name is Alberta Cromwell and you live here in El Templo?"

"Yes, sir."

"And did so live on the night when this crime was alleged to have been committed?"

"Yes, sir."

"You lived at eleven sixty-two Cinder Butte Avenue in an apartment house?"

"Yes, sir."

"The same apartment house where the decedent, Leslie Milter lived?"

"Yes, sir."

"And where was your apartment with reference to his?"

"My apartment was right next to his. There were two apartments on the second floor. He had one, and I had the other."

"Was there any connecting door or any means of communication?"

"No, sir."

"Now, on the night in question, did you see the defendant in this case, Mr. John L. Witherspoon?"

"Yes, sir."

"Where and when?"

"It was about twenty minutes to twelve, perhaps a quarter of twelve. I can't be certain of the exact time. I know that it was after eleven-thirty and before midnight."

"*Where* did you see him?"

"Just leaving the apartment of Leslie L. Milter."

"Are you certain of your identification?"

"Yes, sir. I not only saw the man, but I took down the license number of his automobile. I am certain it was Mr. Witherspoon."

"Now, do you know whether he left the apartment of the decedent, or . . ."

"Yes, sir," she interrupted in her eagerness to answer the question. "I know that he left the apartment. I heard his feet coming down the stairs; then I heard the lower door open and slam, and he walked across the porch."

"How could you see all this?"

"From my window. The house has two bay windows on each side of the second floor. One is on Mr. Milter's side, and one is on my side. From my bay window, I could look down and see the door of Mr. Milter's apartment."

"You may cross-examine," Copeland said.

Mason got slowly to his feet, his eyes boring steadily into those of the witness. "You were acquainted with Leslie Milter in his lifetime."

"Yes."

"You had known him in Los Angeles?"

Her eyes were defiant. "Yes."

"You were his common-law wife?"

"No."

"You were not his wife?"

"Absolutely not."

"Did you ever claim to be his wife?"

"No."

"Did you ever live with him as his wife?"

"Objected to as incompetent, irrelevant, and immaterial, not proper cross-examination," Copeland roared, indignantly. "That question, if the Court please, is asked purely for the purpose of debasing the witness. It has absolutely no bearing on . . ."

"The objection is sustained."

Mason bowed acknowledgement of the Court's ruling, said respectfully, "Your Honor, if I might be permitted to argue the point, I think that the bias of a witness is a material factor and . . ."

"This Court is not going to permit the question," Judge Meehan stated. "You are entitled to ask the witness if she was the wife of the decedent, if she had ever claimed to have been his wife. You are entitled to ask her if she was friendly with him, but having received the answers that you did, the Court rules that you are *not* entitled to place this witness in an embarrassing position in view of the present state of the record. You will understand, Counselor, that the evidence

181

concerning the murder of Leslie Milter is introduced for a very limited purpose. While your right of cross-examination as to the facts which the officers encountered in that apartment is not limited, your cross-examination of this witness as to motivation *is* limited. The Court rules that the relationship called for in your question, even if it did ever exist, would be too remote.''

"Very well," Mason said, "I will make my point in this way. Miss Cromwell, it was possible for you to go out of the back door of your apartment and, by climbing over a low wooden railing, get on the back porch of Milter's apartment, wasn't it?''

"I suppose a person could have done so.''

"Did you ever do so?''

There was something of triumph in her eyes. "No,'' she said flatly and in a tone of cold finality.

"You hadn't done so on the evening in question?''

"Certainly not.''

"You hadn't seen Leslie Milter on that evening?''

"I had seen him earlier in the evening when he entered his apartment.''

"You hadn't been visiting in his apartment?''

"No, sir.''

"And Leslie Milter wasn't fixing a drink of hot buttered rum for you when the doorbell rang, and he didn't then tell you to go back over to your apartment?''

"No, sir.''

"Now, you have mentioned that you saw the defendant leaving the apartment. Had you been keeping a watch on the apartment earlier in the evening?''

"No, sir. I wasn't keeping a watch on it when I saw the defendant leave. I simply happened to be standing there at the bay window.''

"Why were you standing at the bay window?''

"I simply happened to be there.''

"Could the defendant have looked up and seen you?''

"No. I don't think so.''

"Why?''

"Because I was looking *out*. He would have had to look *in*.''

"And he couldn't have done so?''

182

"Certainly not."

"You mean to say that he couldn't have seen you standing there in that window because there was no light behind you?"

"Of course."

"Then the room must have been dark."

She hesitated a moment, then said, "Yes, I guess it was. It *may* have been."

"The lights were not on in that room?" Mason asked.

"No, sir. I guess not."

"And the shades were up?"

"Why . . . I . . . I'm not certain."

"Do you want this Court to believe that you saw the witness through a drawn shade?" Mason asked.

"No, I didn't mean that."

"What did you mean, then?"

For a moment, she was trapped, and there was desperation on her face. Then she thought of a way out and said triumphantly, "I thought your question related to whether *all* the shades were up or down. I knew that the shade on that one window had not been drawn, but I couldn't remember about the others."

She smiled triumphantly, as much as to say, "You thought you had me that time, didn't you? But I got out of it."

Mason said, "But there were no lights in the room."

"No. I'm certain there were none."

"For what purpose did you enter that darkened room?" Mason asked.

"Why, I . . . I just wanted something in there."

"The window at which you were standing was near the door on the side farthest removed from the door?"

"Yes, on the side farthest away from the door."

"And the light switch is near the door, is it not?"

"Yes."

"So that, when you entered this room in search of something, which you can't now recall, you didn't turn on the light switch, but you did walk all the way across this darkened room to stand at the window, looking down at the door of Leslie Milter's apartment?"

"I was just standing there—thinking."

"I see. Now, shortly after that, when I appeared at the

apartment and rang the doorbell trying to get in, you came down the stairs from your apartment, did you not?"

"Yes."

"And talked with me?"

"Yes."

"And we walked a few feet together, up toward the center of town?"

"Yes."

"And you went to the stage office, did you not?"

The district attorney was gloating now. "Your Honor, I *must* object. This examination certainly is going far afield. Where this witness went, or what she did after she had left that apartment house, is certainly not proper cross-examination. It's incompetent, irrelevant, and immaterial, and too remote in point of time to have any possible bearing upon the case. The Court will bear in mind that this entire evidence has been introduced for a very limited purpose."

Judge Meehan nodded, said, "This Court will hear argument on it, Mr. Mason, if you wish to argue it, but it would seem that the position taken by the district attorney is correct."

"I would think so," Mason said. "I should think that it was quite correct, and I think I have no more questions of this young woman. Thank you very much, Miss Cromwell."

Plainly she had expected a pitched battle with Mason, and his calm acceptance of her statements, which were so directly at variance with the statements she had previously made to him, came as a surprise.

She was just about to leave the witness stand when Mason said casually, "Oh, one more question, Miss Cromwell. I notice Raymond E. Allgood is in the courtroom. Do you know him?"

She hesitated, then said, "Yes."

"Do you know his secretary, Sally Elberton?"

"Yes."

"Have you ever made any statement to either of them, claiming that you were the wife of Leslie Milter?" Mason asked.

"I . . . That is . . ."

"Will you stand up, Miss Elberton, please?"

The blond young woman got to her feet very reluctantly.

"Haven't you ever told this woman that you were Leslie Milter's common-law wife?" Mason asked.

"I didn't say I was a common-law wife," the witness said. "I told her to lay off of him, and . . ." She caught herself abruptly in mid-sentence, dammed the stream of words which had started to pour from her mouth.

As she realized the effect of what she had said, as she looked around at the curious eyes focussed upon her, she dropped slowly back into the witness chair as though her knees had suddenly lost their strength.

"Go on," Mason said. "Go right ahead and finish what you were about to say."

She said indignantly, "You trapped me into that. You made me think it was all over, and then got that woman to stand up, and . . ."

"What have you against that woman, as you term her? . . . That's all, Miss Elberton. You may be seated again."

Sally Elberton settled back into her seat, conscious of the craning necks of spectators; then all eyes were once more upon Alberta Cromwell.

"All right," the witness said, as though suddenly making up her mind to see it through, "I'll tell you the *whole* truth. What I told you was the absolute truth except I was trying to cover up on that one thing. I was the common-law wife of Leslie Milter. He never did marry me. He told me that it wasn't necessary, that we were married just as legally as though we'd been married in a church, and I believed him. I lived with him as his wife, and he always introduced me as his wife; and then this woman came along and turned his head completely. She made him want to get away from me. I knew he'd been stepping out on me before, but it had been just here and there, the way a man will. This was different. She'd completely turned his head, and . . ."

The dazed district attorney, suddenly gathering his presence of mind, interrupted to say, "Just a moment, Your Honor. It seems to me this is also too remote and distant, that it's incompetent, irrelevant, and immaterial, and . . ."

"I think not," Judge Meehan ruled sternly. "This witness is now making a statement in direct contradiction to a statement which she made under oath a few minutes earlier. She is admitting that she falsified a part of her testimony. Under

185

the circumstances, the Court wants to hear every bit of explanation this witness wants to make. Go right ahead, Miss Cromwell.''

She turned to face the judge and said, ''I don't suppose you'll ever understand, but that's the way it was. Leslie ran away from me and came down here to El Templo. It took me two or three days to find out where he'd gone. I came on down to join him. He told me that he was here on a business matter, and I couldn't be with him, that it would ruin things if I should try to make trouble. Well, I found there was a vacant apartment next to his, and I moved in. I guess he really was working on a case, and . . .''

''Never mind what you guess,'' District Attorney Copeland interrupted. ''Just answer Mr. Mason's questions, Miss Cromwell. If the Court please, I submit that this witness shouldn't be allowed to make a statement of this nature. She should only answer the questions which are asked her on cross-examination.''

Judge Meehan leaned forward to regard the young woman. ''Are you explaining the contradiction in your testimony, Miss Cromwell?'' he asked.

''Yes, Judge.''

''Go right ahead,'' Judge Meehan said.

She said, ''Then Leslie told me that if I'd be a good girl and not rock the boat, that within a week or so we could go away and travel anywhere we wanted to. We could go down into Mexico or South America, or anywhere. He said that he was going to have lots of money and . . .''

''I'm not particularly concerned with what he said,'' Judge Meehan broke in to say. ''I want to know how it happened that you falsified a portion of your testimony and whether that is the only part in which you failed to tell the truth.''

''Well,'' she said. ''I've got to explain this so you'll understand. Leslie told me the night he was killed that his business was all ready to close up, but that Sally Elberton was coming down to see him. He told me I'd been all wet about her. He said that his relationship with her had been built up just so he could get some information. That he'd been working on her so he could put across this deal. He said she was a vain, empty-headed little brat, and he had to kid her along in order to keep on getting information out of her.''

186

"Were you over in Leslie Milter's apartment that night?" Judge Meehan asked.

"Well—yes. I was. I went over to have a talk with him, and he was fixing me a hot buttered rum. He didn't expect Sally Elberton until right around midnight. Then the doorbell rang, and he got sore and said, 'I gave that little brat keys to my apartment so she wouldn't have to stand out in front of it ringing a bell with all the world to see. I suppose she's lost her keys. You skip over to your apartment, and within half or three-quarters of an hour I'll give you a signal that the coast is clear.' "

"What did you do?" Mason asked.

"I went out the back door and across to my apartment. I heard him lock the back door after I left. Then I heard him going toward the front of his apartment."

"Did you look to see who was coming into the apartment?"

"No, sir, I didn't. She'd have been in by the time I got to my window, anyway. I went in, sat down and listened to the radio."

"Then what?"

"After a while I began to get nervous and just a little suspicious. I tiptoed out to the back porch, and I couldn't hear a thing; then I put my ear to the wall and I thought I could hear someone moving around very quietly. Then I thought I heard voices. Well, I made up my mind I'd go and stand at the window and look down at the door and see exactly when she left. I went into the front room and stood by the window. I saw there was a car parked in front of the apartment, and then this man"—she pointed to Witherspoon—"came out and got in the car. I didn't know that he was expecting any man, and I thought perhaps it might have been an officer."

"Why an officer?" Mason asked.

She said, "Oh, I don't know. Leslie was inclined to take chances at times. I—well, he'd had some trouble. Anyway, I took down the license number.'

"And then what?" Mason asked.

She said, "I thought I'd go down and ring Leslie's bell. I thought that would make him come to the door, and anyone that was upstairs would remain upstairs. I—I wasn't dressed, just had a robe on over some underthings. So I went back into my bedroom and dressed. Well then, I thought I'd try to peek in through the window in the back door. So I went out to the back porch again, climbed over the rail, and gently tried the back door. It was locked. There was a little diamond-shaped glass window up near the top. By standing on tiptoe, I could look through it. I could see that the kitchen was pretty well filled with smoke. I dragged a box over, and stood on it and looked through the diamond-shaped window. I could see a man's feet with the toes pointed up, and could see that the pan of sugar and water had boiled dry. I pounded on the door, and got no answer. I tried the knob, and the door was locked. Well, I moved the box back, climbed over the porch rail, back to my apartment, and went downstairs as fast as I could. You were ringing the bell of his door, and so I didn't dare to show too much interest, or try to force my way in. As soon as I could get away from you, I walked down the street and telephoned the police that something was wrong up at Leslie Milter's apartment. Then I went to the bus depot, and waited—and so help me, that's the truth and every bit of it."

Judge Meehan looked down at Perry Mason. "Any further questions?" he asked.

"None, Your Honor," Mason said.

District Attorney Copeland answered the judge's inquiry by a somewhat dazed shake of his head.

"That's all," Judge Meehan told the witness. "You are excused."

It wasn't until she heard the kindly note in his voice that Alberta Cromwell burst into tears. Sobbing, she groped her way down from the witness box.

The bailiff walked over to District Attorney Copeland, tapped him on the shoulder, and handed him a folded note.

Copeland studied the note with a puzzled expression, then said to Judge Meehan, "Your Honor, I think I have uncovered a very strange and unusual situation. If the Court will permit me, I would like to call a hostile witness."

"Very well," Judge Meehan said.

The district attorney got up, walked across the railed-off enclosure, and paused to stand looking at the black-garbed, heavily veiled figure of Mrs. Roland Burr, who was sitting in the front row of the spectators. He raised his voice and said dramatically, "If the Court please, I now wish to put on the stand Diana Burr, the widow of Roland Burr. She will be my next witness. Mrs. Burr, will you please come forward and be sworn?"

Mrs. Burr was surprised and indignant, but at Judge Meehan's order to come forward, she walked to the witness stand, managing to look very tragic and dainty in her black mourning, and held up her hand and was sworn. She gave her name and address, then waited expectantly while District Attorney Copeland glanced around the courtroom to make certain that he had the undivided attention of the spectators. "Did you ever see a duck drown?" he asked dramatically.

This time there was no levity from the courtroom. It needed but a glance at Mrs. Burr's countenance to make it plain that this was a moment filled with tense drama.

"Yes," Mrs. Burr said, in a low voice.

In the silence which descended upon the courtroom, it was possible to hear the sounds of breathing and rustling garments as people moved uneasily in their chairs, straining to get a better view of the witness.

"Where?" District Attorney Copeland asked.

"At the home of John L. Witherspoon."

"When?"

"About a week ago."

"What happened?"

She said, "Marvin Adams talked about a drowning duck. My husband laughed at him, and Adams brought in a young duck and a fish bowl. He put something in the water, and the duck began to sink."

"Did the duck drown?"

"Mr. Adams took him out before the duck had completely drowned."

The district attorney turned triumphantly to Perry Mason. "And now you may cross-examine," he said.

"Thank you very much," Mason said with exaggerated politeness.

For a long moment, Mason sat perfectly still, then he asked quietly, "You formerly lived in Winterburg City, Mrs. Burr?"

"Yes."

"You first met your husband there?"

"Yes."

"How old are you?"

She hesitated, then said, "Thirty-nine."

"Did you ever know a Corine Hassen in Winterburg City?"

"No."

"Did you ever hear your husband speak of a Miss Corine Hassen?"

She avoided Mason's eyes.

"What is the object of all this?" the district attorney interrupted. "Why don't you cross-examine her about the duck?"

Mason ignored the interpolation. "Did you ever hear your husband speak of a Miss Corine Hassen?" he asked again.

"Why—yes—it was years ago."

Mason settled back in his chair, was silent for several seconds.

"Any more questions?" Judge Meehan asked of Mason.

"None, Your Honor."

District Attorney Copeland said with a sarcastic smile, "I was hoping you'd ask some questions which would throw a little more light on that drowning duck."

"I thought you were," Mason said, smiling. "The drowning duck now becomes your problem, Mr. District Attorney. I have no further questions of this witness."

The district attorney said, "Very well, I'm going to call Marvin Adams as my next witness. I will state, Your Honor, that I hadn't expected to do this, but the Court will understand I'm simply trying to get at the true facts of this case. In view of what this witness has said, I think that it's . . . ."

"The district attorney needs make no statement," Judge Meehan said. "Simply call your witness."

"Marvin Adams, come forward," the district attorney said.

Marvin Adams, obviously reluctant, came slowly forward to the witness stand, was sworn, and sat down facing the hostile eyes of the district attorney.

"You have heard what this last witness said about a duck drowning?"

"Yes, sir."

190

"Did you perform such an experiment?"

"Yes, sir."

"Now then," the district attorney said, getting to his feet and pointing an accusing finger at Marvin Adams, "did you or did you not perform that experiment in the apartment of Leslie Milter on the night of his murder?"

"No, sir."

"Did you know Leslie L. Milter?"

"No, sir."

"Never met him?"

"No, sir."

"Were you ever at his apartment?"

"No, sir."

"But you did perform the experiment of making a duck drown, and explained that experiment to the guests assembled in Mr. Witherspoon's home?"

"Yes, sir."

"And," the district attorney said triumphantly, "the persons present included Mr. John L. Witherspoon, did they not?"

"No, sir. Mr. Witherspoon wasn't there."

For a moment, the district attorney was nonplused.

"Just what did you do?" he asked, trying to cover his discomfiture. "Just how did you make a duck sink?"

"By the use of a detergent."

"What is a detergent?"

"It's a relatively new discovery by means of which the natural antipathy between water and oil can be eliminated."

"How is that done?"

As Marvin Adams explained the complex action of detergents, the spectators were staring open-mouthed. Judge Meehan leaned forward to look down at the young man, his face showing his interest.

"And do you mean to say that, by the aid of this detergent, you can cause a duck to sink?" the district attorney asked.

"Yes. A few thousandths of one per cent of a powerful detergent in water would cause a duck to submerge."

The district attorney thought that over for a few moments, then said, "Now, you aren't as yet related in any way to the defendant in this action, are you?"

"Yes, sir, I am."

"What?"

"I am his son-in-law."

"You mean . . . what *do* you mean?"

"I mean," Marvin Adams said, "that I am married to Lois Witherspoon. She is my wife."

"When did this marriage take place?"

"In Yuma, Arizona, about one o'clock this morning."

The district attorney took time to think that one over too. Spectators whispered among themselves.

District Attorney Copeland resumed his questioning. Now he was asking his questions in the cautious manner of a hunter stalking his prey. "It is, of course, quite possible that one of the persons who saw this experiment performed could have told the defendant about it. Isn't that correct?"

"Objected to," Mason said easily, "as being argumentative and calling for a conclusion of the witness."

"Sustained," Judge Meehan snapped.

"Have you ever discussed this experiment of the sinking duck with the defendant?"

"No, sir."

"With his daughter?"

"Objected to," Mason said. "Incompetent, irrelevant, and immaterial."

"Sustained."

Copeland scratched his head, looking down at some papers, looked up at the clock hanging on the wall of the courtroom, said suddenly to Marvin Adams, "When you left the ranch of the defendant the night of the murder, you took with you a small duck, did you not?"

"Yes, sir."

"One that belonged to the defendant?"

"Yes, sir. His daughter told me I might have it."

"Exactly. And you took this duck for a certain purpose, didn't you?"

"Yes, sir."

"To perform an experiment?"

"Yes, sir."

"Now, are you positive that you didn't go to the apartment of Leslie L. Milter shortly after leaving Witherspoon's ranch?"

"I have never been to Mr. Milter's apartment."

192

"Are you willing to swear positively that the duck which Officer Haggerty found in Milter's apartment was not the same duck which you took from Mr. Witherspoon's ranch?"

Before Adams could answer the question, Lois Witherspoon said in a clear, firm voice, "He can't answer that question. I am the only one who can do that."

Judge Meehan rapped for order, but stared curiously at Lois Witherspoon.

Mason, on his feet, said suavely, "I was about to object to the question, anyway, Your Honor, on the ground that it calls for a conclusion of the witness, that it is argumentative. This Court is not concerned with what a witness is *willing* to swear to. That doesn't help solve the issues before the Court. The statements of *a fact* which a witness makes under his oath are the only pertinent ones. To ask a witness what he *'is willing to swear to'* is argumentative."

"That is, of course, merely a loose way of framing the question," Judge Meehan said. "Perhaps, technically, your objection is correct upon that point."

"And, even if the questions were reframed," Mason said, "it calls for a conclusion of the witness. The witness can testify whether he placed any duck in the fish bowl in Milter's apartment. He can testify whether he was ever in Milter's apartment. He can testify whether he kept the duck in his possession or what he did with it. But to ask him whether a certain duck is one that he had seen or had in his possession earlier, calls for a conclusion of the witness—unless, of course, it is shown there is some distinguishing mark upon that one particular duck which differentiates it from every other duck."

"Of course," Judge Meehan said, "if the witness doesn't *know* that, he may state simply that he doesn't know."

Marvin Adams was smiling. "But I *do* know," he said. "The duck which I left in my automobile . . ."

"Just a moment," Mason interrupted, holding up his hand. "There's an objection before the Court, Mr. Adams. Just refrain from answering until the Court has ruled on the objection."

Lois Witherspoon, still standing, said, "He can't answer that question. I'm the *only* one who *can* answer it."

Judge Meehan said, "I am going to ask Miss Witherspoon

193

to be seated. After all, we must maintain order in the court-room.''

"But don't you understand, Your Honor?" Lois Wither-spoon said. "I . . .''

"That will do," Judge Meehan said. "A question has been asked of this witness, and there is an objection before the Court, a rather technical objection to be certain, but one which, nevertheless, the defendant is entitled to make.''

"I think, if the Court please," Mason said, "more hinges upon this question and this objection than the Court realizes. I notice that it is approaching the hour of the noon adjournment. Might I suggest that the Court take it under advisement until two o'clock this afternoon?''

"I see no reason for doing so," Judge Meehan said. "The objection, as I understand it, is technical; first as to the nature of the question, then as to whether it calls for a conclusion of the witness. Of course, if the witness doesn't actually know, he is free to say so in just those words. I think, therefore, it is not necessary to lay a proper foundation by showing that there was some marking upon the duck or other identification which would enable the witness to know. However, as to the form of the question—I am referring now to the point that the district attorney has asked the witness if he would be willing to swear to a certain thing—I believe the objection is well taken. The Court will, therefore, sustain the objection to this particular question upon this one specific point, and the district attorney will then be at liberty to ask another question in proper form—and I suppose an objection will be made by counsel for the defense. Whereupon, the objection will be in the record in such a clear-cut way there can be no confusion as to the question of law involved.''

"Very well, Your Honor," Mason said. "Pardon me, if the Court please, before the district attorney reframes that question, may I suggest to the Court that the district attorney should be cautioned not to throw away the most valuable piece of evidence in this case.''

Copeland gave a quick start of surprise, whirled to stare at Mason. "What do you mean?''

Mason said suavely, "That bit of paper which was handed to you a few minutes ago.''

"What about it?''

194

"It's evidence."

The district attorney said to Judge Meehan, "I submit, Your Honor, that it is *not* evidence. That was a private, confidential communication handed to me by some person in this room."

"Who?" Mason asked.

"That is none of your business," Copeland said.

Judge Meehan interposed dryly, "That will do, gentlemen. We will have an end to the personalities. And the Court will try to restore some semblance of order. Now, Miss Witherspoon, if you will please be seated."

"But, Your Honor, I . . . ."

"Be seated, please. You will have an opportunity to tell your story later on.

"Now, for the purpose of getting the record straight, let it appear that a question has been asked of this witness. An objection was made to that question. The objection has been sustained."

"And, if the Court please," Mason interposed suavely, "may it appear at this time that I have requested that the district attorney do not destroy the note which was handed to him a few minutes ago?"

"Upon what ground?" Judge Meehan asked. "I am inclined to agree with the district attorney that that is a confidential communication."

Mason said, "It is the most pertinent piece of evidence in this case. I am asking that the Court impound that evidence until I can prove that it *is* pertinent."

"Upon what grounds?" Copeland asked.

Mason said, "Let us list the people who *knew* that Marvin Adams had performed the experiment of drowning a duck, since only such a person could have written that note to the district attorney—a note which, I take it, advised the district attorney to call Mrs. Burr to the stand and interrogate her on this point. The defendant in this case didn't know it. In any event, he didn't write that note. Mrs. Burr didn't write that note. Lois Witherspoon didn't write it. Obviously, Marvin Adams didn't write it. Yet it was written by someone who knew that experiment had been performed at that time and at that place. I think, therefore, the Court will agree with me that this is highly pertinent evidence."

195

District Attorney Copeland said, "If the Court please, the prosecutor in a case, as well as the police officers who are investigating a case, quite frequently get anonymous tips to significant facts. The only way they can hope to get such tips is by keeping the source of information confidential."

Mason interposed quickly, "I think, if the Court please, that, inasmuch as it is approaching the hour of the noon recess, I can discuss the matter in Chambers with the Court and the district attorney, and convince both the Court and the district attorney of the importance of this bit of evidence."

Judge Meehan said, "I see no reason at the present time for asking the district attorney to submit in evidence any confidential communication he may have received from anyone."

"Thank you, Your Honor," Copeland said.

"On the other hand," Judge Meehan went on, "it seems to me that if there is any chance this might turn out to be a significant piece of evidence, it should be preserved."

Copeland said with dignity, "I had no intention of destroying it, Your Honor."

"I thought the district attorney was about to crumple it up and throw it away," Mason said.

Copeland lashed out at him, "This isn't the first time you've been mistaken in connection with this case."

Mason bowed. "Being purely a private citizen, *my* mistakes don't result in the prosecution of innocent men."

"That will do, gentlemen," Judge Meehan said. "The Court will take a recess until two o'clock in the afternoon. I will ask counsel to meet with me in Chambers at one-thirty, and I will ask the district attorney not to destroy that note which was handed to him, until after meeting with counsel in Chambers. Recess until two o'clock this afternoon."

As people began filing out of the courtroom, Mason looked at Della Street and grinned. "Whew!" he said. "*That* was close."

"You mean you were just stalling?" she asked.

"Stalling for time," he admitted. "Lois Witherspoon was going to stand up there and tell the whole business, right out in public."

"She'll do it at two o'clock, anyway," Della Street said.

196

"I know it."

"Well?"

Mason grinned. "That gives me two hours in which to think up a way out, or . . ."

"Or what?" Della Street asked as Mason left the sentence unfinished.

"Or solve the case," Mason said.

Lois Witherspoon came pressing forward. She said, "That was very, very clever, Mr. Mason, but it isn't going to stop me."

"All right," Mason said. "But will you promise you won't say anything to anyone about it until two o'clock."

"I'm going to tell Marvin."

"Not until just before he goes on the stand," Mason said. "It won't make any difference."

"No, I'm going to tell him now."

"Tell me what?" Marvin Adams asked, coming up behind her and slipping his arm around her.

"About the duck," Lois said.

A deputy sheriff, coming forward, said, "John Witherspoon wants to talk with you, Mr. Mason. And he also wants to see his daughter and—" here the sheriff grinned broadly— "his new son-in-law."

Mason said to Adams, "This might be a good time for you to go and talk things over with him. Tell him I'll try and see him shortly before court convenes this afternoon."

Mason caught Paul Drake's eye, and motioned him to join them.

"Have you been able to find out anything about that letter, Paul?" Mason asked in a low voice.

"Which one?"

"The one that I gave you—the one Marvin Adams received, offering him a hundred dollars to show the writer how to make a duck sink."

Drake said, "I can't find out a thing about it, Perry. The telephone number is just as you surmised, that of a big department store. They don't know anyone named Gridley P. Lahey."

"How about the letter?"

"Absolutely nothing you can find out about it. It's mailed in a plain, stamped envelope and written on a piece of paper

197

which has been torn from a writing pad, one of the sort that is sold in drugstores, stationery stores, five-and-ten-cent stores, and so many other places that it's impossible to try and trace it. We have the handwriting to go by, and that's all. It isn't doing us any good now."

Mason said, "It may help later, Paul. See if you can locate the woman who was employed as nurse—the one Burr fired, will you? She—"

"She was here in court," Drake interrupted. "Just a minute, Perry. I think I may be able to locate her."

He strode out through the swinging gate in the mahogany rail, to thread his way through the crowd that was slowly shuffling its way out of the courtroom. A few minutes later, he was back with a rather attractive young woman. "This is Miss Field," he said, "the nurse who was on the job the morning Burr was murdered."

Miss Field gave Mason her hand, said, "I've been very much interested in watching the way the case developed. I don't think I should talk to you. I've been subpoenaed by the district attorney as a witness."

"To show that he asked Witherspoon to get him a fishing rod?" Mason asked.

"Yes. I think that's one of the things he wants."

Mason said, "You don't do any fishing, do you, Miss Field?"

"I don't have time."

"Do you know very much about fishing rods?"

"No."

"Is there any chance," Mason asked, "any chance whatever, no matter how remote, that Burr could have got up out of bed?"

"No chance on earth. Not without cutting the rope which held that weight on his leg, and even then, I doubt if he could have made it. If he had, he'd have put the fracture out of place."

"The rope wasn't tampered with?"

"No."

Mason said, "He didn't want you touching that bag of his. Is that what caused your discharge?"

"That's the way the trouble started. He kept that bag by the side of the bed, and was always delving into it, pulling

198

out books and material to tie flies, and things of that sort. I stumbled over that bag every single time I went near the bed. So finally I told him that I'd arrange the things out on the dresser where he could see them, and he could point out whatever he wanted, and I'd bring it over to him.''

"And he didn't like that?''

"It seemed to make him furious.''

"Then what happened?''

"Nothing right then, but a half hour later he wanted something, and I stumbled over the bag again. I stooped to pick it up, and he grabbed my arm and almost broke it. I can ordinarily get along with patients, but there are some things I won't stand. However, I probably would simply have reported it to the doctor and stayed on the job, if it hadn't been that he ordered me out of the room and told me he'd start throwing things at me if I ever came in again. He even tried to club me with a piece of metal tubing.''

"Where did he get the tubing?'' Mason asked.

"It was one he'd had me get for him the night before. It had some papers in it, some blueprints. It was one of those metal tubes such as maps and blueprints come in.''

"Had you seen that on the morning of the murder?''

"Yes.''

"Where?''

"He had it down by the side of the bed, down with the bag.''

"What did he do with it after he tried to club you with it?''

"He put it—let me see, I think he put it under the bed-clothes. I was so frightened by that time that I didn't notice— I have never seen a man so absolutely furious. We have trouble with patients once in a while, but this was different. He actually frightened me. He seemed beside himself.''

"And you telephoned for the doctor?''

"I telephoned and reported to the doctor that he was exceedingly violent and was insisting that a new nurse should come on the case; and I told the doctor I thought it would be better if a new nurse came out.''

"But the doctor came out without bringing another nurse?''

"Yes. Doctor Rankin thought he could fix everything all

199

up with a little diplomacy. He just didn't realize the full extent of what had happened, nor how absolutely violent the patient was."

"Now, he told you the day before that someone was trying to kill him?"

She seemed embarrassed, said, "I don't think I should talk with you about that, Mr. Mason, not without the district attorney's consent. You see, I'm a witness in the case."

"I don't want to try to tamper with your testimony," Mason said.

"Well, I don't think I should talk with you about that."

Mason said, "I appreciate your position. It's all right, and thank you a lot, Miss Field."

Chapter 21

Despite the fact that the night had been cold and that the season was early spring, the midday sun sent the thermometer climbing up toward the top of the tube, and Judge Meehan, sitting in Chambers, had relaxed into the comfortable informality of shirt sleeves and a plug of tobacco.

Mason entered just a few moments before Copeland arrived. Judge Meehan, teetering back and forth in a squeaky swivel chair behind a littered desk, nodded to them, sent a stream of tobacco-stained saliva into a battered brass cuspidor, said, "Sit down, gentlemen. Let's see if we can find out what this is all about."

The two lawyers seated themselves.

Judge Meehan said, "We don't want to throw away any evidence, and if there's something in this case that makes it look like the district attorney was barking up a wrong tree, we'd like to find out about it, wouldn't we, Ben?"

The district attorney said, "I'm barking up the right tree, all right. That's why you're hearing so many squeaks."

Mason smiled at the district attorney.

Judge Meehan said, "Personally, I'd like to know what this is all about."

Mason said, "Around twenty years ago, Marvin Adams' father was executed for the murder of his business partner, a man named Latwell. Latwell's widow married a man named Dangerfield. The murder took place in Winterburg City. Adams' father said that Latwell told him he was going to run off with a girl named Corine Hassen, but authorities found Latwell's body buried under the cement floor in the basement of the manufacturing establishment."

"So that's where this Corine Hassen entered into the case?" Judge Meehan said.

"I never knew her name," the district attorney announced. "I couldn't understand what Mr. Mason was getting at when he was asking questions about Corine Hassen."

"Witherspoon know anything about this?" Judge Meehan asked, the tempo of his tobacco chewing increasing somewhat.

Mason said, "Yes. He hired the Allgood Detective Agency in Los Angeles to investigate. They sent Milter; then they fired Milter because he talked too much."

Judge Meehan said, "Of course, this is all off the record. If you boys want me to go back in there and just sit down and listen, I'll go back and sit down and listen; but if there's any point about that note being valuable evidence—or if Witherspoon isn't guilty of those two murders and someone else is, it might be a good idea to have an informal chat and sort of pool our information."

"I have nothing to say," Copeland remarked.

Mason said, "Milter was a blackmailer. He was here to collect blackmail. The evidence shows he told his common-law wife he was about ready to make a clean-up. Now whom was he blackmailing?"

"Witherspoon, of course," the district attorney said.

Mason shook his head. "In the first place, Witherspoon isn't the sort of man who would pay blackmail. In the second place, Milter had no means of bringing pressure on Witherspoon. Witherspoon didn't care if all the facts about that old murder came out. He was getting ready to force his daughter to call of the engagement and wipe the thing off his books."

"How about Witherspoon's daughter?" Judge Meehan asked. "Hasn't she got money?"

"Yes."

"Well, how about her then?"

"If Milter had gone to her with that story, she'd have married Marvin Adams, anyway. He certainly couldn't say to her, 'Look here, Miss Witherspoon, I know something about the man you're going with that you wouldn't want to hear. If you'll pay me umpty thousand dollars, I won't tell you.' "

"That's right," Judge Meehan said, "but that isn't what he'd have told her. He'd have said, 'You pay me umpty thousand dollars, and I won't tell your *father*.' "

"Lois Witherspoon wouldn't have paid him any umpty thousand dollars," Mason said, grinning. "She wouldn't have paid him umpty cents. She'd have slapped his damn face, grabbed Marvin Adams, gone over to Yuma, got married, and defied the world.''

"She would, at that," Judge Meehan agreed, grinning.

"Now, mind you," Mason went on, "Milter was going to get a large sum of money. He told his common-law wife it was going to be enough so they could travel anywhere they wanted to. That means he had something that was bigger and better than just the ordinary shakedown. It was connected with something he'd discovered while investigating that old murder case. And the person whom he was blackmailing didn't have the ready cash available to pay off, but was expecting to get it.''

"How do you know that?" Judge Meehan asked.

Mason said, "I'm making deductions now."

"They don't hold water," Copeland objected.

Mason said, "Let's forget that we're on opposite sides of the case. Let's look at this in the light of cold reason. A blackmailer has information. He naturally tries to get all of the money he can for that information. When he's once got it, he clears out—until after the money's gone, and then he's back for more.''

Judge Meehan said, "Keep right on. You're doing fine as far as I'm concerned.''

Mason said. "Let's see where that leaves me. Milter investigated a murder. He uncovered certain information. He came here to blackmail someone. That someone kept him waiting. But on the night he was murdered, he expected to get his money. Now what was the information out of which he expected to make a fortune? Whom was he blackmailing and why?''

"Well," Meehan said, "suppose you answer that question. You don't seem to think it could have been Witherspoon or his daughter. Therefore, it must have been young Adams. Now, where was young Adams going to get the money?''

The district attorney suddenly sat up straight in his chair. "By marrying Lois Witherspoon!" he exclaimed. "And then getting control of her fortune.''

Mason grinned, said to Copeland, "Then your theory is that Adams was going to get married, immediately grab his wife's fortune, and squander it on a blackmailer to keep him

203

from telling something which his father-in-law already knew?''

The smile left Copeland's face.

"Suppose *you* tell us," Judge Meehan said.

Mason said, "The agency Milter worked for was crooked. It ran a Hollywood scandal sheet and wasn't above blackmailing its own clients. Allgood decided that he'd shake down Witherspoon. He was planning the first step in that campaign when I appeared on the scene. He didn't change his plan of campaign because of that, but simply started using me as a means of contact. It was a penny-ante sort of blackmail, something which had to be carried on on a wholesale basis in order to pay off. Milter, on the other hand, was after real big game. As I see it, gentlemen, there's only one thing he *could* have uncovered in connection with that old case which would have given him information that was important enough to be sold for a small fortune.''

The swivel chair squeaked as Judge Meehan, sitting bolt upright, said, "By George, *that* sounds reasonable. I take it you mean the identity of the real murderer?''

Mason said, "Exactly.''

"Who?" Judge Meehan asked.

Mason said, "Mr. Burr was staying out at Witherspoon's house. Mr. Burr had been in Winterburg City at about the time of the murders. Mr. Burr was trying to raise cash. He told Witherspoon he had sent East for some money, that he expected it to arrive the day he was kicked by the horse. The history of that old case shows that Corine Hassen said she had a boy friend who was insanely jealous. Roland Burr would have been about twenty-seven at the time. He knew Corine Hassen. Now put all of those things together, and you can make a pretty good deduction as to whom Milter was blackmailing, and why.''

"But how about this money Milter was going to get from the East?" Copeland asked.

"It arrived, all right," Mason said. "Let's look back at that old crime. More than one person was involved in it. Carrying Latwell's body down into the basement of the old manufacturing plant, breaking a hole in the cement in the cellar, digging a grave, interring the body, placing new cement over the hole, putting a pile of refuse back over that place in the cellar, then dashing to Reno, finding where Corine Hassen was waiting for Latwell to join her, getting her out in a rowboat, upsetting the rowboat, letting her drown, then removing her clothes, and leaving the nude body in the lake—well, I would say all that took two persons, one of whom must have had access to the manufacturing plant. If you were being blackmailed for a murder, and you had an accomplice who had money, you'd naturally send for that accomplice and tell her to pay up, wouldn't you?''

"You mean Latwell's widow?" Judge Meehan asked.

"That's right—the present Mrs. Dangerfield.''

Judge Meehan looked across at the district attorney. "This sounds like it was going to hold water," he said.

Copeland was frowning. "It doesn't account for the facts," he said.

"Now then," Mason went on, "suppose the accomplice decided that it would be a lot better to get rid of Milter than to pay blackmail. In order to do this successfully, the pair would naturally want what crooks would call a 'fall guy,' someone to take the blame, someone who had a motive and an opportunity.''

"Witherspoon?" Copeland asked skeptically.

Mason shook his head. "Witherspoon blundered into it by accident. The one they picked as the logical suspect was Marvin Adams. You can see what a sweet case they could have built up by using circumstantial evidence. When the officers broke in to Milter's apartment, they'd find a drowned duck in a fish bowl. That would be sufficiently unusual to attract immediate attention. Marvin Adams had to go into town to take that midnight train. He had to do some packing. He was planning to come out to Witherspoon's ranch in a borrowed jalopy. That meant Lois Witherspoon couldn't ride back to town with him, because, if she did, she wouldn't have had any way of getting back to the ranch. Marvin had some packing to do. Therefore, it was almost a certainty that, between eleven o'clock in the evening and midnight, Adams would be in El Templo. He'd leave somewhat early to walk down to the train. No one would be with him. He couldn't prove an alibi. His motivation would be obvious. Milter had tried to blackmail him to keep the old murder case a secret. Adams didn't have any money. Therefore, he resorted to murder.''

Judge Meehan nodded, and there was an almost imperceptible nod from the district attorney.

"It was as logical as you could hope to plan out anything in advance," Mason said.

"But how did they know that young Adams was going to take a duck off the ranch?" Judge Meehan inquired.

Mason took the letter Marvin Adams had given him from his pocket. "Because they held out a bait of one hundred dollars," he said, "by the simple expedient of signing a fictitious name to a letter."

Judge Meehan read the letter out loud. "I suppose Marvin Adams gave this to you?" he asked Mason.

"Yes."

"Well," Copeland said, his tone thoughtful, "suppose you tell us *what did* happen, Mr. Mason."

Mason said, "Burr was being blackmailed. He sent for Mrs. Dangerfield to come out and bring money. She had a way of her own that was a lot better than paying money. Witherspoon had some acid and cyanide there on the ranch. Burr got ample supplies of both, wrapped them up in a package, checked the package at the Pacific Greyhound stage office, and mailed Mrs. Dangerfield the check at her El Templo hotel. Then he went back to the ranch.

"Doubtless, he intended to do something else which was either connected with the murder or which would pin the crime on young Adams. But something happened he couldn't foresee. He got kicked by a horse. He was put to bed, given hypodermics, and found himself flat on his back with his leg sticking up in the air and a rope attached to a weight tied around it. That was something he couldn't possibly have foreseen."

"What happened there in Milter's apartment?" Judge Meehan asked. "How do you figure that out?"

"The girl who was working for Allgood telephoned that she was coming down. She had something important to tell him. So Milter, who was playing along with two women—his common-law wife and this blonde—told Alberta Cromwell he was having a business visitor at midnight, and made her think his relationship with the blonde was purely a business one. But it happened that Mrs. Dangerfield came in before the girl from the detective agency. Mrs. Dangerfield probably said, 'All right, you've got us. You want umpty-ump thousand dollars. We're going to pay it, and no hard feelings. We just want it understood that it'll be one payment and no more. We don't want any future shakedowns.'

"Flushed with triumph, Milter said, 'Sure, I was just mixing up some hot buttered rum. Come on back and have a drink.' Mrs. Dangerfield followed him into the kitchen, poured the hydrochloric acid into a water pitcher, dropped in the cyanide, perhaps asked where the bathroom was, and walked out, closing the kitchen door behind her. A few seconds later, when she heard Milter's body fall to the floor, she knew her work was done. It only remained to plant the duck in the fish bowl, and get out. Then the complications started."

"You mean Witherspoon?" Judge Meehan asked.

"First, there was the blonde from the detective agency. She had a key. She calmly opened the door and started climbing up the stairs. That was where Mrs. Dangerfield thought fast. You have to hand it to her."

"What did she do?" Copeland asked.

Mason grinned. "She took off her clothes."

"I'm not certain that I follow you on that," Copeland said.

"Simple," Mason said. "Milter had two women in love with him. One was his common-law wife. One was the girl from the detective agency. Each one of them naturally thought she was the only one, but was jealous and suspicious of the other. The blonde had a key. She started up the stairs. She saw a semi-nude woman in the apartment. She had come to warn Milter that Mason was on his trail. What would she naturally do under those circumstances?"

"Turn around and walk out," Judge Meehan said, spitting tobacco juice explosively into the cuspidor, "and say, 'to hell with him.' "

"That's it exactly," Mason said. "And she was so excited she didn't even bother to pull the street door all the way shut. Then Witherspoon came along. He started upstairs, and Mrs. Dangerfield pulled the same thing on him, making him retreat in embarrassment. Then, with the coast clear, Mrs. Dangerfield walked out.

"Milter's common-law wife had been lulled into temporary quiescence, but she was suspicious. She watched and

207

listened. When Mrs. Dangerfield, standing half undressed at the head of the stairs, argued with Witherspoon about coming up, Milter's common-law wife heard the feminine voice, decided it was her chance to see who the woman was, and poked her head out of the window. She saw Witherspoon leaving the apartment and got the license number of his automobile."

Judge Meehan thought things over for a few moments, then said, "Well, it could have happened just that way. I suppose the common-law wife came downstairs, and saw you at the door. She didn't want to stand there and ring the bell. And, anyway, you were ringing the bell and not getting any answer. She wanted to get to a telephone, so she started uptown. That gave Mrs. Dangerfield a chance to put on her clothes and leave the apartment."

"That's right, because I left then, too."

"All right," Judge Meehan said. "You've advanced an interesting theory. It isn't any more than that, but it's interesting. It accounts for Milter's murder, but it doesn't account for Burr's murder. I suppose Mrs. Dangerfield decided she wasn't going to have a pin-headed accomplice who was always getting her into trouble, so she decided to eliminate him in the same way. But how did she get past the dogs out at Witherspoon's house? How did she get the fishing rod for Burr?"

Mason shook his head. "She didn't."

Judge Meehan nodded. "I was sort of thinking," he said, "that just because both murders were committed with acid and cyanide isn't conclusive evidence they were both done by the same person. And yet that's the theory on which we've been working."

"It stands to reason," Copeland said.

Judge Meehan shook his head. "The means are unusual. Not many people would have thought of committing the first murder that way, but after all the publicity, it's reasonable to suppose the second murder could have been committed by any one of ten thousand people—so far as the means are concerned. Just because two people are killed three or four days apart by shooting, you don't think they must have been killed by the same murderer. The only reason you fall into a trap here is because the means were a little unusual."

208

"Exactly," Mason said. "And in that connection, here's something that's very significant and very interesting. When I came to Witherspoon's ranch, I was carrying with me a transcript of the evidence in that old murder case and some newspaper clippings. I left them in a desk there at Witherspoon's house during dinner, and someone opened that desk and moved the transcripts—someone who evidently wanted to know the reason for my visit."

"You mean Burr?" Judge Meehan asked.

"Burr was then laid up in bed with a broken leg."

"Marvin Adams, perhaps?"

Mason shook his head. "If Marvin Adams had known anything about that old murder case, he'd have probably broken off his engagement to Lois Witherspoon. He most certainly would have been so emotionally upset, we could have detected it. John Witherspoon wouldn't have done it because he *knew* why were were there. Lois Witherspoon wouldn't have done it; first, because she isn't a snoop, and second, because when I finally told her what we were there for, she turned so chalky white that I knew she'd had no previous intimation. That leaves one person, one person who left the dinner table while we were eating and was gone for quite a few minutes."

"Who?" Copeland asked.

"Mrs. Burr."

Judge Meehan's chair squeaked just a little. "You mean she murdered her husband?"

Mason said, "She found out about the old case and about what we were investigating. She'd put two and two together. It tied in with her husband's financial worries and the fact that Mrs. Dangerfield had arrived in El Templo. She ran into Mrs. Dangerfield on the street. Mrs. Burr put two and two together, and she knew. What's more, Burr knew that she knew.

"Mrs. Burr is highly emotional. She doesn't like to stay put. Her record shows that after she's been married just so long, she gets restless. Witherspoon may have thought those embraces were fatherly or platonic, but Mrs. Burr didn't. Mrs. Burr was looking around at the Witherspoon ranch and the Witherspoon bank account. And she'd found out her husband was guilty of murder."

"How did she find it out? Where was her proof?" Judge Meehan asked.

Mason said, "Look at the evidence. The nurse was fired when she tried to unpack the bag which Burr kept by his bed. What was in that bag? Books, flies, fishing tackle—and what else?"

"Nothing else," Copeland said. "I was personally present and searched the bag."

Mason smiled, "*After* Burr's death."

"Naturally."

"Wait a minute," Judge Meehan said to Mason. "That room was full of deadly gas fumes. Until the windows had been smashed open, no one could have got in there to have taken anything out of the bag, so you've got to admit that the things that were in the bag when Ben Copeland searched it were the things that were in the bag when Burr was murdered, unless the murderer took something out."

Mason said, "Well, let's look at it this way. Burr got the acid in the cyanide for Mrs. Dangerfield to use. He got plenty while he was getting it, and he had both acid and cyanide left in his bag. He may have intended to double-cross Mrs. Dangerfield—or perhaps his wife, who was getting altogether too suspicious. Everything was sitting pretty as far as he was concerned, and then he got laid up with a broken leg. As soon as he became conscious and rational, he asked his wife to bring that bag and put it right by the side of his bed. He didn't want anyone else touching it. You can imagine how he felt when the nurse announced she was going to unpack it. Someone who wasn't a trained nurse might fail to appreciate the importance of the acid in the bag with the cyanide. But with a nurse—well, you can see what would have happened."

"Now, wait a minute, Mason," Judge Meehan said. "Your reasoning breaks down there. Mrs. Burr wouldn't have killed her husband. She didn't have to kill him. All she had to do was to go to the sheriff."

"Exactly," Mason said, "and that's what she was intending to do. Put yourself in Burr's position. There he was in bed, trapped. He couldn't move. His wife not only knew he was guilty of murder, but had the proof. She *was* going to the sheriff. The nurse all but made the discovery of Burr's secret. His wife already knew it. Burr fired the nurse. He was hoping that some opportunity would present itself to kill his wife before she went to the sheriff, but he was laid up in bed. He realized he was trapped. There was only one way out for Roland Burr.''

"What?'' Judge Meehan asked, so interested that his jaws had quit moving.

Mason said, "The nurse knew all about acids and cyanides, but she didn't know anything about fishing. Burr got her to hand him an aluminum case, saying that it held some blueprints. He slipped it under the bed covers. That was his fishing rod. He was naturally very bitter about Witherspoon. He knew that his wife intended to get rid of him, and then marry Witherspoon. So Burr decided he would spike that little scheme right at the start. He had only one way out, but in taking it, he intended to have a sardonic revenge on the man whom his wife had selected as the next in line for matrimonial honors.

"He made it a point to ask Witherspoon to get the fishing rod for him in the presence of witnesses. It was a fishing rod he already had concealed under the covers in the aluminum case. As soon as he was left alone, he took out the fishing rod, put two joints together, placed the third joint on the bed within easy reach, screwed the cover back on the aluminum case, dropped it down to the floor, and gave it a good shove. It rolled clear across the room. Then Burr opened the bag. He took out the things he was afraid the nurse would find, the bottle of acid and the cyanide. He put them on a moveable table on wheels which had been placed by the side of his bed. He dumped the acid into a vase that was on the table, dropped the cyanide into it, took the butt of the fishing pole, and pushed the table just as far as he could push it. Then he picked up the tip of the rod with his left hand and held it as though he had been inserting it in the ferrule.''

Judge Meehan was too interested to take time out to expectorate. He held his lips tightly together, his eyes on Mason.

"And then?'' District Attorney Copeland asked.

"Then,'' Mason said, very simply, "he took a deep breath.''

Chapter 22

Della Street said reproachfully to Perry Mason, "You certainly do give a person plenty of scares, don't you?"

"Do I?"

"You know darn well you do. When it came two o'clock and the judge didn't come out to go on with the case, and then the deputy sheriffs began to go around picking up people here and there, I decided they'd nailed you on the charge of tampering with evidence or being an accessory or something."

Mason grinned. "The district attorney was a hard man to sell, but once he got the idea, he really went into action. Let's go pack and get out of here."

"What about Witherspoon?" she asked.

Mason said, "I think I've had about all of Witherspoon I want for a while. We'll send him a bill on the first of the month, and that will wind up our acquaintance with Mr. John L. Witherspoon."

"Has Mrs. Dangerfield confessed?"

"Not yet. But they've got enough evidence on her now to really build up a case. They found the box which was checked at the Pacific Greyhound station, the bottle of detergent and, best of all, where she'd burned a letter of instructions from Burr. The ashes still held enough writing so they can prove the conspiracy. Also they got a few fingerprints from Milter's apartment."

"You'd have thought she'd have worn gloves up there," Della Street said.

Mason laughed. "You forget that she'd put on a striptease act to scare away visitors. A woman doesn't appear at the head of the stairs wearing next to nothing, and with gloves on her hands."

"No. That's right," Della Street admitted. "How about Lois and Marvin?"

"Off on a honeymoon. Did you bring along the papers in that will-contest case, Della?"

"They're in my brief case, yes. I thought you might find time to work on them."

Mason looked at his watch. "I know a desert inn," he said, "run by a quaint old man, and a woman who makes the most marvelous apple pies. It's up at an elevation of about three thousand feet where there's a lot of granite-rock dikes to be explored, interesting groups of cacti—where we'd be completely undisturbed, and could check over the papers in that whole file, dictate a plan of strategy and a preliminary brief . . ."

"What causes all the hesitation?" Della Street interrupted.

Mason grinned. "I just hate to get so far away from an interesting murder case."

Della grabbed his hand, said, "Come on, don't let that hold you back. You don't have to worry about finding cases any more. They hunt you out. My Lord, how frightened I was when Lois Witherspoon got up and started to tell what she knew, and I realized you were just sparring for time!"

Mason grinned. "I sweat a little blood myself. I kept one eye on the clock and tried to stir up a lot of excitement that would take the district attorney's mind off what he was doing. If I had used the usual tactics of objecting to the questions and the witnesses, I'd have simply centered suspicion on myself. As it was, I managed to stall it through, but don't ever kid yourself—it was by the skin of my eyeteeth."

She said, "Your eyeteeth won't have any skin left. Did anyone ask why the duck didn't sink eventually?"

"No," Mason said.

"What would you have told them if they had?"

Mason grinned. "From the time Haggerty arrived in the room, he was in charge of the case. It was up to him to explain why the duck *didn't* drown."

Della Street studied him with the shrewd appraisal which a woman gives a man whom she knows very, very well. "You went into that apartment," she charged. "You saw the drowning duck, and you thought that Marvin Adams had been there. You sympathized with him because his dad had been executed for murder and because he was in love, and you deliberately, willfully, maliciously, and with felonious intent started to juggle the evidence."

Mason said, "You should add, against that peace and dignity of the People of the State of California."

She looked up at him with laughing eyes. "How far is it to this desert inn?" she inquired.

"It'll take us two hours' hard driving."

"I'll telephone the office and tell Gertie," she said. "When shall I tell her we'll be back? How long will it take to get the dictation done in the will contest?"

Mason squinted his eyes thoughtfully, looked up at the cloudless blue of the Southern California desert sky, felt the welcome touch of the sunlight which bathed the metropolis in brilliant warmth.

"You tell Gertie," he said, "that we'll be back when she digs up a *good* murder case for us—and not before. Tell her that just any old ordinary murder case won't do. We want . . ."

Della Street started toward the hotel, Mason striding along at her side, people on the streets craning their necks, turning to watch them.

Della Street looked up at Perry Mason. "Well," she said, "you've contributed to the education of an agricultural community. You've shown them how to drown a duck. City slicker! Now, what else do you know?"